DICKINSON AREA PUBLIC LIBRARY
3 3121 00161 0349

D0394144

Heirs and Graces

BERKLEY PRIME CRIME TITLES BY RHYS BOWEN

Royal Spyness Mysteries

HER ROYAL SPYNESS
A ROYAL PAIN
ROYAL FLUSH
ROYAL BLOOD
NAUGHTY IN NICE
THE TWELVE CLUES OF CHRISTMAS
HEIRS AND GRACES

Constable Evans Mysteries

EVANS ABOVE
EVAN HELP US
EVANLY CHOIRS
EVAN AND ELLE
EVAN CAN WAIT
EVANS TO BETSY
EVAN ONLY KNOWS
EVAN'S GATE
EVAN BLESSED

Specials

MASKED BALL AT BROXLEY MANOR

Heirs and Graces

RHYS BOWEN

BERKLEY PRIME CRIME, NEW YORK

THE BERKLEY PUBLISHING GROUP
Published by the Penguin Group
Penguin Group (USA) Inc.
375 Hudson Street, New York, New York 10014, USA

USA | Canada | UK | Ireland | Australia | New Zealand | India | South Africa | China

Penguin Books Ltd., Registered Offices: 80 Strand, London WC2R 0RL, England
For more information about the Penguin Group, visit penguin.com.

This book is an original publication of The Berkley Publishing Group.

Library of Congress Cataloging-in-Publication Data

Bowen, Rhys.
Heirs and graces / Rhys Bowen.—First edition.
pages cm
ISBN 978-0-425-26002-9
1. Aristocracy (Social class)—Fiction. 2. Inheritance and succession—Fiction.
3. Murder—Investigation—Fiction. 4. England—Fiction. I. Title.
PR6052.0848H45 2013
823'.914—dc23 2013015987

FIRST EDITION: August 2013

PRINTED IN THE UNITED STATES OF AMERICA

10 9 8 7 6 5 4 3 2 1

Cover illustration by John Mattos.
Cover design by Rita Frangie.

This book is dedicated to three wonderful women:
Carolyn Hart, Eve Sandstrom and Jan Giles,
who sat with me all night in an emergency room
last year when I broke my pelvis
and then looked after me until I was flown home.
They helped me get through a horribly difficult situation
and I'll never forget their kindness.

Chapter 1

The Ides of March 1934
15 Cheyne Walk, Chelsea

One thing I should have learned about my mother was that I could not count on her. After all, she bolted from the family home, abandoning my father and me when I was two, and by the time she resurfaced again in my life she had worked her way through a global list of men. These included an Argentinian polo player, a French race-car driver and an English mountaineer. The latter wanted to marry her and to adopt me. I adored him, but Mummy tired of playing second fiddle to mountains. As an actress, Mummy never played second on any bill.

She was in many ways like a cat, only showing interest in people when she wanted something from them, on which occasions she could be devastatingly charming. She definitely saw the universe with herself at the center and lesser beings orbiting around her, waiting for her to turn the full glow of her sunshine on them when they were needed. So I should have realized when she told me that she was taking a house in London, intended to write her memoirs and wanted me to be her secretary that it was too good to last for long. We had started off well enough in a delightful little house in Chelsea overlooking the Thames. Mummy was full of enthusiasm. She bought me a sturdy Underwood typewriter, and I had made some progress at mastering it, reaching a typing speed of several words per minute without getting my fingers trapped in the keys. I won't say it was easy, even then. Mummy would start on some story while I tried to keep up with her, taking frantic notes, only to find that she'd stop with a look of amused horror on that perfect face. "Oh, no. Scratch that, Georgie. I can't possibly let anyone know about what happened that night," she'd say. "It would bring down the government (or create a new world war or even the pope would be furious)," leaving me dying of curiosity.

I was coming to the conclusion that there wasn't much about her life that could be told to the general public, unless the book were to come out with a plain-brown cover, like *Lady Chatterley's Lover*, when the blow fell. We'd been at work for over a month, interrupted only by impulsive visits to her milliner for a new hat or her masseuse for a knot in her shoulder, when she breezed into the breakfast room one morning, waving a letter.

"It's from Max, darling." She sounded breathy, excited. Max von Strohheim, German industrialist, ridiculously wealthy, was her current beau.

"He's still pining for you?"

"More than that, darling. He can't live without me a moment longer." I wasn't quite sure how she knew this, since she spoke no German and Max's English was limited to monosyllables, but she went on, waving the letter at me. "He says he knows that March in Germany is too gloomy for words so he's bought us an adorable little villa on Lake Lugano. He knows that I adore Switzerland—so safe and tidy, and the Swiss are so good at hiding one's money, aren't they?"

"I don't know," I said. "I've never had any money to hide."

She ignored this, still caught up in her own rapture. "A villa on Lake Lugano sounds like exactly what I need right now. I do miss sunshine and good Continental food. And I do miss Max too. The sex was truly magnificent. He's like a rampant stud bull in bed, although I probably shouldn't discuss such things with my daughter."

"Mummy, you've been revealing your intimate secrets to me for six weeks," I said. "And I am twenty-three. So does this mean you're off to Lake Lugano, then?"

"Oh, absolutely," she said. "Tomorrow's boat train, if my maid can get everything packed up in time."

"But what about this house?" I wanted to ask "What about me?" but I was too proud to do so.

She shrugged, as if this had only just occurred to her. "I've paid the rent through the end of the month," she said. "Feel free to stay on if you want to."

That wasn't the response I had wanted. For one heady moment, I had hoped that she'd invite me to Lake Lugano with her and we'd continue with her autobiography on a vine-covered terrace overlooking the lake with a pot of good coffee or maybe glasses of champagne beside us.

"What about your book?" I asked. "Aren't you going to finish it?"

She laughed. "Oh, darling, it was such a silly idea, wasn't it? I don't really want my adoring public to know the sordid details of what I've been up to, and as you saw for yourself there's not much I can divulge without fear of lawsuits. I don't know why I wanted to do it in the first place."

"I do," I wanted to say. You wanted a reason to spend some time in London with your only daughter. I felt a lump come into my throat.

"Come on, get your coat on," she said, attempting to drag me up from the table. "That food isn't fit for man or beast anyway. We'll get something out."

"Where are we going in such a hurry?"

"Shopping, of course. I have nothing to wear that's suitable for a Swiss lake. Harrods or Barker's, do you think? Both so stodgy and English, aren't they? I wonder if I should stop off in Paris for a quick run on Chanel? Of course, Coco won't be there. She's bound to be at her villa in Nice—or on someone's yacht."

My thoughts sped back to the heady time the year before—Mummy's villa, Chanel's dresses; so many adventures. I wondered what it would be like to be the kind of person who mentions casually that she should make a quick run on Chanel. I did at least own one Chanel outfit now, plus some elegant clothes that Mummy had bought me, and it occurred to me that it was rather pathetic of me to feel so let down.

I followed Mummy into the front hall as she threw a blonde mink stole around her shoulders and placed an adorable cloche hat on her head. I shouldn't be relying on my mother, I told myself. I should be making my own way in the world. Actually, there was nothing I wanted more. God knows I had tried. But the world was still in the grips of the Great Depression and there were no jobs even for people with oodles of qualifications. My education at a posh Swiss finishing school had only equipped me to walk around with a book on my head, to curtsy without falling over (most of the time) and snag a suitable husband.

In case you think I was a pathetic specimen unable to attract a man, let me tell you that I was unofficially engaged to an absolutely dreamy chap called Darcy O'Mara. What's more, he was the son of an Irish peer—which should make him eminently suitable for the daughter of a duke like me, except that he was as broke as I was, lived by his wits and made money in dubious ways. So there was no wedding in my foreseeable future, unless Darcy struck it rich somehow. When I last heard from him, he was in Argentina, involved in some kind of secret undertaking—probably an arms deal.

"Come on, darling. Let's go and find a taxicab. I've got absolutely masses to do if I'm to get out of here tomorrow." Mummy yanked at me again as I tried to put on my coat.

"I thought you weren't going to bother with London shops, and were going to stop in Paris," I said.

"One does need some basics," she said. "Good woolen underwear, for example. We might go skiing in the Alps. And Harrods can come up with something tolerable occasionally. Is it too late for cashmere in Lugano, do you think?"

Without waiting for an answer, she dashed into the street and started looking for a cab. I was about to follow her out of the front door when the lugubrious figure of Mrs. Tombs appeared from the kitchen area. "Done with your breakfast then, are you?" she asked in that voice that always implied that life was an unbearable burden.

"Yes thank you, Mrs. Tombs."

"Going out then, are you?"

She did have a talent for stating the obvious. I was on the front step, with my coat on. "Yes, Mrs. Tombs. My mother needs to do some shopping."

"Always shopping, she is. Don't she have enough clothes by now? She's already got both wardrobes full upstairs."

Privately, I felt that my mother would never have enough clothes. Shopping was a major sport for her, but I wouldn't dream of being disloyal in front of a domestic. "I don't think that Miss Daniels's shopping habits are anything to do with us," I said, referring to my mother by her stage name, which she preferred to use over her current legal one. She was still officially married to an American oil tycoon called Homer Clegg, who had so far refused to grant her a divorce, owing to a Puritanical religious streak my mother hadn't known about when she married him.

"So do you reckon you'll be back for your dinner?"

I sighed. She was becoming more annoying by the minute. "Mrs. Tombs, remember I reminded you that the midday meal is called lunch among our type of person, and dinner is served at eight o'clock in the evening."

She sniffed, wiping her hands on her pinny. "Well pardon me for breathin'. Yer lunch, then. Are you going to want lunch?"

"Who can tell?" I said. "Have something ready anyway. Maybe something light like a salad?"

"You won't find no lettuce down the greengrocer's on the corner. Only in your highfalutin sort of shops at this time of year."

"Very well, a—" I broke off. I had foolishly been going to suggest a soufflé or even an omelet, both of which would have been beyond her.

"We'll bring back smoked salmon. Make sure we have brown bread, thinly sliced."

"Right you are then." I had long ago decided that there was no point in instructing her on the correct way to address the daughter of a duke. She wouldn't use it.

She sniffed again and shuffled off to clear the breakfast away. Really, she was a most depressing woman, but she came with the house. "How convenient," Mummy had said. "We won't have to hunt for servants."

She was what was termed a cook general, although the word "cook" was debatable. Her cooking skills were nonexistent and if we'd let her have her way we'd have dined on gray, overstewed mutton and boiled-to-death cabbage. Fortunately Mummy liked to eat well, and a constant stream of deliverymen from Harrods and Fortnum's kept us from starvation.

Mummy had already found a taxicab, one of her many miraculous talents. Cabs just appeared out of nowhere for her. I climbed in beside her.

"Mrs. Tombs wanted to know if we'd be in for lunch," I said.

"That woman should have been drowned at birth," Mummy said. "Isn't it funny how people seem to have appropriate names? She has a face like a gravedigger. And I'm sure all the previous tenants died of her cooking. If I weren't leaving, I'd write to the owner and let him know what a disaster she is. Of course, he doesn't care. He's in Monte Carlo."

"She does clean quite well," I pointed out. "It's not her fault she can't cook."

"You are too nice natured, darling. You won't get anywhere in this world being kind and generous. You must turn into a lioness like me and gobble up people who disagree with you."

"I'm not very good at gobbling," I said. "And I want to like people, and be liked by them."

She sighed. "The sooner you get married and have babies to adore the better." She paused, looking out of the window at the side wall of Harrods. "No news of the delectable Darcy then?"

"Nothing for ages." I sighed.

"You must make him want to come rushing back to your side, my darling. You must learn how to turn into a little tigress in bed. It's a pity I'm going or I could have given you a few pointers."

"Mummy, we're not married yet," I said in a shocked voice.

She laughed merrily at this. "Darling, since when did sex and marriage have anything to do with each other. Our kind of people marry so they can legally get their hands on nice pieces of property and someone else's title and fortune."

I smiled out of the window but said nothing. Mummy was hardly "our kind of people," having been born in a two-up, two-down house in the East End of London to a Cockney policeman and his wife. Fortunately, her acting skills and stunning good looks had snagged her my father—the Duke of Glengarry and Rannoch, who was Queen Victoria's grandson and thus cousin to the king, which made her "Your Grace" for a while, until she bolted. It was the title she regretted giving up most. She still liked to play the role of "Your Grace."

The taxi pulled up outside the front entrance to Harrods. A braided doorman leaped forward to open the door, as if knowing instinctively that Mummy was inside.

"Hello, Albert," she said, turning the full force of her radiance on to him. "How are you today?"

"All the better for seeing you, Your Grace," he said as his fingers closed around the generous tip.

"How sweet of you to remember me," she said. As if he wouldn't.

Then she swept through the cosmetics department, pausing only long enough to request a jar of her favorite face cream to be ready for her on her way out; the glove department, pausing only long enough to ask for emerald green kid gloves and a matching scarf and then she was in the lift going up to the dress department. During the next half hour, she must have tried on at least twenty and discarded them all as too frumpy and too last-season.

So we were off again, at whirlwind speed, collecting gloves, scarf and face cream, and commissioning someone to run to the food hall and have smoked salmon delivered by noon to the house. As usual, I was in awe of her energy, efficiency and the way she took it for granted that every employee of Harrods was there only for her. If only I could have been a little more like her, in temperament and in looks. I sighed. She was petite with huge, blue eyes, giving a quite false air of being helpless and delicate. I was tall and angular with the healthy, outdoorsy appearance of my hardy Scottish ancestors.

"Where to now, do you think?" she asked as another taxicab screeched to a halt beside us. "Not Barker's. Too depressing. Selfridge's? Too common. Liberty's? Too country. Fenwick's? Now, there's a thought. She tapped on the glass. "Bond Street, driver. One should find something there."

And so we set off again. "Have I time to get my hair set, do you think?" she asked. "That adorable young man around the corner from the Burlington Arcade will fit me in, I know. You can wander for a while, darling, can't you, while I have a teeny little shampoo and set?"

Privately, I thought that one of the more depressing things in the world was to wander along Bond Street with no means of buying anything in the shops, but it was only a rhetorical question and a fine enough day for walking. We dashed through Fenwick's, acquiring a Fair Isle skiing jumper, just in case she went skiing, a bathing wrap in case she decided to bathe and a pair of good, sensible, tweed trousers for tramping around the Alps. To this she added a variety of undergarments.

"Of course only the French know anything about underwear," she said in her clear, theatrical voice, which carried to the gods. "The English don't seem to think undies should have anything to do with seduction or sex. What red-blooded man would possibly want to tear off these voluminous English knickers?" And she brandished a particularly large pair. Several ladies up from the country turned around in horror. One fanned herself with her gloves. "But there are times when one would rather be warm, and there's nothing like good English wool for that."

Then we were outside and Mummy rushed off to the hairdresser, who left some poor client, half rolled in curlers, to his assistant while he ushered my mother to the best chair. I came out again, wondering what to do for the next hour. I knew I could have asked Mummy for money but I was like my grandfather in such matters. The money came from Max and I was too proud to ask for it.

So I wandered down Bond Street , half looking in shop windows, imagining what it would be like to go in and say, "I'd like to look at that emerald necklace," when I was grabbed from behind.

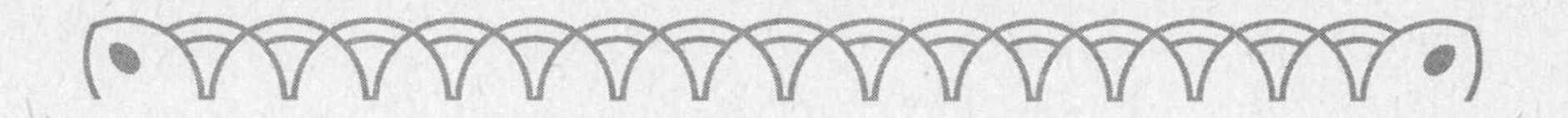

Chapter 2

On Bond Street

Before I could cry out or do anything sensible, I was spun around and a voice gasped in my ear, "Darling, it is you! How absolutely divine."

And there was my best friend, Belinda Warburton-Stoke, looking even more lovely and glamorous than the last time I had seen her. She was wearing a black, tailored, two-piece suit with scarlet-leather trim and a little scarlet hat with a provocative veil. Her dark hair was cut in a chic bob and her mouth was a gash of bright-red lipstick. The whole thing screamed Paris.

"And shopping in Bond Street, no less," she said. "Things must be on the up and up for you."

"I wish they were." I kissed the cheek she had extended to me. "But it's lovely to see you too, Belinda. I've missed you. Where have you been? I called at your mews cottage a couple of times but it was all shut up and deserted."

"Paris, darling. Where else?"

"Another French marquis?" She had been smitten by a dashing marquis when we had been in France together the previous year.

"Not at all. I've been working for Chanel, if you'd really like to know. Remember, she did say that my designs showed promise, so I thought I'd go and learn at the feet of the master—or in Coco's case, the mistress." And she grinned at her double meaning.

"So are you home just for a visit?"

A slight spasm of annoyance passed over her face. "I'm afraid we've parted ways, Chanel and I. A certain Frenchman started to show interest in me, the way they do." (They did, for Belinda.) "He was rather attractive so I didn't exactly repulse his advances. How was I to know he was one of Coco's lovers? It turns out she doesn't like to share. So I was given the boot. Here I am, back in London and dying to start my own clothing line."

"How exciting," I said.

She looked around. "Do you absolutely have to shop or can we go for a coffee? I'd love to chat but these high heels are killing me."

"It will have to be somewhere nearby. I'm with my mother, and she's getting her hair done around the corner."

"Ah, so that's why you're in Bond Street then. Come on. There's a little place on Albemarle Street that manages a non-poisonous coffee." She started off, tottering slightly in enormously high wedges on the uneven pavement. We found the little café and sat, beaming at each other as the waitress brought two demitasses of thick, rich coffee.

"Your own line, Belinda! That sounds thrilling. You wouldn't like an efficient, private secretary, would you?"

"Do you know of one?"

"Me. I've been Mummy's secretary for the past month. I can actually work a typewriter."

"I'm impressed. And I'd hire you in a minute, but frankly, my dear, I can't start my business without capital. I'm almost as broke as you are. My stepmother—you remember, the wicked witch—persuaded my father that I no longer need an allowance. How hateful is that. She said it was my fault I wasn't married, and that I should be standing on my own feet at twenty-four."

"So we're in the same boat," I said. "I was supposed to be helping Mummy write her memoirs."

Belinda almost choked on her coffee. "She'd never tell all, surely. My dear, think of the scandals."

"I know. That's what she decided. Also, Max has bought her a villa in Lugano and she's off to join him, abandoning the project and her only daughter."

"I'd probably abandon my only daughter for a villa in Lugano at this time of year," Belinda said as a great gust of March wind sent newspapers flying outside the window. "So what about you? Where will you go—back to Rannoch House?" (Rannoch House was the family's London house on Belgrave Square.)

I shook my head. "It's all shut up. Binky and Fig decided not to come down to London this winter. Too expensive to move all the staff. They are staying put up at Castle Rannoch."

Binky, my brother, was the current Duke of Glengarry and Rannoch. The dreaded Fig was his wife and current duchess. In spite of owning a castle and a London home they were almost as broke as I was, thanks to our father squandering the fortune, and then subsequent death duties on the property.

"You lived in the London house alone before," Belinda reminded me.

"But I'm not allowed to anymore. Fig begrudges the miniscule amount of heat and light I'd use. I can stay on at the house Mummy rented until the end of this month, but I've no idea what I'll do then. I simply can't go home to Scotland. It's so dreary there, and Fig makes me feel so unwelcome."

"It is your family seat. She's only a Rannoch by marriage. And not connected to the royals the way you are. You should put your foot down, Georgie."

I vigorously stirred the thick, black liquid in my cup. "Unfortunately, it is her house now and not mine. My brother is the duke and she is the duchess, and I'm only a poor relation."

"Goodness, you sound depressed," she said. "I never am. I'm always sure something good will turn up, and it usually does."

"You have skills and talents," I said. "I don't."

"What about the typewriting?"

"I don't think I'm good enough to be anybody's real secretary yet. And anyway, I've nowhere to stay."

"I'd invite you to share my little mews place but there's only one bedroom, and it would rather cramp my style—in case I decided to bring someone home occasionally." She didn't add that the someone in question would undoubtedly be of the male sex.

"I understand," I said.

"Of course, you have one trump card I don't have," Belinda said. "You can always ask your royal relatives to help you." I should probably mention that Queen Victoria was my great-grandmother and thus King George was my first cousin, once removed.

"Belinda, I can't ask them—" I began but she cut me off.

"You've helped them out enough times. What about that princess, or that snuffbox? They owe you a favor, Georgie."

"You're right," I said. "But in their eyes I have two choices open to me—marry a half-lunatic European prince or become a lady-in-waiting to an elderly royal aunt."

"There are one or two rather handsome European princes. Remember Prince Anton?"

"Yes, but I'm not going to marry out of duty. I already have a chap I love."

"How is the divine Darcy?"

I looked down at my cup. "Off on some jaunt again. The Argentine, I believe. I do love him, Belinda, but he's hardly ever here."

She nodded in sympathy. "Well, even the second of those choices you mentioned sounds preferable to living with Binky and Fig at the moment, don't you think? Would it be too odious living in a stately home in the country? There would be good food and maybe hunting, and interesting people might come to stay."

"You really are an optimist, Belinda. But it would be in the depths of the countryside and I'd have to wind wool and walk horrid little dogs that nip my ankles. I want a life of my own, not to be a hanger-on in someone else's life." I looked up at her. "So how do you plan to find the money to finance your clothing line? Any rich men in the picture at the moment?"

"I'm only just back from Paris, but I'm working on it. I've been to Crockfords every night."

"You're going to rely on gambling to come up with the money?"

"Not exactly, darling." She gave me a cheeky smile. "There are still an amazing number of rich men who go there to gamble—Americans, colonials, foreigners. I look sweet and helpless and ask them for tips on how to play roulette. They always put down my stake for me. But I'm really looking for what the Americans call a sugar daddy."

"Belinda—you wouldn't! You wouldn't really let an older man take care of you just for the money, would you?"

She shrugged. "I don't see how else I'm going to get rich. There don't seem to be too many eligible and rich young men around these days. If they are eligible, they are stony broke like Darcy. If they are rich, they are either married or old and flabby. I suppose I might find a ninety-year-old millionaire and marry him."

I had to laugh at this. "Belinda, you are awful."

"Just practical, darling. I'm a survivor like your mother."

I glanced at my watch. "I should probably go. Mummy hates to be kept waiting."

"Well, let's see something of each other, now we're both in town. I may be short of funds but I still have enough for the occasional nightclub or play . . . and I'll spread the word that we are available for party invitations. We'll have fun, won't we?"

As we left the coffeehouse, I really believed that we might. Mummy departed the next day, dressed in her floor-length dark mink and a cloud of Chanel No 5. "Have fun, darling," she said, kissing me about two inches from my cheek to avoid spoiling her makeup. "And come out and stay with us once we're settled."

I watched her go, wondering how any woman could breeze through life so completely unaware of other human beings, even her only child. The taxicab door slammed, she waved and then she was gone.

Mrs. Tombs was standing behind me in the hall, wiping her hands on her pinny. "My rheumatics are playing up something terrible," she said. "You don't mind having the leftover stew for your dinner, do you?"

I stomped upstairs in deep gloom. I didn't think I could endure staying here until the end of the month. I opened my bedroom door and was met by an amazing sight. Someone was sitting at my dressing table—someone with scarlet lips, red cheeks, eyes lined with kohl and hair piled on her head. The effect was like a cheap celluloid doll they sell at funfairs.

"What in heaven's name?" I began.

My maid jumped up guiltily. "Sorry, miss," she said.

"Queenie, what were you doing?"

She hung her head, embarrassed. "Your mum left some of her makeup behind. In fact, she threw it away. Seemed a shame. So I rescued it from the wastebasket for you. I thought you might look better if you tarted yourself up a bit."

"You obviously thought you might look better too," I said, not knowing whether to laugh or frown.

"Well, I ain't never had the chance before to tart meself up," she said. "You never know, I might look good as a vamp."

"Queenie, only ladies of the night wear that much makeup," I said. "And servants none at all. Now go and wash it off."

"Bob's yer uncle, miss," she said. "I only did it for a bit of a laugh. Don't get too many laughs around here, not with her down in the kitchen with a face that would curdle milk."

I shook my head. "Queenie, I don't know why I keep you as my maid."

"I do, miss," she said. "You can't afford one of them posh maids what talks proper and knows how to behave."

"True. But I did hope you might learn to behave like a posh maid."

"I don't burn your clothes when I iron them very often these days," she said defensively.

"But you still call me miss, when I must have told you a thousand times that the correct way to address the daughter of duke is 'my lady.' "

"Yeh, sorry. I always forget that one, don't I? I suppose it's because you don't look like a lady to me. You look dead ordinary." She reached the doorway and turned back to me. "Are we really stopping on here?"

"Until the end of the month, I expect," I said.

She gave a dramatic sigh. "I don't know much longer I can face that miserable old cow downstairs."

"Queenie, it's not up to you to pass judgment."

"Well, you don't have to eat with her. If she had her way, I'd starve—and the way she cooks, I'd rather starve sometimes."

"I tend to agree with you there," I said, "but I've nowhere else to go right now. You certainly don't want to go back to Scotland any more than I do. My sister-in-law is always badgering me to sack you."

"She's another right cow," Queenie said.

"Queenie. I've told you before—that is not the way you should speak of a duchess."

"Well, she is. The way she treats you. It ain't fair that you got no money and nowhere to go while she lords it over that bloody great castle. I think you should get your own little place in London like your friend."

"With what?"

"You got a typewriter now, don't you? You could be a proper secretary with a bit of practice. They make good money."

A small bubble of hope formed itself in my mind. "I suppose I might, if I practiced hard."

"Course you could." She smiled at me encouragingly and I knew why I kept her. "Well go on then," she added. "Get working."

I sat at my typewriter over the next few days and worked away.

The queick brown fox jumps over the lazy dog

Thtqujivk brown box jumpsd over the lacy dobn.

Rats.

Ttj quick briwnficjunbpsobnerthf lax . . .

I wasn't exactly improving at a rapid pace.

I was all right if I went slowly and carefully. I just got flustered if I was in a rush. The end of the month was getting closer. If I could only find a job soon then I could maybe stay with my grandfather for a few days until I got my first paycheck. Then I could look for a flat of my own. I wasn't sure whether the royal kin would approve of my being a typist, or of staying with a retired London policeman in a little semi-detached with gnomes in the garden, but then they weren't paying for my keep either. At least it was better than housecleaning and the escort service I had previously tried.

With time running out, I decided to visit an employment agency. First I used a sheet of writing paper with the Rannoch crest on it to write myself a reference. "This is to recommend Fiona Kinkaid, whom I have recently employed as my secretary. I have found her willing and efficient and satisfactory in every way. I am now going back to the Continent and wish her well." I signed it with my mother's round and childish signature, which was so simple to copy. I decided not to use my own name, just in case the press got wind of it and the family objected, so I used the name of a rather glamorous doll I had once owned. Then off I set to the nearest agency. It was up a flight of stairs, just off Curzon Street. Halfway up the stairs, I heard the clatter of typewriters going at an alarming pace. Suddenly the door opened and a girl stomped down the stairs past me. "Old dragon," she muttered to me. "I only made one mistake and she told me I wasn't up to snuff. They expect automatons, not people."

I turned on my heel and followed her back down the stairs. Face facts, Georgiana. How idiotic and naïve of me to think that a few weeks pecking away at a typewriter would make me into a secretary. I was a hopeless case. Unemployable. I now had no alternative other than to go home to Castle Rannoch with my tail between my legs, unless . . . I paused, remembering what Belinda had said. Surely being a lady-in-waiting to an elderly royal relative would be better than Fig. Anything would be better than Fig.

I found the writing paper again and addressed a letter to Her Gracious Majesty, Queen Mary.

I agonized over whether to start it "Dear Cousin Mary," or "Your Majesty." I opted for the latter. The queen was a stickler for formality. I explained that I would prefer not to go back to Scotland and wanted to do something useful, but unfortunately had nowhere to stay in London as my brother had closed up the London house. Any help or introduction that she could give me would be gratefully accepted.

I finished "I remain Your Majesty's most humble and devoted servant, your affectionate cousin, Georgiana."

Then I took it to the post, held my breath and waited.

Chapter 3

Cheyne Walk, Chelsea, and Buckingham Palace

It was only two days before the end of the month and Mrs. Tombs was dropping not-too-subtle hints that she hoped I'd hurry up and clear out because she had cleaning to do before the next lot came in. I was beginning to despair when I received a reply from Buckingham Palace.

"My dear Georgiana," Her Majesty had written in her own hand. "Your letter arrived at a most fortuitous time. If you would care to come to tea tomorrow, I think I might have an interesting little assignment for you."

It was signed "Your affectionate cousin, Mary R." (the *R* meaning Regina, of course). Even when she was being affectionate she always remained correct.

I stood there, studying the letter, not knowing whether to be excited or worried. The queen's past little assignments had ranged from hosting a visiting princess to stealing a purloined snuffbox. One never knew. At least it would be better than a cold, bleak castle in Scotland. I went upstairs to make sure I had something suitable to wear. I chose the skirt and dusky-pink cashmere cardigan that my mother had given me for Christmas. They were the closest I had to daytime chic. Then

I had to remind Queenie not to pack them with the rest of my belongings.

"So where are we going then?" she asked.

"I have no idea. But somewhere."

"I hope it's abroad again," she said. "I could do with some of that Froggy food again after her downstairs. And sunshine too."

A glorious picture of the villa in Nice swam into my head—the Mediterranean sparkling blue at the bottom of the cliff, the scent of mimosas in the air. It was probably too much to hope for. Then I reminded myself that it had been dangerous too. I hoped this assignment would not involve danger. Excitement was fine, but I'd prefer not to come within an inch of my life again.

"So where are you off to then?" Mrs. Tombs asked, appearing in that uncanny way every time I came into the front hall. "Another bit of shopping?"

"No, I'm going to have tea with the queen," I said.

"Go on with you. Pull the other one, it's got bells on," she said, chuckling.

"No, honestly."

"Why would the queen want to have tea with you?" she asked, her voice dripping with sarcasm.

"Because I'm her cousin," I replied. "I'm Lady Georgiana Rannoch. I'm frequently invited to the palace."

"Blimey." She put her hand up to her face. "And I never knew. I thought your face looked familiar somehow. Wait till I tell her next door that I've been entertaining royalty."

I almost said "And serving her leftover stew," but I contented myself with a smile as I went out.

I arrived at Buckingham Palace on the stroke of four. It always took every ounce of courage to approach those tall, gilded gates and to tell those impossibly tall guards that I was expected for tea. Then I had to cross the forecourt, which always seemed to take forever, with the eyes of passing tourists upon me, before I went under the arch, across the courtyard and up to that terrifying main entrance.

"Good afternoon, my lady," the welcoming footman said, bowing. "Her Majesty is expecting you in the Chinese Chippendale room. Allow me to escort you there."

Oh, crikey. The Chinese Chippendale room. Why couldn't she have chosen somewhere else? Any other room in the palace would have done. But the Chinese Chippendale room was her favorite: small, intimate and decorated with far too many Chinese vases, priceless porcelain statues and her jade collection. There's probably something you should know about me: in moments of stress I tend to get a little clumsy. I remember tripping over the footman's outstretched foot when he bowed to usher me inside once, thus propelling me rather rapidly into the room and nearly butting HM in the stomach. I would be all too capable of turning around and knocking a priceless Ming vase flying.

Still, I put on a brave face as I was escorted up the grand staircase to the piano nobile, where the royal family actually lived and entertained. Along those never-ending, richly carpeted hallways with marble statues frowning down at me from their niches. Then a light tap on a door, the footman stepping inside and saying, "Lady Georgiana, Your Majesty."

I stepped past him, carefully avoiding his foot, pushing the door into an unseen table or tripping over a rug. I stopped in surprise and thought I was seeing double. Two middle-aged ladies with identical, waved, gray hair, upright carriage and lilac tea dresses were sitting on the brocade sofa beside the fireplace. My first thought was that I should have worn a tea dress and the cashmere cardigan was inappropriate, but then one of the ladies held out her hand to me.

"Georgiana, my dear. How lovely to see you. Come and meet my dear friend."

I saw their faces then and realized that the other lady had a more prodigious bosom than the queen, but wore that same imperious look on her face as Her Majesty. The next thought that passed through my mind was that I would hate to be her maid.

"You may tell Mary that she can serve tea now," the queen said to the waiting footman, then she smiled up at me as I took her outstretched hand and tried to curtsy at the same time I kissed her cheek—a maneuver I had never quite managed to accomplish without bumping my nose.

"Edwina, I don't know whether you have met our cousin Georgiana?"

"I don't believe so, ma'am," the formidable lady said, picking up her lorgnette to examine me more carefully, "but of course I was acquainted with her dear grandmama."

I realized she meant Queen Victoria's daughter, not the grandma who bought her fish and chips on a Friday night from the corner chip shop.

"I'm afraid I never had the chance to meet her," I said, not sure whether she was to be addressed as "ma'am" as well. "She died before I was born."

"Such a pity. A great loss."

"Georgiana, this is one of my oldest friends, Edwina, Duchess of Eynsford."

"Dowager duchess these days, ma'am, now that dear Charles is no longer alive."

"Do take a seat, my dear," the queen said, indicating a low gilt chair beside their sofa. "Tea will be arriving any minute."

I sat cautiously. To one side of the chair was a small lacquer table on top of which were several jade statues. The dowager duchess had folded away her lorgnette. "Oh yes, I can see she'd be perfect," she said to the queen.

It looked as if my fears were coming true. I was to be shipped to be a young companion of some sort to a dowager duchess.

There was a tap at the door and a tea trolley was wheeled in, laden with every kind of delectable tiny sandwich and cake imaginable.

"I hope you have come with a good appetite," the queen said. "It looks as though my chef has surpassed himself."

I almost smiled at the irony of this. I had been to tea with the queen often enough to know that protocol demands that one only eat what Her Majesty eats. And Her Majesty eats very little. I had suffered the agonies of watching those éclairs, Victoria sponges and petit fours sitting untouched while we chewed on pieces of plain, brown bread. Still, food was among the least of my worries today. Another, more alarming thought had entered my mind: Did this dowager duchess perchance have a son who needed a suitable wife? Was that why I was deemed instantly suitable?

The maid poured cups of tea and placed them on a low table in front of the ladies. When she handed me my cup, however, I realized there was no space to rest it on the small table beside me. I would have to balance it on my lap somehow. Oh, golly.

"Help yourselves, my dears," the queen said and took a piece of malt bread herself. To my amazement and delight, the dowager duchess leaned across and put two large cakes on her own plate. "I think I'll dispense with the sandwiches and go straight to the good stuff since I have to dine at the Savoy and there's always so much food," she said.

I was trying to work out how I could lean across to take any kind of food without spilling my tea. I hastily drank the top two inches, although it was a little too hot, and managed to take a watercress sandwich.

"Now, Georgiana," the queen said. "I expect you're wondering what you are doing here with two elderly ladies like us. The truth is that a tricky problem has arisen and you'd be just the person to help sort it out. Would you like to apprise Georgiana of the situation, Edwina?"

"Thank you, ma'am," the Duchess of Eynsford said, wiping cream from the corner of her mouth with her napkin. "You see, Georgiana—if I may call you by your first name—it's like this. Two years ago my dear husband, the Duke of Eynsford, died. The title and property passed to my son Cedric. Cedric is no longer in the first flush of youth; in fact, he is approaching fifty."

My heart rose to my mouth. They want to marry me off to a man of fifty!

"Approaching fifty," she repeated, "and has flatly refused to do his duty and produce an heir. He told his father and me outright that he saw no reason to share his bed with an unappealing horse-faced female just to ensure the continuation of an outmoded title."

"It's the current generation," the queen said and they exchanged a look. "No sense of duty. We were brought up to put duty above all things. When I was told to marry the king's older brother, the Duke of Clarence, I agreed, although I found him not to my taste. Between ourselves, I was most relieved when he died of influenza before the wedding, and it was suggested that I marry his brother instead. His Majesty and I have been most content, which proves that duty need not be a chore."

"We suffer together in our disappointment, don't we, ma'am?" the duchess said. "Each of us with sons unwilling to step up and do their duty for the greater good. Although the Prince of Wales is still young enough to marry and produce the heir."

The queen gave a refined little snort. "He has turned forty, Edwina. And as long as that dreadful Simpson woman is in the picture, he won't even look at another woman. Truly, I sometimes wish we were back in the dark ages, where I could dispatch the royal assassin to dispose of her on a dark night. But then he'd probably find someone else just as disagreeable."

"At least you have other sons," the duchess said. "You already have grandchildren."

"And fine little girls they are too," the queen said, beaming. "There would be no shirking of duty with Elisabeth. She has the right stuff, that one. Fell off her pony the other day trying to jump a fence at Windsor. And do you know what she was worried about—whether the pony had hurt himself!" She shook her head, smiling. "Margaret

Rose—well, I'm not so sure about her. Delightful child, but a mischievous strain too. Hid her grandfather's spectacles the last time she was here. He thought it was funny. But we digress."

She turned back to the duchess. "I'm sorry, Edwina. Please continue."

I had been sitting frozen through this dialogue, trying to think what to say when they suggested that I'd be exactly the right person to marry a fifty-year-old woman hater and give him an heir.

"Is the current duke your only child then, Your Grace?" I asked.

"I have a daughter, Irene. She married a foreigner—an absolute bounder, a Russian count she met in Paris. He worked his way through her fortune then took off for South America with an Argentinian dancer, if you please. Leaving her with three children, and no money to raise them properly. They are living with us at Kingsdowne Place at the moment."

The queen leaned closer to me. "Her Grace's younger son was killed in the war on the Somme," she said. "A most valiant young man. Awarded the VC posthumously after carrying several of his wounded men out of the line of enemy fire."

The duchess was now smiling, which completely transformed her face. "My son John. He was always quite a handful but what a charmer. I can't tell you how many tutors we got through before m'husband sent him to Eton. He was nearly expelled for setting the dormitory on fire, smoking under the sheets. Also got into a spot of trouble while he was up at Oxford. Something to do with cheating on an examination. Johnnie always did like to take risks. So my husband shipped him off to the colonies to make a man of him. He spent a couple of years in the Australian outback doing all kinds of manual work on sheep stations, cattle ranches, God knows what. One rather gathers the lifestyle suited him and if war hadn't broken out, he might never have come home. But the moment war was declared, he caught the first boat back to England and enlisted in his father's old regiment. He was killed within the first few months of fighting."

She stopped, and I watched her fight to compose her features. I waited patiently, wondering what might be coming next.

"So will the title die out with the present duke?" I asked. "Is there no other heir?" I had finished my watercress sandwich and, emboldened by the way that the duchess was stuffing cream cakes, I leaned across and took an éclair. It was light as a feather, with cream oozing out of it.

"That was what we all feared," the duchess went on. "There appeared to be no male heir even among the most remote of cousins. Under the entailment, the title would die out with my son and the estate would revert to the crown. But then about eighteen months ago, we received the most extraordinary letter. It was from a doctor working in the Australian outback, of all places. The newspapers from England containing my husband's obituary had just reached him. He saw that my husband's family name was Altringham—Charles Forsythe Altringham, Duke of Eynsford. He said that he knew a young man working on a sheep station who bore an uncanny resemblance to my late husband. He was reputed to be a relation of nobility and his name was also Altringham—Jack Altringham, to be precise."

She paused and looked up, waiting to see the significance of this in my face. "Jack being the common nickname for John, of course.

"Well," she went on, after taking another quick bite of her cake, "we hired investigators in Australia to look into the matter. John had been there for two years, after all. It was possible that he had fathered a child—but as to being a legitimate heir. . . ." She brushed crumbs from her impressive shelf of bosom before she said, "But it turned out to be true. It seemed he had formed an attachment with a young woman who worked as a schoolteacher in a remote community. When he found that he had"—she lowered her voice and coughed with embarrassment—"that she was in the family way," she corrected, "he did the honorable thing and married her. There was a marriage certificate filed away at some county courthouse. Miss Ida Binns to John

Jestyn Altringham. He left out his title, you notice. Typical John. Always wanted to be ordinary, even though his father told him that he was born to the highest levels of nobility and had to accept it whether he liked it or not." And she wagged a finger at us. I had to admire her pluck at wagging a finger at the queen.

"But that's wonderful," I said. "You now have your heir."

"Well, yes," the duchess said hesitantly. "If one must accept the child of a Miss Ida Binns—a young man who works on an Australian sheep farm—I suppose one must. One simply can't let the title die out."

"This is where you come in, my dear," the queen said.

I had forgotten for a moment that I was somehow to be involved in this matter. What on earth could they want from me now? A suitable marriage for the young sheep farmer?

"How old is this Jack Altringham?" I asked.

"Twenty, so we understand—which would make sense, because John left to come home at the outbreak of war in 1914. He may actually have left Australia before the child was born."

Twenty. Did they want to marry him off before he could get into any trouble?

"And what exactly would you like me to do?" I asked. I took a discreet bite of éclair. Without warning, cream shot out and landed on my front. If the queen and duchess witnessed it, they were too well-bred to say anything. All I could think of was thank heavens it had shot toward me and not onto Her Majesty's brocade sofa, or, worse still, onto HM. I was dying to wipe it off but couldn't do so while their eyes were on me. Also I realized that I held a cup in one hand and the éclair in the other. That left no hand free to pick up a napkin. I felt my face turning red.

"The young man will be completely uncivilized, unused to our kind of society," the duchess said. "He will be overwhelmed by Kingsdowne Place and our way of life. We thought that someone his own age—someone who has been brought up to the highest social standards—could show him the ropes and help him to learn his new position in life. He will find you less intimidating than an old dragon like me."

The cream was now sliding down the front of my white blouse. Maybe they hadn't noticed. If they had, I was hardly exhibiting those highest standards of social behavior at this moment. I half expected the dowager duchess to say that she had changed her mind and wanted someone who didn't squirt cream to educate her heir.

"So what do you say, Georgiana?" the queen asked. "Do you feel up to the task?"

"Oh, absolutely," I said. I put the half-eaten éclair into my saucer and reached to set down the cup and saucer on the low table by the sofa.

"Splendid," Her Grace said. "I am delighted. A load off my mind, if you must know. If you are free to travel immediately, I am staying tonight at our house on Eaton Place, dining with friends at the Savoy and return to Kingsdowne in the morning. You can travel down to Kent in the Bentley with me."

Kent, I thought. The garden of England. How lovely. For once I seemed to have fallen on my feet. Surreptitiously I picked up my napkin from my lap and dabbed at my blouse. As I lifted my elbow I must have knocked the table beside me. Out of the corner of my eye I saw the dragon figurine teeter. I reached out and made a successful grab for it as it was about to fall. Then I turned back to the two ladies.

"Thank you. I'll be ready in the morning," I said, giving them what I hoped was a confident smile.

"Jolly good. Splendid," the duchess said.

"Oh yes. Jolly good," the queen echoed. I thought she looked a little pale.

Chapter 4

CHELSEA AND EN ROUTE TO KENT

That evening, I was supervising the packing of my belongings, not wanting to leave anything to the next morning. I had discovered that leaving Queenie to pack my things could be a disastrous mistake. I remembered the time she had wrapped my riding boots, still muddy, with my one good evening gown. And she always managed to leave something out. So I went around the house after her, opening drawers and calling her attention to left objects. Each time she had to reopen the trunk, she said "Sorry, miss," and stuffed the object down the side, not caring what she crumpled in the process. I was becoming more and more short-tempered with her.

"And look, Queenie, here are my best silk stockings," I said. "Careful with them. Where is the tissue paper?"

"All gone, miss. Never mind. I'll shove them inside your shoes."

I bit my tongue and took deep breaths. "And you do have my jewelry case? I think I'd better take it with me in the motorcar."

"Yes, you'd better," she said. "I don't know how I'm going to manage all this stuff as it is."

"I've told you. You hire a porter and have him load it into the train carriage for you. You will be met at Swanley Junction station. You will remember that, won't you?"

"Yes, miss. I expect so."

"And don't fall asleep or you'll wake up in Dover."

"I can't help it, miss. I always get that sleepy on a train." She stopped, mouth open, as her brain digested something. "'Ere. What about that typewriting machine of yours? You can't expect me to carry that. It weighs a bloomin' ton."

"Oh, golly." I'd quite forgotten it myself, sitting forlorn in the study downstairs. "I certainly don't want to abandon it. Maybe the duchess can find a place for it in the boot."

I was just on my way down to examine the typewriter when there was a thunderous knock at the front door. I opened it and Belinda stood there, dressed up to the nines in a startling, floor-length black opera cape, a black, feathered cap over one eye and a long, black cigarette holder.

"Come on, darling. Buck up and get changed," she said. "We're going on the town."

"Belinda, I've just packed all my belongings," I said. "I'm going to the country tomorrow."

"You can unpack them again, can't you? Come on, Georgie. It's going to be fun. An American businessman is taking me to dinner and dancing at the Savoy. And he said he had a friend in town and did I have a friend. So naturally I thought of you. They are dripping in dollars, darling. We'll have a fabulous time."

"It is tempting," I said. "I haven't eaten properly in a week. But I simply can't leave Queenie to finish my packing."

"Of course you can. When are you departing?"

"Tomorrow morning. A dowager duchess is coming for me in her motorcar. I couldn't be late."

"A dowager duchess? Darling, you're not really going to be a companion, are you?"

"Not exactly."

She came into the hall and took my arm. "Come on. Upstairs. You can tell me all about it as you get dressed."

"Belinda," I said hesitantly. "This evening—it does just involve dinner and dancing, doesn't it? These American businessmen will not be expecting more than that?"

"Darling, they are always the soul of propriety. Especially since I told them that you were the king's cousin. They'll treat you with kid gloves and we'll get a slap-up meal. And you never know—one of them may be the sugar daddy that I'm looking for."

"Belinda, you're wicked," I said, laughing.

"So you'll come then?"

"Why not?"

I extracted my good evening dress and shoes, much to Queenie's annoyance. "I got all them things laid in there nice and proper," she said, "and now you go and muck the whole lot up again."

"That maid of yours is becoming too big for her boots," Belinda said as we left in a taxicab. "Familiarity breeds contempt. She'll have to go."

"The trouble is, I can't afford to replace her," I said. "Essentially she works for her keep. I'd never find another maid who'd do that."

Belinda slipped her arm through mine. "Forget about maids. We're going to have a glorious time."

We did. Lovely food, a good band, a man who held me as if I was made of porcelain when we danced and kept calling me "Your Highness." I wasn't in bed until two. So I was a little bleary-eyed when Queenie woke me the next morning saying, "I've managed to stuff your dress and shoes in that big trunk but the old bat won't give me a hand with it down the stairs."

I leaped up, washed, dressed in my traveling tweeds and helped Queenie bring down the trunk. I could hardly let her bump it all the way down by herself. If Mrs. Tombs thought she was getting a tip, she could think again. I saw Queenie off in her taxicab literally one minute before the duchess arrived. I heaved a sigh of relief that they hadn't crossed paths. Somehow I didn't think the duchess would approve of Queenie.

"You're off then, are you?" Mrs. Tombs asked as she appeared from the kitchen. "Righty-o. I suppose I've got to give your room a good clean now."

Then she caught sight of the Bentley with the chauffeur in dark-green uniform standing at the front door. "Blimey," she said.

"Here we are," Her Grace called, waving cheerfully from the backseat. "Wilkins will load in your things. Hop on in."

Wilkins was as elderly as the Bentley and looked frail enough for the wind to blow him away. I felt horribly guilty as I watched him stagger toward the boot, carrying my typewriter.

"What on earth is that monstrosity?" Her Grace asked.

"My typewriter. I'm learning how to type."

"Gracious. What on earth for? It's not as if a girl of your standing will ever need to find a job." She patted my knee. "Take my advice and leave the typing to the lower classes, my dear."

I thought she was going to forbid me to take the machine but Wilkins had already installed it, and even she wasn't cruel enough to ask him to remove it again.

The drive down to Kent was part delight and part terror. I don't think Wilkins's vision was that good and he received constant instructions from the dowager duchess, which made the drive even more precarious.

"I know that silly policeman is holding up his hand to stop traffic," she boomed into her speaking tube from the backseat, "but that can't possibly apply to us. He must see that we're the kind of people who should not be kept waiting. Drive straight past, Wilkins."

And I closed my eyes as we headed at full speed into the path of a lorry, which swerved to avoid us at the last second while we sailed on, the duchess apparently oblivious to the chaos behind her. I believe the policeman blew his whistle, but we were long gone. When we came to a railway level crossing at which the gates were being closed,

I was relieved that Wilkins wisely refused to make the gatekeeper open them again as the express from Dover came thundering through a few seconds later. In fact, I began to wish that I had taken the train with Queenie and the luggage.

The terror was compounded by the close proximity to the dowager duchess, who peppered me with questions and regaled me with comments about people I didn't know.

"So did you go to school or did you have a governess? No point in overeducating girls, that's what I always say. Nothing more dangerous than an educated woman. In my day, speaking French, riding and playing the pianoforte were all that was required of a girl. So you've come out, I take it? Had any interesting proposals? Have you seen anything of the Devonshires recently? Is it true what they plan to do to Chatsworth?"

I stumbled through the answers under the glare of her eagle eye, made larger as she stared through the lorgnette.

"Never met the Devonshires? I thought everybody knew them. And the Westminsters. Where have you been hiding yourself? You must get out into society more if you're to make a good match."

She peered at me through the lorgnette. "And your small talk is sadly lacking. One needs small talk, my dear, if one wants to flourish in society," she said. "I don't hold with idle gossip, but one should be au fait with what is going on. Apropos of which, what do you think about this latest chapter in the saga of the Prince of Wales?"

I was grateful for once that I could join in this discussion and mentioned that I knew Mrs. Simpson.

"You've actually met the woman, have you?"

When I told her that the Simpsons had actually stayed at our Scottish castle, I could see my stock rise in her eyes. "So that she could be near HRH at Balmoral, of course," she said, nodding conspiratorially. "The woman astounds me with her brazenness. And married to someone else too. Has she no shame?"

I replied that I didn't think she had.

"Surely the boy will come to his senses before his father dies," she said. "My son's defiance only means the loss of a title, but in the prince's case it's the whole future of the monarchy at stake. Why couldn't he just do what his ancestors have always done—marry someone suitable and then keep a mistress?" She lifted her lorgnette and stared at me. "He could have married someone like you. It's not as if you're first cousins."

"Much as I like my cousin David, I intend to marry for love," I said.

She snorted. "What a curious notion. Got a young fellow in mind, have you?"

"Well, yes."

"Not the son of the stable boy, one hopes."

"No. His father is a peer."

"Well, that's all right, then. So many young people have the most curious ideas on equality these days. You read about it all the time in the lesser newspapers, don't you? Young men and women of our class marrying typists and jockeys and actresses. Don't they realize that the future of the empire depends on a stable aristocracy?"

I thought it wise not to mention that my father had married an actress. Actually, I'm sure she knew. It would have made good gossip in its day—as would my mother's subsequent bolt. I also stayed silent about Darcy's lack of money or prospects. I found myself thinking about Darcy, wondering where he was and when I would see him again. How would I ever get in touch with him? I wondered. How would he find out I was in the depths of the Kentish countryside? I just wished he was better about writing letters, but then I realized that a lot of his trips were supposed to be hush-hush and he probably couldn't tell me where he was and what he was doing. I sighed. Why did romance have to be so complicated?

I stared out of the window, watching the grimy streets of London give way to suburban rows and then, just after we passed through the town of Sidcup, suddenly we were in the countryside. There were orchards on either side of us, some of them sprinkled with early blossoms. The first primroses were appearing beside the road as we came down a long hill and left the main road at the village of Farningham. Then we were driving through a leafy valley with a stream at the bottom until we came to the village of Eynsford itself. It was the quintessential English village with a pub and village shop, nestled beside an old packhorse bridge that crossed the stream. To one side of the bridge was the even more ancient ford that gave the village its name. Two little boys were standing at the edge of the stream with jars that looked as if they might contain tadpoles. Then we left the village behind, and the valley narrowed. Above us, the skeletons of ancient beech and oak trees were showing new spring leaves.

"Almost there now," the duchess said as we turned off the road and started to climb the hill. "I think you'll like Kingsdowne. Lovely old house. Not been ruined by Victorian opulence and lack of taste, thank God."

We emerged from the woods to more open farmland and then before us was a high, brick wall and in it an impressive gateway—an enormous arch topped with great stone lions. As we approached it, a man came rushing out of the gate house and the wrought-iron gate was opened for us. Then we drove for a good half-mile through parkland before there was any sign of the house. Through the trees I spotted what looked like the antlers of a herd of deer.

"Knole likes to think they have a better deer park than us," she said, referring to another nearby stately home, "but they don't have fallow deer or Chitral deer, which we had shipped back from India when my husband was viceroy."

Then the drive turned a corner, and I think I actually gasped. There was the house—an enormous and elegant building of mellowed gray stone, four stories high and beautifully proportioned, surrounded by manicured lawns and formal gardens. In front of the pillared main entrance was an ornamental lake complete with swans. The house was set on a rising slope of hillside, which at this time of year was covered in a carpet of daffodils. As we came out of the trees, the sun appeared from behind the clouds and suddenly the house was perfectly reflected in the lake. My spirit soared. I was going to be staying at this attractive place for the immediate future, with duties no more onerous than teaching a young Australian which fork to use at dinner. For once I could look forward to an enjoyable time ahead.

As the motorcar crunched over the gravel of the forecourt, the duchess suddenly turned to me. "I think it best if we don't let the family know the real reason for your being here, don't you? They haven't yet come to terms with the fact that a complete stranger will be coming into their midst, which may mean the end of life as they know it."

"So how do you propose to explain my presence?" I asked.

"Suitably vague, I think. Old friends with your royal grandmother and invited you to stay for a while. Maybe recuperating from an illness and needed good, country air. Yes, I think that should do it."

I wondered why we needed a good reason to invite me until I realized that of course it was no longer her house. It was presumably up to her son, the present duke, to do the inviting. And he was a self-confessed woman hater. I wondered what he'd say about my arrival.

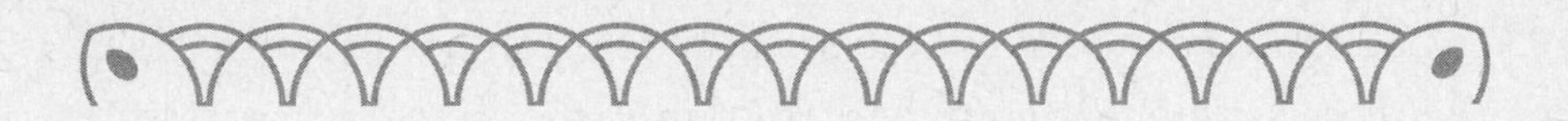

Chapter 5

Kingsdowne Place, Eynsford, Kent

Dear Diary, I have fallen on my feet for once. It's gorgeous.

As the Bentley came to a halt outside the front steps, a bevy of footmen rushed out to open the doors for us.

"Welcome to Kingsdowne Place, my lady," one said, assisting me from the backseat. He was dressed in a smart, black livery with gold buttons. It was almost like being back at Buckingham Palace. Another footman was attempting to assist the dowager duchess from her seat.

"I am not quite an invalid yet, Frederick," she said. "There is no need to lug me from the backseat like a sack of coals."

"Sorry, Your Grace." The boy turned scarlet.

"Come along, my dear," she said to me, using her cane to stride up the steps ahead of me. We entered a magnificent foyer. In the center a broad staircase ascended to a landing, where it divided in two to rise to the next level. The walls and ceiling were painted with enormous Renaissance-style Italianate murals of Greek gods and goddesses. While I tried not to gawp, the duchess said, "I don't suppose your maid has arrived yet with your things, so you won't be able to change for luncheon. But I'll have Frederick show you up to your room so that you can have a wash and brushup after the journey."

Oh, Lord. They didn't change for luncheon here, did they? Did that mean something for the morning, an afternoon tea dress for tea, a dinner gown *and* something different for luncheon?

I was relieved when she added, "One's clothes do get so crumpled on the journey that I always like to have them pressed as soon as possible."

I gave her a weak smile.

"And when you're ready come down to the Long Gallery. I'll have sandwiches and coffee served there. I expect you're famished after that long trip."

It hadn't been much more than an hour, but I'd avoided Mrs. Tombs's earlier, halfhearted attempt at breakfast and was certainly ready to eat. Frederick picked up my overnight bag and jewelry case and set off up the grand stair. I followed, finding it hard to take my eyes off the voluptuous, half-nude figures and cupids that covered the walls and ceiling. At the first landing, we turned to the left and set off down a hallway, which seemed to go on forever. Along the walls the Altringham ancestors glared down at me from their portraits, each one with the bulging, pale eyes that were obviously an inherited trait. From the look of some of them, I wondered if insanity might also be an inherited trait, in which case a breath of fresh air and fresh blood from Australia might be a good thing.

At last Frederick opened a door and I stepped into a spacious and elegant room. No Victorian frou-frou and bric-a-brac here—the furniture had the clean lines of the Georgians, the four-poster bed was covered in a blue-and-white, silken counterpane. There were two chintz-covered ladies' chairs around the marble fireplace, and a pretty little Queen Anne writing desk sat in one of the bay windows. Really it was the most inviting bedroom I had ever seen—a room in which one could easily stay for a month or more.

Frederick put down my cases on a bench. "I don't know if Her Grace will be wanting to move you to somewhere more suitable," he said. "We only heard you were coming last night so we were told to put you in one of the guest rooms for now."

If this wasn't suitable, I wondered what was. And in case you think I wasn't used to staying at the best houses, I'd actually stayed at Balmoral with the king and queen every August. It was a requirement of being related to the royals. And trust me, Balmoral is Spartan compared to this—and one has to endure tartan carpets! I had also stayed at a wide variety of stately homes and family seats, but for sheer opulence and elegance this was going to be hard to beat. It struck me that there was still a significant family fortune connected to this title. As I looked out of the window, I heard the crunch of more tires on gravel and wondered if it could be Queenie arriving from the station. But instead a brand-spanking-new Rolls-Royce was pulling up. A chauffeur in a smart, green uniform leaped out and came around to open the back door. Out of it stepped a portly, middle-aged man. He was dressed in a black-velvet jacket and rather baggy trousers. He stood, looking around and as if on cue, three young men came bounding like colts from behind a high hedge in the formal side garden. They too were dressed in black, form-fitting garments, and the way they moved made me think I was watching a ballet in progress. They greeted the portly man with hugs, dancing around him like a group of greyhounds, greeting their master.

I wondered if I was indeed looking at the master of this house. At least this current scene might explain his refusal to marry! After a sheltered youth such things no longer shocked me. Mummy's good friend was Noël Coward and I had been to parties with his cronies, and I had met plenty of young men who would probably also never marry. Actually I enjoyed the witty banter and the air of urbanity—so remote from the austere halls of Castle Rannoch, where I was raised by a God-fearing, hellfire-breathing Presbyterian nanny.

I remembered that the dowager duchess was probably waiting for me downstairs. There was even a washbasin with hot and cold running water in one corner of the room and I removed my hat, washed my face and hands and brushed my hair. But I was rather in need of a lavatory. I glanced at the bell that hung beside my bed on a brocade pull. One tug would bring a servant running, but surely I could locate the nearest bathroom without help? I had just come out of my door when I heard the swish of starched skirts and a maid came toward me, carrying a pile of sheets.

"Can I help you, my lady?" she asked.

I mentioned that I was looking for the bathroom, having been brought up by Nanny not to mention unmentionable words like "lavatory."

"This way, please. Not far at all. I put you in the nicest of the guest rooms for now," she said. "I hope it meets with your approval."

"It's lovely, thank you. . . ." I gave her an inquiring look.

"Elsie, my lady. Elsie Hobbs, head housemaid. Let me know if there's anything that you need, and I'll take care of it."

She had a pleasant, open face and she was giving me a genuine smile. "Actually there is something," I said. "My maid will be arriving shortly. I'm afraid she's still . . . a little raw around the edges. And in a great house like this, she may need a little instruction in how to behave."

"Don't worry, my lady. I'll take her under my wing. It was terrifying for all of us when we first came here."

"Have you been here long, Elsie?"

"Fifteen years, my lady. I came as a girl of fourteen, right after leaving school. My dad was killed in the war so I had to go out to work to support my mum."

"I'm sorry."

"Oh, I'm not. I landed on my feet here. Her Grace may be strict and demand a high standard from us, but she's a fair mistress."

"What about the present duke?"

"His Grace doesn't show that much interest in the running of the household—unless we do something wrong. Then we hear about it.

He sacked poor William on the spot last week because he tidied up the papers on His Grace's desk so he could dust it, and apparently he changed the order of pages. I mean, how was he to know?"

I nodded in sympathy.

"And he'd been here longer than me as well. Came here right after being sent home wounded from the Somme."

She stopped and pushed open a door, showing me a bathroom containing a tub almost big enough to swim in, and a next-door lavatory. I made use of this before I retraced my steps back to the grand staircase. I was standing in that central foyer, wondering where the Long Gallery might be when a most imposing figure in a black frock coat appeared. I'd been in enough great houses, including our own, to know that butlers often look grander than their masters.

"Welcome to Kingsdowne, my lady," he said with a small bow. "I am Huxstep, His Grace's butler. I must apologize for not being here to greet you on your arrival. I did not hear the motorcar, as I was in the wine cellar and my hearing is not what it used to be. Her Grace asked me to escort you through to the Long Gallery."

I followed him through an archway to the right and found that the Long Gallery was well named. It stretched away in front of me with great, arched windows that sent in shafts of slanting sunlight at intervals. It was wood paneled with an exquisite gilded and carved wood ceiling. I guessed that it had been the great hall of the original house. In the center of the long wall, an enormous marble fireplace, big enough to roast an ox, rose to the ceiling, a log fire burning merrily in the grate. There were clusters of sofas and chairs placed at intervals along the length of the room and at one of these clusters, close to the fireplace, the dowager duchess was now seated, working her way through a pile of sandwiches and biscuits. She motioned for me to join her.

"Is the room to your liking?" she asked. "It was all so very last-minute that I didn't have time to think where you would be most comfortable."

"Thank you, it's a lovely room. I shall be quite comfortable there, I assure you."

"The view is better from the other side of the house," she said, "but that seems to have become our bachelor wing—my son's guests, you understand."

"I think I saw them just now. They came running up when a Rolls appeared."

"Did you?" She pursed her lips in disapproving fashion. "That would be my son returning from town. He went up to London to see a show in the West End. He was a benefactor, so I understand. He sees himself as a Medici—a great patron of the arts." She gave a contemptuous sniff. "Hasn't an ounce of talent himself, of course, but that doesn't stop him from composing dreadful music and painting dreadful pictures and surrounding himself with those obnoxious young men." She looked up from her sandwich. "The Starlings, they call themselves. I haven't decided whether they think they are future stars in terms of the arts, or whether they simply dress in black and twitter a lot."

I had to smile.

"Black or white?" Her Grace said, indicating to a maid that she should pour coffee.

"Oh, white please, at this time of day."

A cup of milky coffee was placed in front of me and I reached forward to take a ham sandwich. One thing was clear—I was not going to starve in this place. After Fig's austerity measures and then Mrs. Tombs's cooking, I felt like I was in heaven.

Her Grace looked up at the sound of heavy footsteps. "That will be my son now. No mention of why you're here. He's not the easiest of people, and he doesn't take kindly to my meddling."

I looked up as the Duke of Eynsford came toward us. He was probably once a moderately good-looking man, now gone to seed. His face was podgy, with extra chins and his black velvet jacket was buttoned tightly over an impressive paunch. His hair was already thinning but combed across his bald spot, making him look older than his forty-nine years.

"Hello, Mother," he said. "Opening night was a resounding success. The critics loved it. I shall reap a handsome little amount for my investment, as well as introducing the world to a brilliant new playwright." He stopped as he suddenly noticed me. "Hello," he said. "I see we have visitors."

"Just one visitor, Cedric," the dowager countess said. "This is Georgiana Rannoch. You remember that her grandmother, Queen Victoria's daughter, was most kind to me when I was a new lady-in-waiting."

"Oh yes. Right." He could not have looked less interested, and I wondered if it crossed his mind that I might have been brought down here in a last, desperate attempt to marry him off to someone suitable. He came over and held out a limp hand. "How do you do? I'm Cedric, as I'm sure she's told you. Your brother is the present Duke of Rannoch, isn't he? I don't think I've ever seen him at the House of Lords."

"Binky rarely comes down from Scotland," I said. "He's not very comfortable in a big city."

"Can't think why not," Cedric said. He reached over, grabbed a sandwich and stuffed it into his mouth in one go. "Cities are where all the action is—the pulse of life of a nation. Art. Culture. Theater. They are what make a nation come alive." He looked at me appraisingly. "So, are you just passing through? Paying a courtesy call upon Mama?"

Before I could answer this, the dowager duchess said for me, "She may be staying for a while, Cedric. The poor little thing has been under the weather. I told her she needs good food and country air to build her up again."

"Oh, I'm sorry to hear that," he said, leaving it to me to judge whether he was sorry I'd been under the weather or sorry that I'd be staying. I rather thought the latter.

"And it might be helpful to have another young person in the house when your nephew arrives," she said glibly, as if this had just occurred to her. "He'll find it overwhelmingly strange and I presume quite terrifying, poor boy."

"My nephew," Cedric said with a snort of contempt. "If he *is* my nephew. I'm still not convinced. Those Australians would sell their grandmother for tuppence."

"I'm sure we'll know when we see him," the dowager said. "Supposedly he has a strong family resemblance. And since you're not doing your part to produce an heir . . ."

"Don't start on that again, Mother," he said. "You know my sentiments. And I don't see why I can't leave my fortune as I choose. I'd much rather a new concert hall or theater than the continuation of a dreary dukedom."

"Fortunately you have no choice in the matter," she said in a clipped voice. I was beginning to feel uncomfortable when Cedric looked out of the window and said, "Good God. What on earth is that?"

An estate car had drawn up and out of it stepped Queenie. She was wearing a red hat that looked like an overturned flowerpot and an old overcoat made of the spiky fur of God knows what kind of animal—hyena would be my best guess. The dowager duchess turned to the window and raised her lorgnette in surprise.

"Oh, it's my maid with the luggage," I said.

"Your maid? You let her go around looking like an oversized hedgehog with a flowerpot on its head?" Her Grace demanded.

"She will be wearing her uniform underneath, but I haven't yet got around to buying her a new overcoat," I said, not wanting to confess that I had no money for such items.

"Oh, she's new, is she?"

"Fairly," I said.

"Then, my dear, the sooner you take her in hand and train her, the better," Her Grace said. "You can't let maids ape their betters in fur coats. It simply isn't done. And a coat like that . . . well, it reflects on you in the end. I will ask the housekeeper if we have a suitable discarded black overcoat in the servant's cupboard that she can wear if she has to leave the building again."

Queenie was now looking up at the imposing façade, her mouth wide open, as an estate worker hauled my trunks from the back of the vehicle. I rose to my feet. "I think I had better go and show her where to put my things."

"And be firm about suitable attire," the dowager called after me. "It is never wise to give servants any leeway in the matter of individuality or they abuse it, as your girl has done." She pronounced the word "gell," as did all the women of her era, and she wagged a finger at me. "Their job is to be invisible and to conform at all times."

I hurried out to bustle Queenie away from the dowager's critical eyes and up the stairs.

"Blimey," she said as we entered my bedroom. "We ain't half fallen on our feet 'ere, eh, miss? Now this is how real toffs are supposed to live. Not like your bloomin' sister-in-law and her one piece of toast per person."

"Queenie, remember what I have told you?" I said. "If you can't speak politely of your betters, I might have to let you go."

"Garn," she said, digging me in the ribs. "I know you can't afford a proper maid."

"I'm sure I could find one less improper than you," I said with a frown. "Now, please unpack my things. Ask the servants where you can find an ironing board and iron and make sure everything is well pressed. Oh, and Queenie—remember, one does not iron velvet on the right side, and please, no more burn marks on my white blouses."

"Bob's yer uncle," she said.

At the door I remembered something and turned back. "Oh and one more thing—this is a great household of the highest social order. The servants here will be well-trained and refined, so please do try to behave like a real lady's maid and don't let me down."

"Don't worry, me lady. I can talk posh and walk around with me bleedin' nose in the air with the best of 'em if I want to."

"And Queenie—no swear words."

I left her to it and went downstairs again. As I approached the Long Gallery, I heard Cedric's clipped voice saying, "Exactly why is she here, Mother? This had better not be one of your little schemes."

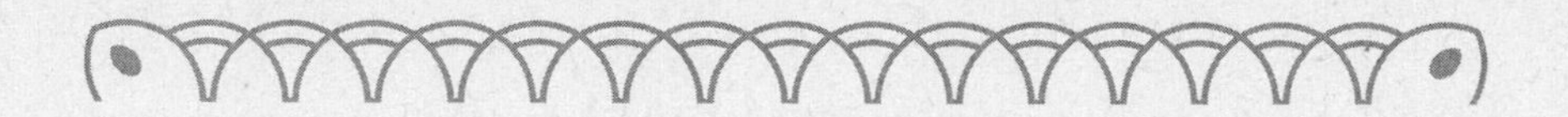

Chapter 6

Kingsdowne Place

Instead of entering the Long Gallery, I turned quickly on my heel and went down the front steps and out into the fresh air. A stiff breeze had now come up and the sun had vanished behind a bank of rather threatening clouds. I wondered if I was being foolish in striking out across the grounds but I didn't want to be part of the unpleasantness in the Long Gallery. If I'd known my presence would cause disruptions in the family, I wouldn't have come. Then I corrected that sentiment. I would still rather be here than up in bleak Scotland with Fig.

I followed the edge of the lake, admiring the easy way the swans drifted across the black water, until I came to a little stream that entered, bubbling over rocks. I heard the sound of rushing water and followed the stream down from the lake until I came to a series of pretty cascades in a rocky glen. It reminded me of my native Scotland until I realized that this whole landscape must be an artificial creation as such glens are not normally part of the Kentish scenery.

Above the cascades I spotted a round, white temple, half hidden amid dark yew trees. Some former duke with an eye for the dramatic had obviously been at work here. I was finding my way out of the cascade glen when I heard the distant sound of a clock chiming noon.

I remembered what the dowager duchess had said about changing for lunch and realized I had better get back.

As I crossed the lawn I heard voices behind me—young voices. Before I could turn around, one of them called out, "You there!"

I stopped and turned to look back. Two children, a boy and a girl, were running together up the slope toward the house, followed by a worried, youngish man in a tweed jacket who was striding out to keep pace with them. They were around ten or eleven, both with pale blonde hair and rather surly faces.

"Yes, you." It was the boy addressing me. "I left my history book on the bench under the big oak tree. Go and fetch it for me."

The worried-looking man had caught up with them. "Really, Nicholas, you can go back and get it yourself," he said. "You can't expect people to fetch and carry for you."

"Of course I can. What else is she doing right now?" the boy demanded. "And I'd be late for luncheon if I went to fetch it myself, and you know that makes Grandmama cross."

Initially I had been too stunned to react. Now I didn't know whether to be annoyed or amused. "Do you always order around your grandmother's guests?" I said.

"I say—you're not a guest, are you?" His expression faltered. "We thought you were her new companion. She was talking about finding a new companion when she went up to town and we saw you arrive with her, so naturally we assumed . . ."

"Never assume," I said. "I'm actually Lady Georgiana Rannoch, and your grandmama invited me to stay."

"You've really put your foot in it this time, Nick," the girl said, nudging him and looking pleased at his red face.

"Sorry," the boy said easily. "But my father is a Russian count, you know. He had to flee for his life during the revolution. And my grandfather was a duke, so I have to get used to ordering people around."

"My grandmother was a princess," I said, "and my great-grandmother was Queen Victoria, so I think I win on that count. And my cousins the king and queen are always most polite in the way they address their staff."

He turned beet red now. "Crikey," he said. "Then you're royal. Does one have to call you ma'am?"

I was very tempted to say yes. And that he had to bow every time he saw me, but since he was now squirming with embarrassment I said, "Actually I'm not an HRH, I'm only a lady. And since we are social equals it would be fine for you to use my first name."

"Oh, jolly good," he said. He stuck out his hand. "I am Nikolai Gregorovitch, son of Count Streletzki, formerly of Russia."

"And I am Ekaterina," the girl said, holding out her hand too. "But Uncle Cedric said it was pretentious to have such names and we have to be called Katherine and Nicholas."

"It probably is easier if you're to go to school in England," I said.

"But so ordinary, don't you think?" Nicholas said. "Our father was not at all ordinary."

"He was a very handsome man," Katherine added.

"So you're Irene's children," I said. "Don't you have another sister?"

"Sissy," Nicholas said. "It's really Elisabeth but everyone calls her Sissy. It was too cold for her to be out today, and none of the servants was free to push her wheelchair."

"Wheelchair?" I asked.

"She fell off her horse and broke her back," Katherine said. "Now she can't walk. It's terribly boring for her."

"Poor thing. It would be. Perhaps I can keep her company while I'm here."

"Mummy wants to take her to Switzerland where there's a good doctor, but Uncle Cedric says it would be a waste of time and cost too much money," Katherine said. "I don't think he likes us very much and he doesn't really want us here."

"I think it would be a waste of money too," Nicholas said. "I mean, we all know she won't walk again. The money should be spent sending me to a decent school."

"What about me?" Katherine said. "I want to go to school too."

"There's no point in educating girls," Nicholas said. "Uncle Cedric said so. They only get married and don't do anything useful."

"I'm as clever as you!" Katherine said. "In fact, I'm cleverer. Uncle Cedric is stupid."

"Both of you stop talking such rubbish and hurry up," the man said. "Or your grandmother will blame me again. And she'll make you go without your pudding."

They ran on ahead at this dire news. The man gave me an embarrassed grin and held out his hand. "I'm Carter, the tutor, my lady. They've been running wild for years before I was engaged. No sense of discipline or decorum, and hopelessly uneducated. You've heard the family history, I suppose. Their mother dotes on them. Their father alternately spoiled them and ignored them, and of course then deserted them. So it's no wonder that Nick's such a confused little boy. His uncle, the duke, isn't exactly helping to provide a good male role model. So I'm trying to do what I can, but it's uphill work."

"I'm sure it is," I said. "I'll see what I can do to help while I'm here."

"You're most kind, my lady," he said and gave me a very nice smile.

As I came into the hallway, I saw Huxstep sorting the post, which had just arrived.

"Did you have a good walk, my lady?" he asked. "A brisk morning. I hope you were not too cold without your overcoat."

"I come from Scotland. This is considered a balmy day," I said.

He managed a polite twitch of the mouth as he carried the tray of letters through to a study. I went upstairs and changed into a kilt and white blouse, which, while not fashionable, were at least clean and presentable. I had just finished dressing when a gong sounded. We were being summoned to luncheon. I gave my hair a final brush then set off down the hallway. As I approached the staircase, two elderly ladies were coming toward me, arm in arm, from the other direction. They looked at me in surprise.

"I say, we've got a visitor. How jolly," one of them said. My mother's phrase "mutton dressed as lamb" came to mind. The one who had spoken was wearing clothes that would have been risqué ten years ago—a flapper dress that showed too much leg, long strings of beads and far too much makeup. "Did you come down from town with Edwina?"

"Er—yes," I said.

"You see, what did I tell you? The spirits never lie," the other one said. She was still dressed in the fashion of the good old days, such as my grandmother would have worn—a long, black dress with a high collar, an impossibly small waist and several rows of good pearls around her neck. Her luxurious, gray hair was piled high on her head in coils and held in place with tortoiseshell combs. She was looking at me with interest. "They said a stranger was coming into our midst, didn't they?"

"We thought that meant the boy from Australia, didn't we?" the painted one said. "Didn't the spirits say the stranger in our midst meant danger?"

"Oh dear, yes. The cuckoo coming into the nest. How worrying." She peered at me. "But this young lady doesn't look at all dangerous, does she? Quite charming, in fact. What is your name, my dear?"

"Georgiana Rannoch."

"You see, I knew. The spirits said something about being reunited with an old friend, and I used to know her grandfather, the old duke. What a terrifying fellow he was. There was some talk of my marrying him, but then the queen snapped him up for her daughter. I was rather relieved, actually. Much happier with poor Orlovski." She held out her hand to me. It was shrunken and wrinkled like a claw, and absolutely dripping with rings. "How do you do. I am Princess Orlovski, Edwina's sister."

"How do you do, Your Highness," I said, not quite sure if I was supposed to curtsy.

"And I am the Countess Von Eisenheim, the youngest sister," the painted one said. "By far the youngest. Actually Mummy and Daddy's afterthought. I can't tell you how glad I am that you've come to visit. Life is so incredibly dull here after the society of Vienna and Paris that one was used to. Our sister's husband became an awful stick-in-the-mud in his later years, and his son is even worse. The only people he invites down here are dreadful, common young men who are artists or writers. We haven't had a decent ball in years, have we, Charlotte?"

"Not in years," the princess said with a sigh.

While we talked we had been making our way slowly down the broad staircase, the sisters arm in arm and taking little, careful steps. We had just reached the bottom when Huxstep appeared in the foyer and sounded the gong again.

"The second gong, Charlotte. We mustn't be late," the painted one said, and they picked up the pace to a speed that made me fear for them—flying down the steps on dainty, little feet. They arrived safely, however, and I followed them into the dining room. The dowager duchess had already taken her place at the far end of an enormous table that would easily have seated fifty.

"Ah, Georgiana. Do come and sit down. Over here beside me. You've met my sisters, I see. Charlotte had a narrow escape from Russia when the revolution broke out. Her husband, the prince, wasn't so lucky."

"Hacked to pieces in front of my eyes," the princess said. "I'll never get that image from my mind. Never. And I was to be next, but a loyal retainer snatched me up into a carriage and galloped off with me. I left with the clothes on my back, nothing more."

I gave her a sympathetic nod.

"And Virginia came to live with us after the war. Her late husband's money was in German banks and of course it became worthless." The duchess gave me a knowing look. "Until then she had been quite the merry widow, hadn't you, Virginia?"

"I've had my moments, Edwina," Virginia said. "Oh yes, I've certainly had my moments."

"And I'd prefer that you didn't recount them to my grandchildren in such detail," Edwina said. "I was shocked to the core at what Katherine came out with the other day."

Virginia laughed. "Oh, yes. That little incident with me and a regiment of Hussars. She was rather impressed with it, I could see."

The duchess gave an embarrassed cough. "Speaking of my grandchildren, I see they are late again. As is their mother."

"No we're not, Mama. Right on the stroke of one." A younger woman came into the room, followed by two subdued children. She was more than slim; she was gaunt, with her collarbones showing above the neck of her dress. She looked flustered and her forehead was creased in a worried frown. "Go and sit down, children," she said.

They scrambled into their seats.

"Where is Elisabeth?" Edwina asked.

"Not feeling too well today, Mama. Nanny is having a tray sent up to her room."

"She needs to get outside more, Irene. You can't mollycoddle her like this. Good, fresh air every day."

Huxstep, the butler, appeared behind the dowager duchess. "Should I have the soup brought in, Your Grace? Will His Grace and friends be joining you?"

"I have no idea, Huxstep," she said. "My son does not consult me in his comings and goings. So yes, please do go ahead and have the soup served. If they come now, they will just have to miss the first course."

Tureens were brought in by two footmen, and a clear consommé was ladled into the Royal Doulton bowl in front of me. I sensed Irene looking at me with interest and I nodded a smile.

"How do you do," I said. I was about to introduce myself when the dowager duchess said, "Irene, Nicholas, Katherine—you haven't met our guest. Georgiana Rannoch—her grandmother was very kind to me when I was a young lady-in-waiting to the old queen. I've invited her to stay for a while."

"We already met her outside," Nicholas said, as if scoring a point.

"Really, Mama, you're wasting your time, you know," Irene said.

"What on earth do you mean?"

"If you're thinking of her as a potential bride for Cedric, there is no chance."

"I assure you I have no interest in becoming Duchess of Eynsford," I said. "My taste in men is very different."

"I agree with you, my dear," Virginia said. "Why would one want to look twice at an unattractive man when there are so many handsome ones in the world?"

"When I was young, we married out of duty," Edwina said. "We were told whom we should marry and we did so. "

"I married Orlovski for love," Charlotte said.

"Nonsense. You liked the idea of being a princess." Virginia chuckled.

"How did you meet a Russian prince, Your Highness?" I asked.

"Our father was ambassador at the court of the Hapsburgs," Edwina answered for her. "The prince was visiting and was taken with my sister."

"I was considered a great beauty at the time," Charlotte said.

"The fact that Father had arranged a generous dowry for each of us didn't hurt either," Virginia added.

"Sit up, Nicholas, and don't slurp your soup," Edwina interrupted sharply. "Really, you children still eat like savages."

"He gets nervous in your presence, Mama," Irene said. "Most children of his age take their meals in the nursery."

"I've always thought it was important for children to learn civilized manners and the art of conversation well before they are taken out in society. Since yours have apparently learned nothing before they came here, I am taking them in hand."

"That's really not fair, Mama." Irene's face had turned red. "They've had to suffer very upsetting things in their young lives. We've all had to suffer."

"Nonsense. You should talk to Billings, the estate manager, about his son, who came home from the war so shell-shocked that he still cries like a baby every night. Or the gamekeeper's son who lost both legs. Or that family in the village who lost all three sons on the same day. That is suffering, Irene. Not going without a new hat every season."

She paused and looked up as Cedric came into the room.

"You're late again, Cedric," she said.

"Since it is I who now should set the time for meals in my own house, I might say that you are early, Mother," he said. "But in fact I am too wound up after last night's triumph to think of joining the bean-feast. I've told Mrs. Broad that we'll have sandwiches and a bottle of bubbly in my study." He looked around the table. "And I don't see what those brats are doing here again. I've made it clear that I have no wish to see my sister's offspring more than once a day. A nursery is the place for children."

"They are learning manners, Cedric. A skill in which I clearly failed lamentably in your upbringing."

Cedric snorted, went to stride from the room, then spun around again and said, "I only came in to tell you that I've received a telephone call from our solicitor. The ship is scheduled to dock in Southampton tomorrow. He will escort the boy up to London for a briefing and plans to bring him down here at the weekend."

"Cedric!" Edwina said in horror. "How many times have I told you that I find that common Americanism deplorable. People of our class do not have 'weekends,' because we do not need to take two days off from our weekly toil. We'll have Nicholas and Katherine using it next."

"Since they will obviously have to work for their living, they had better get used to it," Cedric said.

"I'm sorry. Which boy is he talking about?" Irene asked.

"I assumed you'd all heard the rumors," Cedric said. "Our dear mother has sent out her spies and managed to dig up a possible heir for me. A young man from Australia, who is supposedly Johnnie's legal child. Naturally, I am employing my own agents to have all of his credentials checked and double checked. But he is being brought from Australia as we speak and will be in this house by—by the end of the week."

"And I hope you will all do your best to make him feel welcome," Edwina said. "In spite of what Cedric says, we have to accept that this boy is indubitably Johnnie's son, and thus the rightful heir. He comes straight from a sheep farm in the wilds of Australia and will be overawed by the grandeur of this place. It is up to us to groom him to take over the dukedom someday."

"Someday in the distant future, we hope," Cedric said. "I'm not intending to pop off yet, Mother. And who knows what changes may occur in the next forty years."

With that, he made a dramatic exit from the dining room.

Chapter 7

Kingsdowne Place

"What did I tell you?" Princess Charlotte wagged a finger at Cedric's departing figure. "The spirits never lie. A stranger who means danger. That's what they said, and that same night I dreamed of a cuckoo. A cuckoo sitting on the top of the roof, cuckooing away like mad. And someone in the house called, 'Somebody make it stop, for God's sake. It's driving me insane. I'll pay you to get rid of it.' "

"I don't think we take your spirit messages and dreams as gospel truth, Charlotte," the dowager duchess said. "I remember you dreamed the Derby winner last year and we all put money on a horse that came last."

"The spirits do not like information to be used for monetary gain," Charlotte said.

Irene, I noticed, had turned quite white. "Then it's true that the boy is coming here. And he'll get all of this someday. A common Australian who knows nothing of our heritage and traditions . . . when my own children come from the purest aristocratic blood." She broke off with a little hiccup.

"I think it's jolly unfair," Nicholas said loudly. "And jolly stupid too. Why can't the children of a female inherit anything?"

"Because that is not the way things are done, Nicholas," Edwina said. "None of us is thrilled that the heir to Kingsdowne Place will have no social graces and does not deserve to inherit, but we have to accept that it is the only solution and do our best to make him welcome."

"Well, I don't intend to make him welcome," Nick mouthed to his sister when his grandmother wasn't watching.

The soup plates had been whisked away during this interchange, and turbot in parsley sauce had been placed in front of us. I looked across at Irene and her children as I ate. Of course this stranger coming into their midst might mean everything to them—life, death and survival. If Cedric were to die and Jack Altringham became the duke, then the estate and the fortune would be his, and he could expel unwanted relatives without a penny. I thought that if Nicholas was sensible he'd make his new cousin as welcome as possible.

Steak and kidney pie followed the turbot, then a steamed ginger pudding with custard, followed by a good Stilton and biscuits. At least the food was going to make up for the complicated situation in which I found myself. During the meal, it had occurred to me why I had been asked to come here—only the dowager duchess wanted the Australian boy to be here. The rest were going to go out of their way to make life as unpleasant for him as possible.

Luncheon ended with coffee, and the family dispersed—the older members for an afternoon snooze and the younger back to the nursery and their tutor. I was left alone, unsure what to do with myself. I wanted to pay a visit to the injured girl. I felt rather sorry about the way her brother had dismissed her as if she was not worth talking about. But first I felt I should get an idea of the layout of the main floor. These old houses can be infernally complicated. And if I was supposed to show Jack Altringham around when he arrived, I needed to be au fait with the place myself.

I peeked into the drawing room, then a charming corner morning room with windows overlooking both the front and side of the house.

Then a grand library, a pretty music room with a black grand piano and a harp, and a super view across the formal gardens to the valley below. I wished my talents ran to playing an instrument.

Then I came back through the Long Gallery, now deserted, and passed through several smaller salons and rooms with no particular purpose other than to display collections of various sorts—Roman pottery, porcelain figures and enamel boxes. I presumed these were the fancies of various past dukes. One room was small, square paneled in dark wood in which the glass-topped display cases were filled with butterflies. I stood looking at them with a mixture of fascination and pity. It seemed so cruel that the bright, delicate creatures should end up with a pin through them for some gentleman's pleasure.

I came out into a hallway that turned a corner into a new, narrow and rather dark corridor. This clearly wasn't a main thoroughfare and I felt a little uneasy with all those closed, paneled doors. Ahead of me I could hear the faint clatter of dishes, and had no wish to stray into the servants' domain. That would be too embarrassing. I turned around and decided to retrace my steps. Only I couldn't remember how I had reached this corridor in the first place. I tried a door and found it to be locked. I opened another into a small room, its contents shrouded in dust sheets. I felt uneasiness growing. I began to have an absurd feeling that I was being watched, and quickened my pace.

On my left was a door set back into an alcove. That looked promising, as if it might lead through to the main hallway I had left previously. I was about to open the door when a voice behind me said, "I wouldn't go in there if I were you. People have gone in there and never returned."

My heart did a complete flip-flop. I spun around to see one of the young men in black was standing there. "Cedric's secret passion—his photographic darkroom. God knows what goes on in there but he doesn't allow anyone else in. He'd have an absolute fit if he saw you even standing at his doorway." He gave me a conspiratorial smile. His accent still bore traces of a line north of Birmingham. "He sees himself as the next Cecil Beaton," he said. "Frankly, I don't think he has an artist's eye but of course we wouldn't dare tell him." He looked at me with interest. "Now, you're not one of the staff dressed like that. And your clothes are definitely too frumpy to be anything but an aristocrat, so one can only assume you're a visiting relative. But definitely not the Australian heir, unless you're a cross-dresser—in which case, how delicious."

I had to laugh at this. "I'm not a cross-dresser and I'm not a relative," I said. "I'm a guest of the dowager duchess. She was a friend of my grandmother. I'm Georgiana Rannoch."

"Oh, my my—then I've seen you in the society pages," he said. "I remember when you came out."

"Do you go to any of the deb balls?" I asked.

"Oh, no, duckie. I am far, far below the level to be considered suitable, although I would look lovely in a backless white dress and a tiara." He held out his hand to me. "I'm Adrian, one of Cedric's protégés. I'm a painter of sorts. Not particularly good but it beats going down a coal mine." His hand held firmly on to mine. "Come and meet the other boys. They'd love to be cheered up by a new face. Ceddy has been in a foul mood since he found out about this long-lost nephew. I don't know why. It's not as if he's going to claim the family fortune until Ceddy's pushing up daisies, is it? And I'm sure he'll be a delightful addition to our happy family—all rugged and tanned and primitive." And he gave a tiger-like growl.

Adrian led me at a great pace along a hall lined with weapons. "Don't be afraid," he said. "The family hardly ever uses them these days."

"Actually I feel quite at home," I said. "Our Scottish castle has a pretty formidable collection of weapons too."

"Oh, of course, I keep forgetting that you're almost royalty," he said. "And you seem so nice and normal too. Listen." He paused and cocked his head like a spaniel out shooting. "I think they've moved to the ballroom, cheeky devils. I hope you're not easily shocked.

God knows what they'll be doing in there. They do tend to get carried away."

At the end of the hall we turned a corner, and Adrian thrust open the first door on our left. We stepped into a glorious room. French windows, framed with blue-velvet drapes revealed a view of lawns, giving way to parkland and distant hills on which tiny dots of sheep were grazing. The parquet floor glowed with loving care, and a row of impressive chandeliers was suspended along the length of the ceiling. At the far end was a raised dais for an orchestra. It was currently occupied by another slim young man in black operating a gramophone, which he was in the process of rewinding.

"Do it again, Jules," he said. "And this time try to imagine you're Fred Astaire."

"He'll never manage it, he has too much hair, Simon," Adrian called.

"Then pretend you're Ginger Rogers," the dark young man he'd addressed as Simon said.

The person they were talking about stood in the middle of the room, wearing a leotard and tights. He really did have lovely hair—a honey-blonde color, which curled over his ears. I was quite jealous.

"It's no good, Simon. I just don't feel it," he said. "There's something not quite right about the music."

"What are you two doing in here? I'm sure Ceddy wouldn't like you wandering all over the house without his permission," Adrian said.

"We're working on the new play, silly," Simon said. "If he wants to have an original Simon Wetherington creation for his festival this autumn, I have to get a move on. And Jules is being difficult and can't seem to get what I want him to do."

"I just don't see myself as a dancing Welsh coal miner," Jules said.

"It's a dream sequence, Jules. You're an actor. Put yourself into the role. Work with me."

They seemed to notice me standing in the doorway for the first time. "I don't think we're ready for outside observers yet," Simon said.

"This is Georgiana Rannoch. You know—Lady Georgiana Rannoch from the society pages. Pally with the royals."

This was a slight exaggeration. I'd made the society pages a few times during my season but hardly ever since then. But they all came over to me excitedly nonetheless.

"She's going to be staying for a while," Adrian said.

"Lovely. Can you dance? You could be Ginger Rogers for poor Jules, who hates dancing alone."

"I'm afraid I'm a hopeless dancer."

"Pity," Simon said. "You've got the right color hair for the part."

"So are you creating a musical comedy?" I asked.

"It's going to be darker than that, darling—a combination folk opera, Shakespearean drama and musical revue, all rolled into one."

"Quite an innovation," Adrian said. "The boy's brilliant, of course. Ceddy snapped him up when he saw his last play being performed in Edinburgh."

"And he's promised to put on the extravaganza at his new festival, if Simon can finish it in time," Jules said.

"What festival is this?"

"Haven't you heard?" they twittered at me excitedly, making me think how apt it was of someone to have dubbed them the Starlings.

"Ceddy's planning to have an outdoor amphitheater built down below the cascades," Simon said. "He wants to hold a festival here, like Glyndebourne. He wants Kingsdowne to become *the* mecca for the arts."

"Goodness," I said. "How ambitious."

"Oh yes. Cedric wants his name to go down in history. The Medici of mid-Kent," Adrian said.

The other two boys glanced around nervously. "You shouldn't say things like that, Adrian. You'll get us all slung out on our ear," Simon said.

"Fiddlesticks," Adrian said. "Ceddy adores me, and you know it. I can do no wrong in his eyes."

"This week," Julian said. "Ceddy is notoriously fickle, as you very well know."

"Absolutely not. He must adore me for myself because I admit my painting is not up to Picasso standards."

"If he adores anyone, it's Marcel," Julian said coldly.

"Who is Marcel?" I dared to ask.

"His valet. French; terribly dark and brooding and Continental," Adrian said, rolling his eyes. "What is not to adore about him. Every time he speaks with that French accent I absolutely melt into a puddle."

"Enough dallying," Simon said. "Come on, people. Back to work or this play will never finish. And, Lady Georgiana, darling, couldn't you please be Ginger Rogers—pretty please? How can I choreograph a duet with one person, and Adrian has two left feet."

"Very well. I'll try, but I can't promise dancing prowess."

"Isn't she duckie?" Adrian asked, and they all agreed I was.

So for the next hour I was dragged and swung around the ballroom by an enthusiastic Julian. Actually it was a lot of fun until Cedric's bulky form loomed in the doorway.

"What is going on? What are you doing in my ballroom?" he demanded like a schoolmaster who has discovered pupils misbehaving.

"Working on the play, Cedric," Simon said. "We've almost mastered the dream sequence with the Welsh miner."

"What's she doing here?" He glared at me.

"She's standing in for Ginger Rogers," Simon said. "And doing a splendid job."

"Well, stop that now. I need you now to come and look at the site with me," Cedric said. "I've just been down there, and I'm afraid I was right. Those cottages will have to go."

"But they are so picturesque, Ceddy. You can't just knock them down," Simon said.

"I can do what I bally-well like on my land," Cedric said. "The amphitheater needs a backstage area and they are simply in the way. Come and see." He opened one of the French doors and they followed him out obediently, leaving me standing alone in the ballroom.

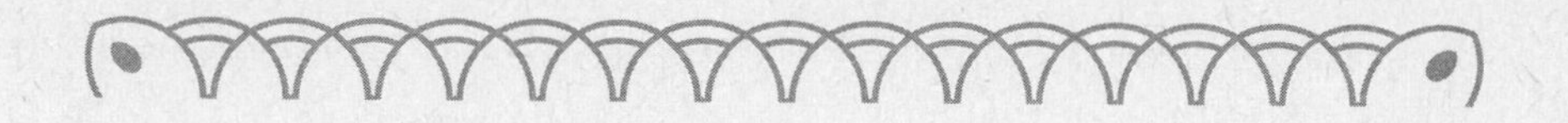

Chapter 8

Kingsdowne

I came out into the hallway and was just making my way back to the main staircase when I met the housemaid Elsie coming toward me with a tray on which there was a teapot and cup.

"Countess Streletzki has another of her migraines," she said. "And she's a great believer in chamomile tea."

I started up the stairs with her.

"I wonder if it would be all right if I visited the countess's daughter Elisabeth," I said. "It must be awfully lonely for her, stuck in her room all the time."

"It is, poor thing," she said. "And such a sweet-natured child she is too. Let me just deliver this to the countess and I'll take you up to the nursery."

"I won't be disturbing her lessons, will I?"

"Oh, no, my lady," she replied. "Miss Sissy is supposed to rest after luncheon."

I waited until Elsie returned from delivering her tray to Irene, and then she led me up another flight of stairs and along the full length of a hallway. Now that we were no longer on the important floors, the décor was not as grand. The walls were whitewashed and plain with the occasional vase in a niche. Elsie tapped at the very end door then opened it.

"Miss Sissy?" she asked. "Are you resting?"

"Why should I rest? I've done nothing all day to make me tired," said a clear voice.

"I've brought you a visitor."

"Oh. I don't know if I'm well enough for visitors," she said hastily.

"I promise not to stay long and tire you," I said and stepped past Elsie into the room. "I just wanted to say hello and introduce myself. I'm Georgiana Rannoch, and I'm staying here for a while so I thought you might like some company."

The girl was sitting in a bath chair at a window, a rug over her knees and a shawl over her shoulders. There was a strong resemblance to the other two children but her face was less sullen and much prettier; she was older than I thought she'd be—around fifteen, maybe. Almost white-blonde hair spilled over her shoulders, and when she saw me her face broke into a charming smile.

"How lovely. Please, do come in," she said. "I thought the visitor might be Grandmama or one of my aunts, and I do find them so tiresome. But another young person—well, that's quite different."

I noticed that this was a corner room with tall windows on two sides, giving a spectacular view over the estate. From the front window, where Sissy now sat, one looked down on the forecourt, the lake, driveway and lawns. Out of the side window, one could see the cascades and the temple peeping out of the trees of the glen before the formal grounds gave way to thick woods, all the way down to the valley. Smoke was rising from unseen chimneys, curling up into the cold air.

"You have a lovely view here," I said.

"I know. At least I can get a glimpse of what is going on. I just saw Uncle Cedric and his funny young men going down past the cascades. I expect they are going down to the village."

"The village?"

"My brother says there's a footpath on the other side of the glen. It's a shortcut to the village and a perfect way to sneak off unobserved. But do come and sit down."

I pulled up a chair from the writing desk and sat in the window, facing her.

"So do tell me—what are you doing here?" she asked.

"Everyone seems surprised that there is a guest in the house," I said. "Do you not get many visitors?"

She shook her head. "I'm told that in the old days, my grandparents used to entertain very grandly all the time, but then my grandfather became ill and died. And now the house belongs to Uncle Cedric, and he only invites his type of people. I think they look quite fun, but I'm never allowed to meet them."

"Why not?"

She made a face. "Not suitable, that's what Mummy says. Too common, for one thing, and of a different moral standard from us. I'm not quite sure what she means or how she knows about their moral standards."

I thought I should probably not elucidate.

"Your grandmother invited me," I said. "And anyway, you are to have another young person in the house from Saturday onward. Your cousin is arriving from Australia."

"The heir? He's actually coming?"

"He is."

"I wonder what he'll be like." Her face was hopeful but guarded. "They say he's young."

"He's twenty, so one gathers."

"I wonder if he's good-looking. Uncle Johnnie was very good-looking, from his photographs."

"So what do you do all day?" I asked.

"When I'm not having lessons, I read a lot." She held up the book on her lap. "Sherlock Holmes. Mr. Carter lent it to me. It's very good.

Mr. Carter is very kind, and he's a really good tutor too. He's awfully brainy, you know. He's a scientist really; an Oxford man. He was planning to be a professor. But he was badly shell-shocked in the war and he can't take any kind of noise or upset, so he's had to settle for teaching boring old us. Nick and Kat are awful to him, and it's impossible to learn with them around. Nick thinks if he's bad enough, he'll be shipped off to school, but Uncle Cedric doesn't want to pay for him, and we have no money." She looked up at me. "You've heard about our tragic circumstances, of course?"

I nodded.

"It's terrible for Mummy, because she was brought up to be so proud and she's so embarrassed that Daddy bolted and left her penniless. She hates being dependent on Uncle Cedric but what choice does she have?"

"I'm also penniless, so I know how she must feel," I said.

"Are you? Golly." She looked at me in silence then said, "At least you're young and pretty and healthy. Someone will marry you. No one will ever want to marry me."

"Oh, surely—you mustn't think like that."

She tossed her head proudly. "Who'd want to marry a penniless cripple?"

"You may walk again."

"Mummy has heard about a doctor in Switzerland who can work miracles with cripples like me, but it costs an awful lot of money and Uncle Cedric won't pay for it." She turned to stare out of the window. "So there's no hope, really."

I wanted to say something encouraging but I couldn't think of any words that would ring true to her. I was in a similarly hopeless situation myself, except that I could still use my legs and I did have Darcy.

Suddenly she leaned forward as a man came running up the hill toward the house. He was dressed like a countryman—old corduroy trousers, a jacket patched at the elbows, a shapeless cloth cap on his head and big boots. When he came close to the house he stopped and looked up at it, frowning. As we watched, the butler came out to him. We couldn't hear voices but the young man was obviously in a state of great agitation. He waved his arms a lot while the butler tried to put a calming hand on the man's shoulder. He shrugged it off, turned away and stomped off down the driveway.

"What was that all about, I wonder," I said.

Sissy shook her head. "I've no idea. I couldn't see him clearly but I think it looked like William, who was one of the footmen here. He was very angry, wasn't he?"

We went on talking for a while, about how she'd loved to ride and hunt and the ways that she filled her days since the accident. "Mr. Carter tries to teach us science, of course," she said. "Nick and Kat are quite keen on doing horrid chemistry experiments but I'm useless."

Her loves were literature, languages and painting. She showed me some of her watercolors, which were good.

"You should show these to your uncle," I said. "He sees himself as a patron of the arts."

She laughed. "Oh, I'm afraid my tame little efforts are not what would impress him at all. He likes modern art with great splotches of color. You know, they look like a spilled nursery meal. Or what he really likes is to take strange photographs of people's nostrils or toes."

There was a tap on the door as we watched Cedric and his retinue return to the house, and in came a well-padded and pleasant-looking nanny.

"Ready for your tea, Miss Sissy?" she asked, then stopped. "Oh, I see you've got company. How lovely for you."

"This is Lady Georgiana, Nanny. She's going to be staying here."

"What a treat," Nanny said. She turned to me. "Miss Sissy gets awfully lonely stuck up here."

"I suppose there is no lift to take you downstairs?"

"There isn't," Sissy said. "Someone has to carry me. And Mummy doesn't like anyone uncouth, like the gardeners or grooms, handling me. So it's hard. But I have a nice tea in the nursery with the twins and Mr. Carter, don't I, Nanny?"

"You do, my love," she said.

Far below, a gong sounded.

"That's downstairs tea," Sissy said to me. "I suppose you'll be going down now." She looked wistful. "Or you could always join us, if you like. We have a jolly tea up here, you know."

"Why not," I said, thinking how much nicer it would be to avoid the formality of tea below, with its added risk of dropping crumbs or squirting cream. I walked behind Nanny as she wheeled the bath chair through to an adjoining room. With a big bookcase, desks, a globe on the front table and currently a science experiment set up with test tubes and Bunsen burners, this was now the schoolroom. But one could see that it had been the nursery. There was still a lovely old dollhouse in a corner; ragged, stuffed animals in an old wagon, and a magnificent rocking horse had pride of place in one of the windows. Nick and Katherine were seated at a low table on which there was a tray of sandwiches, scones and a Victoria sponge.

"Here we are. Here's Miss Sissy and a visitor for you," Nanny said, parking the bath chair beside the table and then picking up the teapot. "Help yourself, my lady. And you others, go easy. I expect sandwiches to be eaten before you attack that cake."

"Oh, but, Nanny, it does look awfully good," Katherine said. "I don't know if we can bear to wait that long."

"You need to learn patience, young lady," Nanny said. "Now, you make a good impression on our guest, or they'll hear about it downstairs."

"You wouldn't tell, would you, my lady?" Nick asked.

"Only if you were about to blow up the house," I said, smiling. "And you can call me Georgie."

"Whizzo," Nick said, and started attacking the sandwiches as only an eleven-year-old boy can.

"So where is your tutor?" I asked.

"We're done with lessons for the day. He's always glad to make a quick getaway." Nick grinned. "Back in his own room—recovering from a morning of us, I expect."

"Actually, they were jolly good lessons today," Kat said. "We were doing wizard science experiments. He let us use the Bunsen burners, and he showed how you could start a reaction with potassium."

"And we made volcanoes yesterday," Nick said, "Only we can't let him see that we're enjoying things. He has to think that we're beyond hope and that we should be sent off to school."

"You want to go to school?" I asked.

"Oh, yes," Katherine said. "It's deadly dull here with no friends and only boring old Nick."

"I am not boring. I'm more interesting than you!" Nick said angrily.

"I find you both boring and I'm stuck with you," Sissy said. "At least you'll be able to get out one day."

"Maybe you will too," Katherine said kindly. "Maybe you'll go to that doctor."

"Maybe." Sissy stared out of the window.

I actually had a jolly time with them and promised I'd visit again.

"I know how hard it can be, stuck up in a nursery," I said. "I went through the same thing when I was a child. At least you have each other."

"And we find ways to sneak around," Katherine said with a wicked grin. "You'd be amazed at some of the things we overhear that aren't meant for our delicate little ears."

"Shut up, Kat," Nick said, giving her a dig in the ribs.

I went downstairs and came out into the Long Gallery at the same time as Huxstep.

"Ah, there you are," the dowager duchess said. I thought she was addressing me and sounded cross, but then she went on, "I saw some kind of altercation going on, Huxstep. You were outside with someone who was gesticulating a lot. What on earth was that about?"

"It was William, Your Grace. You remember the footman whom the duke recently dismissed."

"And what did he want? His job back?"

"He wanted to speak to you, apparently, Your Grace," he said. "He had just found out that his parents' cottage is to be razed to the ground to make way for the new amphitheater. They have lived there all their lives, Your Grace. William was most distressed."

"My son intends to destroy that row of cottages?" she asked incredulously. "That is an outrage, Huxstep. Those cottages have been part of this estate since the sixteenth century. And where does my son intend to put the tenants who currently live in them?"

"Nowhere, Your Grace. He told them, apparently, that they had been living on the grace and favor of this family for too long and this was now the twentieth century and such customs were outmoded."

In the manner of the true aristocrat, her face remained composed. "We shall see about this," she said coldly.

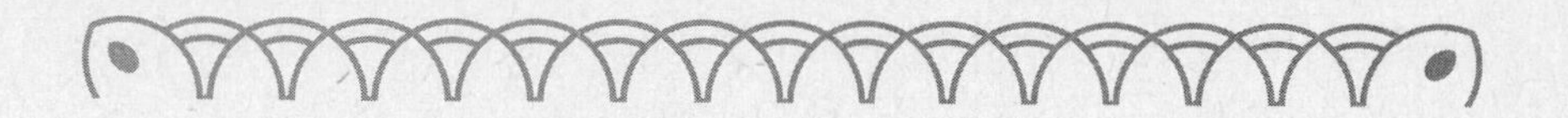

Chapter 9

Kingsdowne

I wasn't exactly looking forward to dinner that night, fearing a gigantic family row. I was even more reluctant to go down once I started to dress.

"I've laid out your best frock, my lady," Queenie said demurely.

"Thank you, Queenie." I looked at the gown, wrap, gloves and stockings all laid out neatly on my bed. This was obviously the new and improved Queenie. Kingsdowne was already rubbing off on her.

"And where are my shoes?" I asked innocently.

"'Ere's one of 'em," she said, handing me a slim, satin slipper.

"And the other?" I asked with growing unease.

"Ah, well. You know how you wanted all your stuff out again at the last minute to go gallivanting on the town with Miss Belinda? And then you made me pack it again next morning?"

"Yes. . . ." The dread was clutching at my throat.

"One of the shoes must have rolled under the bed and I didn't see it."

I stared at her in open-mouthed horror. "You mean I only have one evening shoe?"

"'Fraid so."

"Queenie, you idiot. What am I going to do?"

"It's a long frock. Nobody will notice."

"They'll notice if I walk with one high-heeled shoe on and one off," I said. "I have no other high-heeled shoes suitable for evening. I'm doomed."

"You could wear your bedroom slippers, I suppose."

"They are fluffy. They have feathers around them."

"Better than nothing," she said. "Or I could sneak in to someone else's room and nick a pair of shoes for you."

"You will do nothing of the kind," I said. "I'll have to wear my black town shoes and just pray that nobody looks down. And I'll write to Mrs. Tombs in the morning to have the other shoe sent on. Knowing her, she has probably thrown it out with the rubbish."

"Sorry, miss," she said. "But I did have it all packed up lovely when you wanted it opened up again."

I sighed.

I timed my arrival in the anteroom for sherry so that I came in with Princess Charlotte and her misnamed sister, Virginia. Safety in numbers. I tried to bend my knees a little so that the gown hung over my shoes. But a glimpse of myself in the long, gilt mirror showed that I looked extremely strange, like a walking duck. The sisters did not appear to notice anything wrong with me and led me over to the sherry decanter. I swigged down a couple of glasses to boost my courage.

"Irene will not be joining us," the dowager duchess said, coming over to take a glass of sherry that the footman had just poured. "Another of her migraines, I fear. That poor girl does suffer so."

"It seems to me that her migraines are most convenient," Virginia said almost to herself, but Edwina heard her.

"What a cruel thing to say, Virginia. Just because you have been blessed with the constitution of an ox, you could at least have a little sympathy for those of a more delicate nature."

"A healthy amount of sex. That's what the girl needs," Virginia said, knocking back another glass of sherry in one gulp. "So she's lost one man. So what? Plenty more fish in the sea. Did I weep and wail when my husband found himself a Viennese ballet dancer? Of course not. I simply moved on to bigger and better things. And I do mean bigger and better."

"Virginia. You go too far," Princess Charlotte said. "We have young and innocent ears in this room."

"Nonsense. She needs to know what life's all about. If Irene hadn't been such a pathetic virgin when she came to Paris, she'd never have fallen for Streletzki."

Mercifully, we were saved by the dinner gong. We went through, just four of us, myself and the three weird sisters.

"I see that Cedric is not going to grace us with his presence," Edwina said. "That really is too bad of him, especially on your first evening here, my dear. But never mind. We'll enjoy a good evening without him, won't we?"

"We could have a séance afterward, do you think?" Princess Charlotte suggested. "Our guest could find out what the spirits have in store for her."

"Really, Charlotte. This séance nonsense has to stop," Edwina said. "You are becoming obsessed. And if the two of you behave this way when John's son arrives, then he'll think he's come to a lunatic asylum."

Cedric's young men came to join us as we went in to dinner. It wasn't the easiest meal I have attended. Edwina behaved as if they weren't there, and the three elderly ladies focused their attention on me, peppering me with questions. Princess Charlotte offered to find out what the spirits had in store for me, and Virginia tossed off the names of so many men in so many countries with whom she had enjoyed wild affairs that my mother's autobiography would have read like a girl's school story in comparison.

IN THE MORNING, we got news that Cedric had gone up to town again and was staying in his club, obviously waiting for his mother's wrath to diffuse. Wise man. While he was gone, the household entered into preparation for the arrival of the young Australian. A prime suite of rooms, facing the lake, was prepared for him. Servants whispered about him. The dowager duchess remained impassive but one could tell that she too was a little excited. I suspected that, for her, it would be like seeing her beloved son again. Cedric returned but kept well away from his mother. I'm not sure if they had a confrontation but I did hear his voice once saying loudly, "It's my house now and you'd better not forget it."

Not the most pleasant of men. I was rather glad no young woman was going to be stuck with him.

The day of Jack's arrival approached. We had eaten luncheon and the sisters had retired for their afternoon siesta. I was sitting in the Long Gallery with the dowager duchess, halfheartedly reading the *Horse and Hound* when we heard the sound of tires crunching on gravel.

"Here they are," she said, rising to her feet.

A lovely Rolls-Royce motor came up the drive. "Our solicitor's motorcar," she said. "He obviously does very well for himself writing wills."

The Rolls-Royce drew up. Footmen descended on it like ants on a dead beetle. The chauffeur hurried around to open the back doors of the motorcar. A most distinguished-looking, silver-haired man, dressed in an impeccably tailored suit, extracted himself from one side. Then a young man got out and stood waiting, his back toward us. He was tall and well-built with a shock of black, curly hair not unlike Darcy's.

"I thought he'd be fair like Johnnie," Edwina said. "He's a strapping lad for twenty, isn't he?"

Then he turned toward the house and I let out a little gasp. It wasn't a young Australian I was looking at. It was Darcy himself.

"Oh, no," I heard the dowager duchess say. "Of course that's not he. I expect that's his escort. Here he comes now and he's the spitting image of John. I'd know him anywhere. We must go to welcome them."

And she almost broke into a run. I was breathing so fast that I stood rooted to the spot. What on earth was Darcy doing here? When we'd parted right after Christmas, he had told me that he thought he'd have to go back to Argentina. So how had he become involved with a young Australian boy? I watched the duchess descend the steps to them, shake hands with the solicitor, then nod to Darcy. Finally she held out her hand to a rangy lad dressed in a plaid shirt, khaki trousers and a bush hat. He shook the hand, looking around with wonder, as if he was observing creatures from Mars.

"So what do you think of your first glimpse of Kingsdowne?" I heard the dowager duchess's voice as they came up the steps into the house. "Is it how you imagined it?"

"Strike me," he said. "It's bigger than the bloomin' hotel we stayed in. How many people actually live here?"

"Just us. Just the family."

"Only one family? What a waste. You could rent out rooms. Make some money."

"We have no need to make money, young man," the duchess said in a clipped voice. "We have all we need to live in the lifestyle to which we are accustomed."

The voices were coming closer. "Stone the flamin' crows!" I heard Jack exclaim. "Look at that ceiling. They don't have any clothes on. That wouldn't be allowed at home."

"It's a fresco by a famous eighteenth-century artist," Edwina's voice replied. "In the classical period, they frequently painted nude figures."

"My oath," he said. "My old gran would have boxed my ears if she caught me looking at smutty pictures like that."

The dowager countess was now entering the Long Gallery. Her face was a stony mask.

"I saw some funny little cows as we came up the track." The

Australian came into view beside her. "Is that how small cows are here in England?"

"Cows?"

"Yeah. Skinny, brown, little things among the trees."

"Those are deer. We have a famous deer herd here at Kingsdowne."

"Oh, are they good tucker?"

"Tucker?"

"Yeah. We shoot the roos at home. Usually feed them to the dogs but the tails make good eating."

"We keep the deer to be ornamental, not to eat."

"You wait till there's a drought year. Then you'll be glad enough to eat them." The young man had come out of the shadows of the foyer. He had sandy, sun-streaked hair poking out from under his hat, bright-blue eyes and tanned skin. He almost walked with the rolling gait of the sailor and he wore riding boots.

"Ah. Here you are, Georgiana, my dear." Her Grace looked relieved to see me. "John, let me introduce you to our houseguest, Lady Georgiana. She comes from a most distinguished family, and she will be staying with us for a while."

"Good day," the young Australian said with a nod as he tipped his hat. "And my name's not John. It's Jack."

"Jack is only a nickname for John—which was your father's name and is more suitable for a future duke," the duchess said. She looked around to see if the rest of the party was following into the room. "And may I present the family solicitor, Mr. Henry Camden-Smythe."

"How do you do?" I said in what I hoped was a steady voice. We shook hands.

The duchess now turned her attention to Darcy. "And I'm afraid I don't know your name, young man, but I'd like you to meet Lady Georgiana."

"Darcy O'Mara," Darcy said. "Lady Georgiana and I are already acquainted." He took my hand and held it, his eyes smiling into mine.

"O'Mara? Lord Kilhenny's son. Of course. Your father had a fine racing stable, I remember."

"Not anymore, I'm afraid," Darcy said.

The duchess sighed. "I heard. How my husband loved to go to Ascot. Nothing is the same anymore."

Darcy was now deemed to be acceptable, which was more than could be said for the Australian heir.

"Do sit down," the duchess said. "Tea will be served shortly. I expect you're hungry."

"Too right," the boy said. "I haven't had a decent-size meal since I left home."

He sank into one of the armchairs, not looking at all intimidated by his surroundings. I took a seat on the sofa and Darcy slid into place beside me. I glanced at Darcy and he winked. He didn't seem as shocked to see me as I was him.

"Are you expecting rain, John?" the dowager duchess asked.

"Rain? No. Looks quite fine to me."

"I wondered, because you are wearing your hat in the house, so I thought you might be afraid the roof would leak."

"Oh, no. Looks all right to me," he said easily.

Edwina rang the bell and the butler appeared. "Huxstep, would you please find His Grace and tell him that our guests have arrived, and would he please come to welcome them." She turned back to Jack, who still hadn't taken his hat off. "So you have come from the Australian countryside. Quite different from this, I'd imagine."

"Too right," he said. "Where I come from, we run one sheep per acre. No rain, see. And the bloody rabbits and roos eat what grass there is."

I saw the duchess stiffen at the swear word but she kept quiet. A trolley was wheeled in, and tea was placed on the table in front of us.

"Please do help yourself," the duchess said.

Jack looked at the tiny sandwiches and cakes. "Is this all you have for tea here?"

"It seems quite adequate to me," Edwina said. "What do you have at home?"

"Oh, usually a roast and two veg. Sometimes it's a meat pie."

"That would be what we eat for dinner," Edwina said stiffly.

"You have another meal after this then?"

"We most certainly do. At eight o'clock. And we dress for it, John."

"Well, I wouldn't expect you to sit down in your underwear." He grinned.

"I mean formal dress. Dinner jacket. Do you have one yet?"

"I think so. They took me shopping and bought me some poncy clothes."

We all looked up as Cedric came into the room.

"Ah, this is your uncle Cedric now, John," she said. "He is the current Duke of Eynsford. You are his heir."

"Right-oh." Jack didn't get up but stuck out his hand. "Pleased to meet you, mate."

Cedric looked rather green. "Mother just called you John. Is that your name then?"

"No, just Jack. The blokes on the station called me Jacko, or Blue sometimes."

"Blue? Why was that?"

"On account of my red hair." He looked around at the silence. "Aussie joke, I suppose," he added.

"But you were christened John, surely?" Edwina said.

"I don't think I was christened anything. The parsons don't come around too often out where I was."

"Not christened?" I thought Edwina might faint. She swallowed hard then took a good sip of tea. "My dear boy. We must remedy that. I'll contact the vicar immediately."

"Did your mother ever speak to you about your father?" Cedric asked.

"Yeah. She said he was a bonza bloke. Not at all toffee nosed like his relatives. He promised to come back after the war, and she didn't hear for years that he'd been killed so she kept hoping. She said you lot wouldn't want anything to do with us so she never wrote to you."

"And where is your mother now?"

Jack had been working his way through the plate of sandwiches. "She died when I was a nipper. I went to live with my gran, who was cook on a station."

"On the railway, you mean?"

"No. A sheep station."

Darcy leaned forward. "It's the Australian word for a ranch," he said.

"So you lived on this sheep station?" Cedric asked.

"Yeah. When I was fourteen, my gran died and I went to work riding the boundary fence, until I got crook and had to give it up."

"Crook? You mean you went to jail?"

Jack laughed. "No. Crook. In bed with a bad wog."

Edwina actually choked on her macaroon. "With what?"

"A wog. You know. I caught diphtheria. I was really crook for a while there. But I recovered."

"So you've had very little education?" Cedric said. His voice sounded tight and clipped like his mother's.

"Not much. I know how to read and write. That's about it. And sums. I can do sums all right."

"We must see if Mr. Carter can devote some time to him," Edwina said, then turned to me. "And Georgiana, maybe you can help too."

Jack looked amused. "Do you need education to be a duke? I heard you had servants to do everything for you."

"One needs an education to move freely through the highest levels of society," Edwina said. "All of this will seem very strange to you at first, but you will have to learn to take your rightful place here. We will naturally give you time to settle in, won't we, Cedric?"

Cedric gave a grunt.

"And after tea," the duchess went on, "I'll have Frederick show you to your rooms. He was my late husband's valet, and will help you dress."

"Help me dress?" The boy looked amused. "I've been dressing myself since I was knee-high to a grasshopper."

"Help you dress in a correct manner," she said.

"Is there a pub nearby?" Jack asked.

"I think there is a public house in the village," Edwina said.

Jack turned to Darcy. "So how's about us blokes go down to the pub in time for the six o'clock swill then?"

Edwina picked up the copy of *Horse and Hound* and fanned herself.

"I'm afraid I have to drive back to London," the solicitor said hurriedly.

"Jack, our class of person does not frequent public houses," Cedric said.

"Crikey. You don't drink?"

"We have sherry, and then wine with dinner," Cedric said.

Jack gave Darcy a despairing glance.

"More tea, John?" Edwina asked.

Jack regarded the pot and shook his head. "No, thanks. I'm right."

"Then we'll have you shown to your quarters. Frederick, would you take Viscount Farningham to his room?"

"Viscount Farningham—who is he?" Jack asked.

"You are. It is the title given to the heir to this dukedom. You are now a viscount, Jack. Please try to behave like one."

"Blow me down," Jack said. He followed the valet out of the Long Gallery. Edwina and Cedric sat in stony silence.

"Now you've done it, Mother," Cedric said at last. "Now do you see where your interfering has got us? It's like having Tarzan in the house."

"I do admit that he's a little rough around the edges at the moment," Edwina said.

"Rough around the edges? He couldn't be less civilized if he was a chimpanzee. Hopeless. Clearly untrainable. He'll have to go."

"He is the only heir we have, Cedric. This would not have been necessary if you had done your duty and married."

"Don't start that again." Cedric stood up. "You should have ignored that blasted letter when it arrived from Australia. You were so set on finding darling Johnnie's offspring."

"I was doing my duty—unlike my son, who has neglected his," she said stiffly. "We had to find an heir."

"*You* had to find an heir. I'd have been quite content to let the title die and have the estate sold off."

"We will work with the boy," Edwina said firmly. "Educate him in our ways. Georgiana is here. She can help make him see what is required of him. And maybe Mr. O'Mara can stay for a while too?"

"I'm afraid I'm due back in town," Darcy said, "but I'll try to come down whenever I can."

Cedric started to walk away then turned back. "My young friends were joking that I should adopt one of them and save us all a lot of trouble," he said. "We laughed at the time. Now it doesn't seem like such a bad idea."

With that, he strode from the room.

Chapter 10

Edwina stood up too. "Oh, dear," she said. "How trying. Still, the boy will learn, won't he? He'll have to learn. He does look so like Johnnie." And with that she also walked away, leaving Darcy and me alone.

"I can't believe you're here," I said, taking in every inch of that beloved face—those alarming blue eyes and roguish smile. "What an amazing coincidence."

"Not really. It was I who suggested you might be the person to help the lad settle in."

"But how did you get involved in this?"

"I was asked to go and find this boy right after I left you at Christmas. I couldn't tell you, as I was sworn to secrecy."

"You went all the way to Australia to find Jack?"

"I did."

"But how did you get to Australia and back in three months?"

He grinned. "I flew."

For a moment I thought he was teasing me. "In an aeroplane?" I asked.

"In a series of aeroplanes. London to Basel, train to Genoa, flying boat to Alexandria, another plane to Karachi, then stops along the way to Singapore, over to Darwin and a couple of puddle-jumpers to the sheep station in South Queensland. All in all, it took eighteen uncomfortable yet fascinating days, but was much quicker than a boat."

"Golly," I said. "And did you come back by aeroplane too?"

"No. Too dangerous. Planes have a habit of crashing. On the flight out, we had to put down in the Arabian Desert in a sandstorm, which was a bit unpleasant."

"Darcy." I put my hand over his. "I wish you wouldn't always do such dangerous things."

He took my hands and held them. "A fellow has to make a bit of money any way he can," he said. "And I rather enjoy it." Then he added, "God, you're a sight for sore eyes." Then his arms came around me and he was kissing me passionately. A small voice in the back of my consciousness was whispering that it wasn't wise to be found making love in the Long Gallery of someone else's house, but I couldn't help myself. I found myself responding to his kisses with a fervor and urgency equal to his own. When we finally broke apart, his eyes were smiling into mine. "I must go away more often. You've turned into a hot little piece. I hope someone else hasn't been giving you lessons."

"I have been living a life of absolute purity and boredom, if you must know," I said. "But it is so wonderful that you're here. I do hope you can stay for a while. I have a feeling this won't be a very comfortable place. Poor Jack. None of them wants him here."

"He didn't want to come, either. He's not at all keen to be a duke. He suggested I impersonate him and take over the role instead."

"I wonder what will happen if he turns them down?"

"He's still the heir, whether anyone likes it or not. He'll get the money, the title and the estate. It's up to him what he does with it."

He stood up, taking my hand. "Come on. Let's go for a stroll before it gets dark. Somewhere a little more private."

And we went to explore the interesting scenery of the glen. As to what went on there—modesty forbids a description. But let me just say that it was worth the months of waiting.

MY LOST EVENING slipper had still not arrived from London. I had now written to Belinda asking her to collect it from Mrs. Tombs, but I wasn't hopeful. So I came down to dinner in my town shoes again, knowing that nobody would be paying any attention to me. They would all be looking at Jack. When I arrived in the antechamber, the three elderly sisters and Irene were already present and knocking back the sherry. Cedric and his cronies strolled in soon after me.

"God, I could do with a cocktail," one of them said. "Ceddy, you'll have to install a proper bartender for us. We simply cannot exist on sherry."

"If you'd learn to make the bally things yourself, I could hire you as my bartender, Julian," Cedric said. "Perhaps I could train Marcel. He's such a bright young lad. I'm sure he'd pick it up quickly."

"I'm sure he'd pick anything up quickly," I heard one of the Starlings mutter to another as they came to stand close to me. I don't think Cedric overheard.

Anyway, this topic of conversation was broken off by the arrival of Darcy and Jack, both wearing proper dinner jackets and both looking rather handsome. Jack's red-blonde hair had been slicked into submission, and he looked highly uncomfortable in his new attire.

"Here they are at last," Edwina said. "Come and meet your aunt and your great-aunts, John." It was clear that Edwina was not going to give up calling him by her son's name.

Irene glowered. Princess Charlotte held out her hand in regal fashion but Virginia almost fell upon Darcy and Jack. "Two divine young men," she said. "What fun! If I'd been a few years younger, I'd have given you both the key to my room and had you both at the same time."

Edwina raised her lorgnette. "Really, Virginia, you go too far," she said.

"Edwina. You're such a prude." Virginia grinned at her sister's face. "Look at this gorgeous, dark-haired boy. He wouldn't mind a roll in the hay, I can tell. One can see that he's had his share of thrilling encounters with the opposite sex."

Darcy simply looked amused. "If I had, I wouldn't mention them in present company," he said.

Virginia had seized his hand in her own claw-like ones. "Isn't he a gem?" she said. "So is this the new heir?"

"No, Virginia. He is Mr. O'Mara—the one who escorted John from Australia." She went over to Jack, who was standing as if he wished the floor would open and swallow him. "This is your great-nephew John. Isn't he like his father?"

"One can see a likeness, I suppose," Princess Charlotte said dubiously. "We should have a séance, young man, to see whether your father wishes to contact you. Also to find out if you're the one the spirits warned us about. And for whom there is danger."

"You and your spirits, Charlotte. Such rubbish," Edwina said. "You'll have the boy thinking we're all mad."

The second gong rang, and Huxstep announced, "Dinner is served, your graces."

"Isn't he marvelous?" Adrian whispered to me. "Like a butler in a West End farce."

"This whole thing feels a little like a farce to me," I replied.

"As long as it stays amusing and doesn't turn into melodrama," Adrian said. "Ceddy is absolutely at boiling point, I can tell you. Personally, I think the boy has potential, don't you?"

Darcy had taken the arm of Princess Charlotte, so Adrian escorted me into dinner. I sat beside Jack, thinking he might need some help. Sure enough, he looked down at the lines of cutlery then glanced up at me. "What's all this in aid of?" he muttered.

"Different knives and forks for each course. The round one is the soup spoon. The oddly shaped knife and fork are for fish. One works from the outside inward. Just watch what I do."

"You mean we're going to eat all this food? It's a wonder you folks don't explode."

"We only take a few mouthfuls of each course," I said.

Jack shook his head. "Stone the flaming crows," he said. "Tucker at home starts when someone throws a dead sheep on the back porch, then someone skins it, cuts it up and puts in on the barbie. And we eat it with our fingers, mostly."

Soup arrived. Everyone tipped soup plates away from them except Jack, who also slurped loudly.

"I don't see the rolls. Frederick?" Edwina looked in annoyance.

"They're down here. You want a roll?" Jack said amiably. "Here you go then." And to my utter amazement he threw one down the table in her directions. "You want butter with that?"

"No, thank you!" Edwina said hastily, clearly expecting the butter dish to be lobbed in her direction.

Whitebait followed and Jack was intrigued about eating little fishes whole. "They should let them grow bigger before they catch them," he said. "More meat on them then."

When the spring chickens came, one to each person, Jack immediately pulled it apart with his hands and picked up a leg to gnaw. I tapped him gently. "We don't use our fingers," I whispered.

"How do you get the meat off the bones then?" He looked perplexed.

"We don't, really."

"What a waste."

"I don't think this family worries about waste," I said.

"John—do you ride?" the dowager duchess asked from the head of the table.

"A horse, you mean? My word—I've been riding horses since I could walk."

Edwina looked pleased that there was something they might

actually have in common. "Then we'll have to take you to the hunt that's coming up," she said.

"What do you hunt here?"

"Foxes."

"With guns or what?"

"Certainly not with guns," she said. "We chase them on horseback. It's a sport."

"A barbaric sport, chasing defenseless foxes," Cedric said. The Starlings shuddered.

"It is part of your heritage, Cedric," Edwina said. "You let the whole family down when you say such ridiculous things. Georgiana will no doubt want to hunt, and she can take John with her. I may even join in myself, although I fear my hedge-jumping days are over."

"I'd be happy to take Jack hunting and show him the ropes," I said. I looked across at Darcy. "Will you come down and join us?"

"I'll do my best," he said.

"It's time Nicholas and Katherine learned how to hunt," Irene said, "but since they don't have their own ponies, they obviously can't join you." And she gave a meaningful glare at Cedric.

The meal ended and Edwina led the ladies to the drawing room. I didn't somehow think that the men would linger over their port and, true enough, Darcy and Jack came to join us before we'd had our first cup of coffee. When the party broke up, Darcy waited for me by the stairs and drew me into the alcove behind the staircase. "Since they've put me way over in the bachelor wing and I have to catch an early train tomorrow, I'd better say good-bye now," he said. "I'll come down to see you as soon as I can."

"I'm so glad you're safely home," I said.

"You don't have to worry, you know." He stroked my cheek. "I've got my lucky charm, remember?" And he reached inside his shirt and produced the silver pixie I had given him for Christmas. "I wore it all the way to Australia and back."

"Oh, Darcy." I flung my arms around his neck and kissed him.

"I think the dowager duchess might ship you straight back to London if she witnessed such wanton behavior," he said, laughing. "But don't stop."

I floated into my room on a cloud. Even the sight of Queenie, lying on my bed, snoring, could not dampen my mood. Whatever turmoil there was in the Altringham household, Darcy was home and that was all that mattered.

Chapter 11

Kingsdowne Place

I awoke early next morning, hoping to catch a glimpse of Darcy as he left for the station. Mist swirled around the lake and hung over the shrubbery. I stiffened as I spied a figure walking in the mist then saw from the hat that it was Jack Altringham. I dressed hurriedly and went downstairs to join him. I found him at the stables, stroking the nose of one of the horses.

"Got some bonza-looking horses here, haven't they?" he said. "No expense spared, although I doubt these could go all day through the bush the way our horses do."

"That's a hunter," I said. "They are bred for stamina. You'll find out when you come on the hunt."

He nodded then turned to stare up at the house. "None of it makes sense, does it?" he asked. "I suppose you take it for granted, but to me it all seems bloody silly. This dressing up for dinner and using one fork for this and another for that. What's it all for?"

"Tradition, I suppose. We behave in a way that sets us apart from ordinary people, to remind us that we're special. And you're right. It really is silly."

"If my gran could see me now." He looked up at the house and laughed. "My old gran in Australia, I mean. The one who used to skin the sheep for tucker. Not the one who wants me to call her Grandmama."

"I have the same experience," I said. "I had one grandmother who was a princess and one who was a London policeman's wife. I never met either, unfortunately. But I've always felt suspended between two worlds and never wholly belonging in either of them."

"But you're a real toff," he said. "Anyone can tell that by looking at you. But I'm glad you've got a common side too. You're the only one who hasn't talked to me as if I was a piece of dirt. You and Darcy. He's all right too, even though he is a toff."

"I'll show you around the grounds, if you like," I said.

"Right-oh."

We started to walk, through the formal gardens, past the fountain, past the maze, down through the glen and up to the temple.

"What's this for then?" he asked. "Some sort of religion?"

"No, just for decoration, like everything else," I said. "I know. Another silly thing." And we laughed. I was beginning to like him a lot.

"What time is breakfast?" he asked. "I'm starving. And please don't tell me it's little squares of toast."

"No, there's always a pretty good spread. What do you eat for breakfast at home?"

"Staked necks," he said.

"What sort of necks?" I asked in surprise.

"The ordinary sort. From chooks."

I shook my head. "I thought we spoke the same language, but obviously we don't."

"You know. Chooks. Like we had for supper last night." And he mimicked a chicken.

"Chicken necks?" I made a face.

He laughed. "No, eggs. You know, what they lay?"

"Oh, you said steak and eggs." I laughed too. "Well, there will be eggs, but we don't eat steak for breakfast in England. Too expensive, even for dukes."

We walked back to the house. As we approached he looked up, studying the imposing edifice rising out of the mist. "They don't really want me here, do they? That bloody Cedric hates my guts."

"I can't disagree with you. But try hard to learn and fit in and they'll come around."

As we came into the house I added, "Oh, and I'd take my hat off, if I were you. Hats are not worn inside houses like this, and it only upsets your grandmother."

He looked at me, grinned then removed his hat as we went into breakfast. We were the first ones there and the dishes in the tureens on the sideboard were still piping hot. We both ate heartily and Jack even tried items new to him, like kedgeree.

"I must say, the food is not bad at all," he said.

"And you don't have to go out to ride the boundary fences right after breakfast."

He leaned back in his chair, surveying the carved ceiling above us. "I've never minded hard work. I'm used to it. So what do people like you do all day?"

"Good question," I said. "Usually fight off boredom or do charitable works. But you're a man. You can take an interest in the estate and the home farm. Maybe you can teach the estate workers a thing or two about raising sheep. And we can always go out riding."

He brightened up at this, until Edwina entered. "I hope you're both ready for church," she said.

Oh, Lord. I'd forgotten it was Sunday. So we had to change into our best clothes and march down the footpath to the village church, where the family had their own pews at the front. Nicholas and Katherine, looking remarkably demure in their Sunday clothes, eyed Jack with interest as we crossed the grounds together.

"So you're the one who is going to inherit everything from Uncle Cedric one day," Nick said. "You know, it's jolly unfair. Our mother is also the child of a duke but she can't inherit anything because she's a woman. Don't you think that is stupid and outmoded?"

"I expect it is," Jack said. "But life's not fair, is it? They tell me you've got a sister who can't walk. That's not fair either. And my mum died when I was a little kid. That wasn't fair. The way I see it, you just have to get on with it."

"You're not going to like it here," Katherine said. "You won't know what to do and you'll make a fool of yourself."

"It won't be the first time," Jack said. "You should have seen me try to shear a sheep. I ended up with a bloody great ram lying on top of me. Now, that was really making a fool of myself."

They watched him walk ahead with a mixture of hate and respect. I also realized that they had underestimated Jack Altringham.

As we returned home, Jack asked to meet Sissy. Nick and Katherine reluctantly took him to the nursery, and he didn't come down again until the luncheon gong sounded. Sunday lunch was a magnificent affair that even Jack couldn't complain about, starting with mock turtle soup, then a huge joint of roast beef, Yorkshire pudding, roast potatoes, parsnips and Brussels sprouts followed by trifle. The adults retired to rest after this meal and the children went outside to play. I followed and found Jack showing them what looked like a large hunting knife. Thinking that it would be a step in the right direction if they got on well together, I wandered off on my own, in the other direction through the formal gardens—the rose garden was still just barren stumps at this time of year—then up through those wonderful meadows of daffodils until I found myself at the top of the North Downs, with a view on either side and sheep grazing on grassy slopes.

I was making my way down again and had just reached a copse of beech trees when I heard a scream. I started to run. The descent seemed to take forever, and as I came out to the lawns in front of the house I could see a group of people gathered beneath one of the magnificent old copper beeches.

"It's all right. They are quite safe." I heard Edwina's powerful voice. "Do stop making such a fuss, Irene."

"But he was throwing a knife at Katherine," she said. "He missed her by that much."

I joined the group. Jack was standing sheepishly off to one side with the twins nearby. I went over to them. "What's going on?" I asked.

"Jack was demonstrating how he could throw a knife," Nick said. "It was brilliant, actually. So Kat said could he hit an apple on her head, like William Tell. And he told her to stand still and then he threw the knife into the tree right above her head. Pretty impressive, only Mummy was looking out of her window and absolutely had a fit."

"I might have done too," I said. "It was rather silly, Jack. If you want to make a good impression, you don't try and kill your relatives."

"They were perfectly safe. I didn't even throw it that close to her."

"And what's more . . ." Irene was still shrieking. "He was teaching them to sharpen sticks and spear fish in the koi pond. He's dangerous, Mother. You know how impressionable the children are. For God's sake, send him away before he does anyone real harm."

"Irene, do calm down. I remember your brother Johnnie doing rather the same sort of thing when you were young."

"Yes, and look what happened to him—fathered a child with a nobody in the back of beyond, and then got himself killed by being too damned heroic."

"He acted honorably in both instances, which is more than can be said for your husband."

"That's a cruel blow, Mama. I'm not staying here any longer. I want the children away from this place right now. We're going up to London. Nicholas, Katherine, come with me."

And she stalked off into the house.

Tea had been brought out to the lawn, because the afternoon was a fine one, but it seemed that nobody had much of an appetite—and not just because of the size of the luncheon. Irene did not put in an appearance, nor did Cedric and his Starlings. The princess complained that it was too cold to be outside, so it was just Edwina, the naughty countess Virginia, Jack and me, and we made a halfhearted attempt to enjoy scones, cream and strawberry jam.

"I can't imagine what you were thinking, John," Edwina said to Jack. "Throwing a knife at your cousin."

"I missed, didn't I? And I've done that stunt a million times."

"But, my dear boy, what if she had moved at the last second or you had stumbled? All sorts of things could have gone wrong. Now, please understand that this is a civilized household. We do not go in for violence here."

"I thought we were about to go out hunting foxes," Jack said. "And I've seen all kinds of weapons and animal heads on the walls."

"That is quite different. Those things are acceptable violence. The English nobility has always hunted and served in honorable battles."

"Georgie said I should try to get along with my cousins, so that's what I was trying to do." Jack shrugged.

"In the future, John, please ask me or even Georgiana if a particular pursuit is acceptable before undertaking it," Edwina said.

"I do wish you'd stop calling me John," Jack said. "That's never been my name, and I keep thinking you expect me to be my father and not me."

Edwina drew herself up in her seat and took a deep breath before answering. Maybe she realized that what he was saying was true. She wanted him to be her John, returned from the grave. "It's just that John is a more suitable name for a viscount," she said. "And one has never heard of a duke called Jack. And I expect you to call me Grandmama."

"Right-oh," he said.

I felt for her at that moment. She was going through the same exasperation I often felt in my attempts to educate Queenie. I was glad when tea was cleared away and we walked back into the house. I decided to find something to read in the library. As I passed Cedric's study, I heard raised voices and suddenly a door opened and Irene stormed out, her face bright red.

"That man is impossible," she said to nobody in particular as she disappeared down the hallway in front of me. "A nasty, spiteful miser. He'll get his just deserts someday."

I found a book and retreated to my room, where I read peacefully until it was time to dress for dinner. There was a full complement of guests at the dinner table, but talk was at a minimum until Cedric said, "I understand there was a bit of a ruckus this afternoon. Something about young Jack throwing knives at people?"

"John was merely demonstrating his prowess with a knife," Edwina said before anyone else could answer, "and I must say it was most impressive."

"Most impressive?" Irene demanded. "He missed my daughter's head by inches."

"Too bad," Cedric muttered loudly enough for the Starlings to grin.

"Anyway, the incident will not be repeated," Edwina said. "I have told John that his knife will be kept in the tack room and not brought out without my permission in future. Since there are no brigands in the neighborhood and our food comes to us on a plate, he will actually have no need of it here. So you may stop fretting, Irene. The matter is forgotten."

We went back to our soup until Irene blurted out, "Mama, I have to tell you that Cedric has refused to let me take the children to stay at the London house. He is not using it. He always stays at his club. It's just sitting there, and it is the height of spite and selfishness not to allow my family to use it."

Edwina looked up from her oyster bisque. "It is his house now, Irene. He may use it or not use it as he chooses and there is nothing you or I can do about it."

"Of course you may always stay there overnight if you go up to town to a show or to visit friends, Mama," Cedric said. "But that is very different from Irene wanting to set up home there with her brood. Where does she intend to find servants to run it properly? She has no money to pay them, and I certainly don't want her to take any of our servants. Nor do I want to pay for servants for Irene. It's not my fault that she made a bad decision in her choice of a husband. I warned her that foreigners are always trouble and can't be trusted."

"I object to that remark, young man," Princess Charlotte said. "Prince Orlovski and I were extremely happy and well-suited."

"Until he was murdered by peasants and you barely escaped with your life," Cedric said. "And Aunt Virginia's husbands all died under mysterious circumstances. Doesn't that prove that foreigners cannot be trusted?"

I thought it proved that someone should have questioned Countess Virginia more thoroughly, but Irene waved this aside and went on. "This is all beside the point, Cedric. All I am asking is to stay at the house at Eaton Square with my children—the house I grew up in and where I have many happy memories. This does not seem unreasonable to me. I have already asked you to help send your nephew and niece to decent boarding schools and you have refused. So my only alternative is to move them to London, where at least they can go to good day schools. It is not healthy for them to be stuck out here with only a tutor and no friends their own age."

"There's a school in the village," Cedric said. "They can always go there."

"A village school?" Irene's voice rose dangerously. "Are you mad? You want them mixing with ordinary village children?"

"Since we're led to believe the future Duke of Eynsford's mother was a barmaid or something equally lowly, it might be a good idea to prepare them for what this title may become in the future."

Jack rose to his feet. "My mother was not a barmaid," he said in a voice that was icy cold. "She was a decent woman who earned an honest living to support me."

"Doing what, may one ask?" Cedric said, his voice laden with sarcasm.

"If you must know, she was a schoolteacher in an outback school. You've talked down to me from the moment I walked in, but you'll not insult my mother. If you weren't such a sorry, flabby excuse for a man, I'd invite you to step outside right now to settle this."

"Really," the dowager duchess said strongly. "Well, really."

"Really what?" Jack asked.

"Really," she said again. "This is not acceptable conversation for the dinner table. And, Irene, you were wrong to introduce this subject in the first place. Eaton Square is your brother's house. You are fortunate that he gives you a home at the family seat and a tutor for your children. We are all fortunate that he allows us to continue to live here. Let us never forget that. Now, we will go on with the meal like civilized individuals. Is that clear?"

And she went back to her smoked salmon.

Chapter 12

Kingsdowne

The morning of the hunt dawned red. I suppose I should have taken that as an omen. As Queenie helped me to dress, I found that I was anticipating the day with equal mixture of excitement and dread. I have always adored hunting. One feels sorry for the poor fox, I suppose, although the fox is so rarely caught and killed. But hunting is in one's blood. Setting out on a crisp morning, the horse's breath coming out like dragon's smoke, the sound of the hooves echoing through a silent village, and then the moment when the hounds pick up the scent and off they go, tails in the air and baying—from then on it's pure adrenaline with fields and copses flying by, ditches and walls to be leaped. Normally I would need no excuse to join a hunt, but today I would be responsible for Jack. And hunts are absolutely laden with protocol.

I had long ago given up hoping that my morning tea might arrive when I wanted it, but I reached across and tugged hopefully on the bell pull. Almost immediately there was a tap on my door. I began to feel more charitable about Queenie as I called, "Come in."

Instead of Queenie, a shy maid I hadn't seen before came in with my tray.

"Your tea, my lady," she said and put it on the bedside table.

"Thank you. What happened to my maid?"

"I don't know, my lady. I haven't seen her yet this morning, so Mrs. Broad said I should bring your tea as you'll want to get going for the hunt."

"Most kind," I said, knowing full well that Queenie had overslept once again.

"Do you want me to stay and help you dress, my lady?" she asked.

"I think I can manage," I said. She curtsied and left.

I washed and got into my riding attire. I had my breeches and boots with me, but not a hunting jacket or hunting whip. These had been lent to me by Irene, who declared herself too frail and upset to think about hunting, and not having a horse of her own anyway. As I went downstairs, I saw a man standing in the hallway, smartly turned out in hunting attire. For a second my heart leaped that Darcy had come for the hunt after all.

"Good morning," I said. "Fine day for a hunt, isn't it?"

"Good day, Georgie." He turned around and I was shocked to see it was Jack. He grinned. "I look like a right ponce, don't I?" he said. "That Frederick said this is what I had to wear. The blokes at home would laugh themselves silly if they saw me like this."

"You look perfect," I said. "Just right."

"I thought people wore red jackets for hunting, but Frederick said that black was correct."

"It is," I said. "Pink jackets are an honor bestowed by the master."

"Pink?" He laughed. "You wouldn't catch me wearing pink."

"It's really red. Only it's called pink."

"This really is a bloody silly country," he said.

"You said you were called Blue because of your red hair," I pointed out. "So Australia must be just as silly."

"You got me there." He laughed. We went into the dining room and grabbed an early breakfast. The dowager duchess joined us just as we were finishing, looking terrifying in full hunting gear. "I couldn't turn down the chance to hunt once more," she said. "But I had to promise I would not take the jumps."

We went out to find three magnificent horses waiting for us. Jack looked at his and laughed. "What kind of saddle do you call that little thing? It doesn't look big enough for my bum, let alone yours."

"Well, really!" Edwina exclaimed. "That is a perfectly normal riding saddle, although when I was a gell a lady always rode sidesaddle."

"Do you mind if I take it off and ride bareback?" he asked.

"I most certainly do mind." Edwina allowed the groom to help her into her saddle, the poor man straining and red-faced as he hoisted that considerable weight. "You must learn the rules, John. You must learn to uphold the family honor at all times."

Jack swung himself easily into the saddle and I followed suit.

"We join the hunt down in the village," Edwina said. "It will give you a chance to get the feel of the horse."

"All I can feel right now is this bloody saddle digging into my arse," Jack said. "How can you ride with anything so uncomfortable?"

"What sort of saddle do you use?" I asked. "Or do you ride bareback?"

"Sometimes," he said. "But when I was riding the boundary fences, we had big, Western saddles with a pommel in front. Sort of like sitting in an armchair and hard to fall off if you're trying to rope a calf."

Our hoofbeats echoed in the still, morning air. A flock of rooks rose, cawing from the copper beech. The horses danced nervously, and I noticed how comfortable Jack was in the saddle. Here was someone who really knew horses. Finally his grandmother would have something to be impressed about. A large crowd of riders and spectators on foot had gathered at the pub, while the hounds milled around, wagging tails.

"What are the dogs for?" Jack asked.

"They're hounds, and they track the fox for us. They pick up the scent, chase it and corner it for us."

"It sounds like a lot of bother for one little fox," Jack said. "Wouldn't it be easier to find its den, wait until it comes out and then shoot it?"

Edwina had turned pale and was clutching the gold tie pin at her neck.

A man in a white apron was going around, handing out stirrup cups.

"We get something to drink, do we? Good-oh," Jack said. He took a cup, took a good swig and made a face. "Port? Is it port?"

"Probably. That's what's traditional."

"Struth," he said. "You don't even get a decent beer before exercise. What a country."

The master of fox hounds, resplendent in his red jacket, came up to greet us. "Your Grace, such an honor," he said, tipping his velvet cap to the dowager duchess.

"My guest Lady Georgiana, and my grandson, Viscount Farningham," she said with a certain amount of pride in her voice.

"Delighted to have you join us," he said. "Welcome aboard. Should be a good day for it. Drink up, everyone. Time to be off."

The horn sounded, and we set off up the hill and out of the village. Soon we were crossing fields of stubble, passing sheep and cows. Jack trotted beside me with the easy grace of one used to a life in the saddle. I relaxed and started to enjoy myself. My mount moved smoothly and easily, reacting to my commands as if we'd been together all our lives. We had just crossed a little brook when there came the shout, "View halloo!" as a streak of bright copper fur broke from cover. The hounds were suddenly in full cry, and off we went. It was glorious—the countryside flashing past in a blur, the jingle of harness, thud of the hooves, a hedge coming up at us and the impression of flying as we soared over it. Jack was beside me, matching my horse stride for stride.

"There it goes," someone shouted. "Crafty little devil. It's crossing the stream. The hounds will lose the scent if we're not careful."

At that, Jack took off. One second he was beside me, the next his horse was in a flat-out gallop. It cut through the pack of hounds and splashed through the stream, sending up a sheet of water on either side, and vanished into the woodland beyond.

"What the devil does he think he's doing?" the master bellowed.

I had no idea. It didn't look as if his horse had bolted with him. We could only follow his trail across the stream and into the woods, where the hounds started baying again. We caught up with him in a clearing, his horse surrounded by excited hounds.

As we approached he held up something for us to see, making the hounds go wild with excitement. It was the fox, quite dead.

"Killed the little bugger for you with me bare hands," he said. "Now we can all go home."

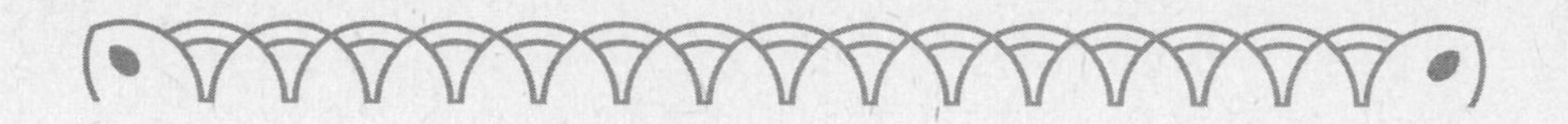

Chapter 13

After the hunt

We rode back in silence. Jack could sense he was in disgrace but couldn't quite see why.

"We went to kill a fox. I killed the fox and saved you a lot of trouble," he said. "I don't see what the fuss was about."

"It's supposed to be done the traditional way, Jack. And they nearly always let it go in the end."

"Let it go? Then what's the purpose?"

"A day's fun," I said. "It all started to keep knights in training for battle during peacetime. It's an English tradition, and it's really tradition that keeps us going."

"Bloody silly," he said. He moved closer to my horse. "Maybe the old cow won't want me here after this, and I can go home where I belong."

I looked at him with compassion, wondering how I'd fare my first week on a sheep station in Australia. "Jack, you have to stay and give it a chance," I said. "Nobody expects you to learn all the ropes at once. And you'll be a duke someday. That's really important. Your father gave his life being awfully brave in the war. Don't you think he'd want you to make the most of your chances?"

Jack shook his head. "From what my mum told me, he thought this whole duke-and-title stuff was bloody silly too. He'd have been quite happy to stay down in Australia."

"At least give it a chance," I said. "You really know nothing about England yet. It's lovely in summer—cricket and cream teas on the lawn . . ."

"Cricket?"

"Yes, it's a game that . . ."

"I know all about cricket. It's the Australian national sport. I'm a great fast bowler. You should see my googlies."

We dismounted, and grooms took the horses away. It will be all right in the end, I thought. Jack will play on the village cricket team and everyone will adore him. . . .

When I went into the house and up to my room Queenie was now awake but unapologetic, and I had her run me a bath before luncheon. At luncheon the children were anxious to hear all about the hunt, but Edwina remained tight-lipped.

"Was the fox killed?" Katherine asked. "Did Jack get blooded?"

"I believe he did," Edwina said.

"I do wish you'd buy us decent ponies, Uncle Cedric, so that we could join in," Nick said. "It's really not fair."

"Ask your father to buy you ponies," Cedric said. "You're his responsibility, not mine."

"How can we ask him? We don't even know where he is," Kat said.

"Precisely." Cedric went back to his meal.

"It's not their fault that their father ran off," Irene said.

"The spirits might tell us," Princess Charlotte said excitedly. "We haven't had our séance yet, have we? Let's do it tonight, after dinner. Then Jack can contact his father, and we can track down Irene's wandering husband."

Cedric stood up. "Really, this family is too ridiculous for words. Not a word of intelligent conversation among you. Babbling and dotty old aunts, a domineering mother and a whining, complaining sister.

I've had enough. It's time you all moved out and left me in peace. I'm under no obligation to feed you, let alone listen to your twaddle." And he stomped out of the dining room.

"Oh, dear. We've upset him," Charlotte said. "Do you think he really will throw us out, Edwina? Where would we go?"

"I'm afraid my son is behaving like a spoiled child," Edwina said, her voice cracking with emotion. "He needs reminding that this is the family seat of which he is caretaker for a while. It is not his house."

"I don't know what I'd do if we couldn't live here," Irene said. "I'd have to take a job, but what am I qualified for? Nothing. You brought me up to be a lady, Mama. I have no skills, no prospects and no hope."

"Don't worry, Mummy," Katherine said. "Nick and I will be brilliant and go to university and earn scads of money."

"Who's going to pay for us to go to university, Kat?" Nick asked.

"We'll be so brilliant we'll both get scholarships," Katherine said.

"Not from what Mr. Carter tells me," Edwina says. "He commented that you were both hopelessly behind for your age. Unlike your sister, who is a most diligent student."

"Such a pity for her. A life blighted before it's begun," Irene said. "I know that doctor in Switzerland could help her."

All in all, it was a gloomy luncheon. Jack and I went up to visit Sissy afterward, and she laughed and laughed when Jack recounted the story of the hunt to her. They were getting along so well, I thought. And she's not really a child anymore. Maybe, who knows what the future will bring? I glanced across at Jack. It wouldn't be sensible for him to marry someone who couldn't ever have children.

THE SUBDUED MOOD still hung over us as we gathered for dinner that night. We worked our way, in near silence, through a leek and potato soup, filets of plaice and roast pheasant. We had just started on the savory—anchovy toast—at the end of the meal when Cedric tapped on his wineglass.

"I have a couple of announcements to make," he said. "In the morning, I will be meeting with the architect who is coming to design my theater. I'm hoping that work will begin almost immediately so that we can plan an autumn season for this year."

He paused. "And my second announcement is that I've decided to end this farce and take matters into my own hands. I have made my own choice of heir and I shall be meeting with my solicitor to find out the procedure for adopting him."

Edwina rose to her feet. "What did you say?" she demanded.

"You have been badgering me for years to produce an heir, Mother, so I have finally granted your wish. I have decided to adopt the person I wish to be my heir. I will not let this dukedom go to an uncouth, uncivilized member of the hoi polloi."

"You're really going to do it, Ceddy?" Adrian asked, his face alight with excitement. "We thought it was just a joke. We never dreamed you'd go through with it. What a coup."

"Who is this person you have decided to adopt?" Edwina asked.

"Yes, who is it, Ceddy?" The Starlings were looking at each other with excited anticipation.

"It's Marcel," Cedric said.

"What?" Adrian shrieked.

"And who might Marcel be?" Edwina demanded.

"His valet," Simon said, sounding near to tears. "A nasty, common, little Frenchman. How could you, Ceddy? We thought at least it would be one of us."

"You just like me for the sort of lifestyle I can give you," Cedric said. He had a self-satisfied grin on his face now. "Marcel is truly devoted to me."

"A French valet?" Edwina demanded. "Are you mad?"

"Better a French valet than an Australian farm worker. He comes from an aristocratic family that lost everything in the revolution. He has good blood."

"Good blood." Edwina spat out the words. "At least John is your own flesh and blood—your brother's child."

"So his mother claimed," Cedric said. "Obviously John was the best choice among the many contenders for father of her brat."

"How dare you!" Jack leaped up. "I warned you before not to insult my mother. You take that back."

He started round the table toward Cedric.

"Stop him," Cedric said to the footmen standing behind us, who were staring at us in horror and fascination. They made a halfhearted grab at Jack, who attempted to fight them off.

"Sit down, John," Edwina said in her powerful voice. Jack hesitated then backed off, standing undecided at the back of the room. Edwina drew herself up to her full height, sticking out that impressive bosom. "This is madness, Cedric. It cannot be allowed to happen."

"I don't think there's much you can do, Mother. There are legal precedents aplenty."

"We will have you declared insane if we have to."

"Good luck. Try it. I'll enjoy the fight," Cedric said. "You and Father always claimed I was spineless and lacked imagination. Now I suspect that I'll have the last laugh."

With that, he strode from the room.

The Starlings had also risen to their feet and watched him go, half wanting to run after him, but not daring to.

"That conniving little minx Marcel." Julian sounded near to tears. "Pretending to be so humble and subservient, when all this time he's been plotting against us."

"He can't really do it, can he, Mama?" Irene asked. "I mean, one can't really adopt someone who is over twenty-one, surely?"

"I have no idea," Edwina said. "And we don't actually know that he is over twenty-one, do we? Your brother selected him. I know nothing about him."

"If he was going to adopt anyone, he should have adopted Nick."

Irene glared at the doorway through which Cedric had departed. "If anyone deserves to be the rightful heir, it is surely one of my children. We have the blood of the dukedom in our veins, don't we? But a common valet, and a Frenchman at that—it's too much to bear. Get on to our solicitor now, Mama. Summon him here immediately, before something awful happens."

"I will telephone our solicitor in the morning and ask him to come down and meet with us, Irene. The wheels of the law move slowly. Cedric can't just adopt someone overnight. And it may just be an idle threat. It wouldn't be the first time your brother did something stupid out of spite then regretted it. Give him time to see the absurdity of his threat."

"We must not give him time, Mama. We must stop it before it's too late. You must go to the House of Lords, if necessary. Daddy's old friends. They will surely help, and Cedric won't be able to oppose the might of the English parliament against him."

"I said give him time, Irene. We do not need to expose this family to ridicule unnecessarily. It will be hard enough to live down the shame of an heir from Australia, but an heir who is a French valet—it would be unendurable." Edwina's voice wavered just the slightest. Then she shook her head violently, as if to gain control of her emotions. "I will speak with the boy. Make him see sense, if it's the last thing I do."

"Séance!" Princess Charlotte stood up and clapped her hands excitedly. "That's what we need to cheer us up. Our séance. The room is all set up for it."

"I hardly think that most people find séances cheerful, Charlotte," Edwina said.

"But Jack will have a lovely chat with his father, and maybe the spirits will be helpful in suggesting a way to get rid of this Marcel. They have the wisdom of the ages, remember."

"Then I'm in," Adrian said, glancing at Julian. "How about you, Jules? Let's see if the spirits can tell us how to bump off Marcel without being caught."

"Adrian, you're terrible," Julian said. "But it might be fun. There's certainly no point in trying to talk to Ceddy tonight. Come on, Simon. Stop sulking. He'd never have adopted you anyway."

"I've just remembered what a gorgeous Polish officer and I once got up to during a séance in Vienna," Virginia said dreamily. "So naughty. Such fun."

"Then come along, everyone. It's all set up in Lady Hortense's sitting room." Princess Charlotte tried to herd everyone out of the dining room.

"Who is Lady Hortense?" I asked as we filed out of the dining room.

"The wife of an eighteenth-century duke," Charlotte replied. "A very powerful medium, apparently. Had ectoplasm floating around all over the place, and violins playing themselves in midair. I have felt her presence most strongly in that room, and I'm sure she'll help with this dreadful Marcel business."

"I am certainly not attending your ridiculous séance," Edwina said. "Come, Irene."

"But, Mama, what if the spirits do have a suggestion for making Cedric see sense?" Irene hesitated, unsure whether to disobey her mother then followed her aunts in the other direction, with the Starlings in hot pursuit.

Jack glanced at me. "Are you going along with this mumbo-jumbo?" he asked.

"I've never been to a séance before," I said. "I played around with a Ouija board at school and it was rather frightening, so I have to confess to being a teeny bit curious. What about you?"

"No, thanks. I don't go for stuff I can't explain."

"Don't you want the chance to connect with your father, perhaps?"

"You really believe that could happen?"

"But if it could—wouldn't you want to hear his voice once?"

He stared hard at me. Then he said, "All right. What have I got to lose? And if I can't go to the pub, there's nothing else to do here."

We fell into step, side by side, and hurried after the disappearing forms of the older women. Lady Hortense's sitting room was a small, square and rather cluttered space, made smaller by the circle of chairs around a table, and by the heavy, brocade drapes, closed at both windows. On the table was a solitary candle in a tall candlestick, a pencil and pad and a Ouija board.

"Everyone, take a seat around the table," Charlotte said. I pulled up a chair between Irene and Jack.

Charlotte lit the candle and had one of the Starlings turn off the electric light. How different faces looked in the flickering flame. Those heavy drapes now seemed to hang ominously close. I began to wish I hadn't come.

"All hold hands on the table," Charlotte commanded.

Irene's hand was icy cold. Jack's was reassuring.

"Isn't this exciting?" I heard one of the Starlings whisper. "Feel my hand. It's all aquiver."

"Spirits from the other side, we call upon you," Charlotte began in such a dramatic voice that I had to suppress the need to giggle. I wished Belinda had been present so that we could have kicked each other beneath the tablecloth, or that Darcy had been sitting across the table to give me a reassuring wink. "Come to our aid, dear spirits. Lady Hortense, are you present among us?"

A long silence was followed punctuated only by the sound of a grandfather clock, ticking away solemnly somewhere outside in a hallway.

"Are you with us, Lady Hortense? Will you be our guide?"

The candle flickered and I felt a cold draft pass over me. I glanced over my shoulder. The door and the curtains were still closed. I thought I detected the faintest of voices whispering, "Yessss."

"She's here," Charlotte said excitedly. "I knew she'd come. Lady Hortense, we'd first like you to find John Altringham for us. You remember your great-great-grandson, who died so bravely in the war?

His son is here with us now. Do you see him? He'd like to hear his father's voice."

Again we waited what seemed like an eternity. Then Irene said, "Listen. Someone is laughing."

We strained to hear and it sounded indeed like distant laughter, very far away.

"It's Ceddy, having a good laugh at our expense," Julian whispered.

"That's not Ceddy's laugh," Adrian said.

"That's Johnnie," Charlotte said. "Don't you remember how he loved to laugh, Irene?"

"Yes," Irene whispered. "Johnnie loved to laugh."

"Is that you, John?" Charlotte said. "Can you show yourself to us? Can you say something to your son?"

Again we waited but the laughter faded into silence. "It's no use. He's choosing not to speak to us," Charlotte said. "I can feel he's here. Maybe what he has to say to Jack is private and he doesn't wish us to overhear."

"We could try the Ouija board," Virginia suggested. "Perhaps he is a voiceless spirit. They are sometimes."

"We could." Charlotte picked up the planchette. "Jack, put your hand on this with me. And Irene. You are both Johnnie's relatives. He'll feel comfortable communicating with you."

Jack gave me a questioning glance before placing his finger on the little disk. Slowly it started to move across the table. "*B . . . U . . . G . . . G . . . E . . . R.*" We repeated the letters as the planchette went to them. "*O . . . F . . . F.*"

"He said, 'Bugger off,' " Jack said delightedly.

"That definitely sounds like Johnnie," Irene said. "Always was rude."

"Anything else you'd like to say, John?" Charlotte asked. But the planchette did not move again. "Apparently not." She looked around the room. "Let us move along then. The problem of Marcel. Spirits from the other side, we need your help. Tell us what will happen. Tell us what we should do to stop a stranger from taking over Kingsdowne."

She looked at us as she pushed the Ouija board into the middle of the table. "Place one finger each on the planchette," she said. We did as she commanded.

"We await you, oh spirits," she said. Slowly the planchette began to move.

"*D*," we said in unison.

It shot across the board. "*E*," we chimed.

"*A*."

Suddenly there was a great gust of wind. The curtains billowed out. The candle was blown out and we were plunged into darkness. Irene and Virginia rose to their feet with a cry of fright. I think the Starlings screamed as well. My own heart was hammering in my chest.

"Death," Charlotte whispered. "It was going to spell out 'death.'"

Chapter 14

Kingsdowne

We went up to bed in uneasy silence. I didn't quite believe in Princess Charlotte and her spirits but I had felt the cold draft in a small, closed room. I had seen the planchette race around to spell out "bugger off." And I had heard the distant laughter. Now, it was possible that this was Jack's idea of a joke, but his expression had also looked wary. And whose idea of a joke would it have been to spell out "death"? Of course, again, maybe we were reading too much into it. The word had not finished before the candle was blown out. It could have been "dear" or "deal." But I had felt the fear in the room.

Queenie was waiting for me, for once cheerful and inclined to be chatty.

"You won't believe what we had to eat in the servants' hall," she said. "Bloody good food they have here, don't they? I'll end up as fat as a pig. Come on, turn around. Let me undo your dress."

"Queenie, I think I can manage from now on," I said. "If you don't mind, I'd rather be alone tonight."

"I don't know about you," she said. "When I don't turn up on time you're always grousing, and when I do turn up you don't want me anyway."

I had to turn and smile at this. "I'm sorry. You're right. I am normally delighted when you turn up at the right time to perform your duties. It's just that I'm a bit unsettled tonight and I really don't want to talk."

"Oh, in that case just tell me to shut me gob," Queenie said. "My old dad was always saying that to me. I'm used to it."

"I don't think I could ever bring myself to tell anyone to shut her gob," I said cautiously. "My great-grandmother Queen Victoria would turn in her grave."

Queenie chuckled and proceeded to undress me in silence, hung up my clothes and even handed me my toothbrush, so that I felt quite guilty for my uncharitable thoughts about her.

"Will that be all, my lady?" she asked.

I nodded. "Thank you, Queenie. You're coming along quite nicely."

"Am I really?" She went quite pink and tiptoed out. I curled up in bed, listening to the moan of the wind down my chimney. Eventually I must have fallen asleep, and I awoke to a wild morning with clouds racing across a sky heavy with the promise of rain. The fire was already burning merrily in my grate, having been lit by an unseen, unheard housemaid, but the prospect outside was so unappealing that I lay under the covers until Queenie arrived with my tea.

"Sorry, miss. It's so bloomin' dark that I overslept again," she said. "Shall I run you a bath? And what will you be wearing?"

"My kilt again with a jumper, I think, and yes, please do run me a bath."

The clock in the great central foyer was chiming nine as I made my way down to the breakfast room. My nanny back in Scotland would say that I was heading down the slippery slope getting up at such a late hour. The three sisters were sitting together at one end of the table, but there was no sign of the other members of the household. They were involved in some kind of heated discussion when I came in, but broke off when they saw me, nodded then went back to devouring kidneys.

"So what do you think it means, Edwina?" Charlotte asked. "It was such an ominous presence and after last night's séance . . ."

"I'd say it meant that you overindulged at dinner last night," Edwina said. "Too much cream in the pudding, maybe."

"Don't mock, Edwina. You know I've had prophetic dreams in the past. Why, I even dreamed of our downfall in Russia. I saw a horde of black ants swarming all over our beautiful picnic, and Orlovski said, 'Everything is ruined.' Then the ants turned and swarmed all over him. And look what happened only a month later."

"Hmmph," Edwina said.

"So maybe Cedric is the evil presence I saw in my dream—although why he should take on the shape of a black panther, I don't know."

"You had a dream last night, Your Highness?" I asked.

"I did. Most real and vivid. I looked out of my window and I saw this huge, black cat stalking through the grounds. Some kind of black panther or leopard, I'd say. And I knew it meant danger for the family and I believe Edwina's voice said, 'How did it get in here? It's dangerous.' And someone else replied, 'The family let it in.' "

Virginia shuddered. "What with that and the Ouija board spelling out 'death' last night."

"Fortunately, there are no panthers wandering about Britain as far as I know," Edwina said. She looked out of the window. "Beastly day. Serves Cedric right for bringing down that architect chappy for his wretched amphitheater. I hope they both get soaked to the skin."

"I can't think what the boy was thinking," Princess Charlotte said. "Hordes of people tramping over the estate. Not a moment of privacy. Didn't you try to talk him out of it, Edwina?"

"Of course I did, but he wouldn't listen. I'm utterly appalled by the whole thing, especially by his callous attitude toward the tenants in those cottages. People have lived there for generations—our estate people—and he simply couldn't care a fig. I don't know how I could have raised such a selfish son. His father would give him a good talking-to. A good thrashing would have been even better."

"Maybe we should have summoned his father during the séance last night," Virginia suggested.

"Please, Virginia, no more about that séance," Edwina said. "News of it has quite upset the servants. In fact—" She broke off at the sound of an anguished wail. "Now what?" she demanded. Far off, we could hear what sounded like a hysterical outburst.

"You see what I mean, Charlotte?" Edwina said. "You've got them all frightened."

We sat there, poised as in a tableau until we heard the sound of feet running in our direction. Elsie, the head housemaid, came bursting into the breakfast room. "Beg pardon, Your Grace," she said.

"What is it, Elsie?" Edwina had risen to her feet. "Who is making that ridiculous noise?"

"It's Lady Irene's maid, Your Grace. She says she can't wake Lady Irene."

Edwina was clutching the jet brooch at her throat. "That silly girl. She can't have . . ." she said. "Elsie, go to Mr. Huxstep and tell him to telephone Dr. Bradley at once. Tell him Lady Irene might have tried to kill herself."

She started out of the room, her hand clasped to her prodigious bosom.

"I'll come with you," I said, and she didn't turn me down.

Up the grand staircase we went, along the front hall with its magnificent views of the rain-swept lake, toward the sound of uncontrolled sobbing. A thin woman with an unmistakably French profile, dressed in severe black, was cowering in the hallway, a lace handkerchief pressed to her mouth.

"Pull yourself together, Francoise," the dowager duchess said. She pushed the maid aside and flung open the bedroom door. Irene lay pale and unmoving in her big, white bed. She looked much younger without her perpetual, worried frown, and I could see she must have been quite a beauty once. I went over to her and put my face close to her cheek. I felt the warmth of breath. "She's still alive," I said.

"Thank God for that," Edwina answered. "I hope that wretched doctor will hurry up."

She sat on the bed beside Irene and took her hand. "Irene, darling, can you hear me? It's Mama. Time to wake up now, darling." Then she shook her. Irene didn't stir.

The duchess looked up at the cowering, sniveling maid. "Did you only just discover her like this?"

"Yes, milady," the girl answered in her strong French accent. "The countess say last night that she is getting one of her migraines and she will take a sleeping powder, so I must not wake her at her usual time in the morning. But when it was past nine o'clock I wonder if perhaps she would like some tea. So I peek in. And she lies there, so pale, not moving. I am afraid. I try to wake her but it is impossible." And she started sobbing again.

Edwina looked at her with distaste. "Show me these sleeping powders," Edwina said. "Do you know how many she had and how many she might have taken?" she asked.

"I do not know, Your Grace," the girl said. "I am not allowed to touch her medicines that the doctor prescribes. She keeps these shut away in her bathroom cabinet."

The duchess's two sisters arrived on the scene, breathing heavily. Charlotte let out a little moan. "You see, I was right. The spirits never lie. I told you they said 'death.' "

Edwina spun on her, eyes blazing. "Be quiet, Charlotte. Enough of your nonsense. Irene is still alive and breathing, and I intend to keep her that way." She broke off, collecting herself as the butler tapped on the bedroom door.

"Your Grace, the doctor is on his way," he said. "Is there anything I can do?"

"Someone should subdue that hysterical French girl," Edwina said, "and, Huxstep, I think you had better wake the duke. He should know about his sister, and he needs to be up anyway, if he is to meet this architect fellow."

"Very good, Your Grace," Huxstep said. "And should I perhaps bring up the brandy decanter and some glasses? You have clearly had a shock."

"Very thoughtful of you, but no, I do not think alcohol is needed. I will stay at my daughter's side until the doctor arrives, and I'd appreciate it if the rest of you left us for the present."

I followed the butler and the two elderly sisters out of the room.

"Do you really think Irene tried to take her own life?" Virginia asked in a stage whisper as we came out into the hall.

"She always did go in for melodrama, even as a child," Charlotte said. "And she was upset last night. I do feel for her. It's terrible when one has lost everything—status, power and money—and is dependent on the goodness of relatives."

"If you're talking about Cedric," Virginia replied, "I don't think there is a large font of goodness to depend upon."

Charlotte nodded. "Cedric has always thought only of himself. I believe he'd turn out his own mother if it suited him."

As we walked down the hall, Huxstep was tapping on a pair of gilded double doors set back in an alcove. The door opened to reveal a rather beautiful young man with big, dark eyes and a Mediterranean look about him.

"Mr. 'uxstep?" he asked. "What is zee mattaire?"

"Her Grace requests that you wake your master and tell him that Lady Irene has been taken ill," Huxstep said.

"But 'e is not 'ere," Marcel said. "He rises early, and he say he have urgent matter to attend to. He instructs me to bring him a cup of coffee to his study."

"Ah, thank you, Marcel," Huxstep said. We followed him down the stairs and I watched him tap on a door then open it cautiously. "Your Grace?" he asked.

Then he pushed the door open wider. "He doesn't appear to be in his study after all," Huxstep said to me, coming out again and shutting the door behind him. "Perhaps he went into breakfast."

"Ah, breakfast. That's what we need," Charlotte said, taking Virginia's arm. "I never did finish my kidneys."

We were on our way to the breakfast room when we passed Frederick.

"Have you seen His Grace recently?" Huxstep asked.

"Not recently, Mr. Huxstep, but I saw him heading for the front door a good hour or so ago. I asked if I should fetch his overcoat or a brolly, as the weather looked most threatening. He said he'd be fine in his tweed jacket and that he wouldn't be gone long. He was just going to take another look at the possible building site, and he had a letter in his hand."

"A letter?"

"Yes, Mr. Huxstep. I asked him if it needed posting but he said he'd pop it in the letter box in the lane as he was going that way and it was important that it catch the first post. I then suggested that the chauffeur could run it into the village, but he said it wasn't necessary and that a walk would do him good."

"I see," Huxstep said. He paused, frowning. "And did any of his young friends accompany him, do you know?"

"I couldn't tell you that, Mr. Huxstep. I didn't see anyone else. I shut the front door behind him then I went back to my duties."

"And this was some time ago, you said?"

"A good hour or more."

"Was it not raining when he set out?"

"I don't believe so, Mr. Huxstep, although the sky certainly looked nasty enough."

"Then I think you'd better put the brandy decanter in His Grace's study," Huxstep said. "He will be exceedingly wet and cold by the time he returns. He will need reviving."

I walked with the sisters and the butler to the breakfast room. Cedric was not there. Mr. Huxstep left again but the two sisters resumed their meal immediately. I poured myself a cup of coffee, but I was too upset to think about food. I came out into the hall again, wondering what I should do with myself. I wanted to be of use, but

I'd been banished from Irene's bedroom. I wondered if I should go up and speak to her children, but decided that was the prerogative of their grandmother. There was also no sign of Jack, so I went through to the morning room, expecting to find the two sisters there. But it was deserted. A lovely fire was burning in the hearth, and I sat in one of the armchairs. Outside the tall, arched window, great squalls of rain were now sweeping across the forecourt. It was certainly a day for a book beside the fire, and I was rather glad that the obnoxious Cedric was getting soaked as he planned to evict his tenants.

I picked up a copy of *The Lady* and was about to start reading when I heard the sound of tires on gravel. I looked up to see a sporty Armstrong Sidley come up the driveway. This had to be the doctor arriving. I watched one of the footmen run out with a large umbrella and escort a small, chubby man up to the front door. A few seconds later our door was opened and the footman came in.

"Begging your pardon, my lady, but a gentleman has arrived to see His Grace. A Mr. Smedley—apparently His Grace is expecting him. Would you happen to know where His Grace might be?"

"I gather he went out to take a look at the site he is considering for his theater project," I said. "This man must be the architect he was expecting."

"That's right, my lady. He did mention that he was from a firm of architects. So His Grace is out on the estate?"

"I think so. He doesn't appear to be in the house."

He looked dubiously out of the window. "So someone should take this gentleman down to find His Grace."

I read in his face that he didn't fancy that someone being himself. I got up. "I'll take him if you like. I'm used to rain like this up in Scotland."

I saw the relief flood across his face. "Would you, my lady? That would be most kind of you. It seems that—" He broke off. "That would be the doctor's car now. I'd better go and escort him into the house, if you'd excuse me."

I followed him out into the hall and introduced myself to the architect. The man didn't look too cheerful about an expedition onto the grounds in this weather. I put on my own coat, tied a scarf around my head then off we went. It certainly was as miserable as any day in Scotland, and as we crossed the forecourt, we got the full force of the wind in our faces.

"Is it far? Should we take the motor?" he asked. "My umbrella would be useless in this wind."

"There's only a footpath, I'm afraid," I said.

"Maybe this may make the duke change his mind about having an open amphitheater," the architect shouted against the force of the wind. "I did suggest that we incorporate the possibility of inclement weather into our design, but he's got this idea of a classical Greek amphitheater in his head."

We skirted the lake and followed the stream downward. The path narrowed as we came into the glen where the stream, swollen with the current downpour, swirled and foamed and splashed over its banks as impressively as any burn at home in Scotland. The architect tried to tread daintily beside me to avoid stepping in puddles, and I noticed that he was wearing highly polished city shoes. I wondered if Cedric had picked the right man for the job.

Then the path turned a corner and the architect stopped short. "What's that?" he said.

Something was lying amid the bushes beside the stream. We made our way toward it, and Mr. Smedley gave a little yelp and exclaimed, "Oh my God."

Someone was lying beside the path, his head and torso half covered with a tweed jacket, while water from the swollen stream splashed up against him as against a large rock. I went up to him, my heart racing, and lifted off the jacket. Cedric was lying sprawled on his face, his white shirt spattered with mud, with what looked like Jack's knife sticking from the middle of his back.

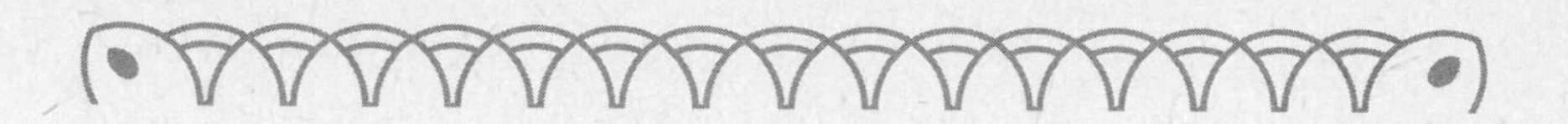

Chapter 15

Mr. Smedley grabbed me and tried to turn me away. "Please, avert your face. Do not look, my lady. It's too horrible for words," he said.

I didn't like to tell him that I had seen dead bodies before. Not that one ever gets used to the sight of gray, lifeless flesh or sightless eyes open wide in surprise. Knives sticking out of backs take a bit of getting used to as well.

"If you feel as if you're going to faint, my lady, do hang on to me," he said, but he was actually clinging on to me and even through my thick, tweed coat I could feel his hands shaking.

"It's all right. I'm not going to faint," I said.

"Is it—is it the duke?" Smedley asked.

"Yes, it is," I said. "It was." I couldn't take my eyes off that knife.

"What do we do? I suppose he is definitely dead?"

"Definitely," I said.

"Then we shouldn't linger here. The murderer could well be lurking behind one of those rocks."

"Only if he doesn't mind getting really wet," I said. "Come on, Mr. Smedley. We have to go back to the house and call the police."

"Should we move him?" Smedley asked. "He's getting awfully wet there."

"I don't think he minds anymore." I looked down at Cedric,

feeling a wave of pity. True, he hadn't been the most pleasant of men, but nobody deserved to end up like this. I picked up his jacket and covered him again. "The police will want to see the crime scene exactly as we found it," I said.

We started back up the path with Mr. Smedley hurrying so fast he was almost running.

"Oh, dear," he said. "Do you think my name will have to come into it? So bad for business anytime one's name is mixed up with the police."

"I'd have thought it would be wonderful publicity for your firm. The papers will be full of the murder of a duke. As an eyewitness, you'll be invited to dinner parties all over London."

"Oh, but I don't think I could bear to talk about it," he said. "I don't think I'll ever get that horrid sight from my mind. Who could have done it? There must be a madman loose in the neighborhood."

Who could have done it? I asked myself as we trudged back up the hill and came out onto the gravel forecourt. Was it possible that Irene's overdose of sleeping medicine was not an attempt at suicide but another attempt at murder? Could the same person be responsible for both? But that didn't make sense—one was so sneaky, and one was so obvious and violent. And I wondered if I should leave it to one of the family members to identify Jack's knife. Where was he, I wondered. It would not look good for him if he had disappeared at this very moment. Surely he couldn't have done this. Not easygoing, affable Jack. But then I realized how very little I knew about him—how little any of us knew.

As we reached the house, Huxstep came out to meet us, carrying a huge umbrella. He looked around. "Did you not find His Grace down there?"

"We found His Grace all right," Mr. Smedley blurted out. "He's dead."

"Dead? His Grace is dead? He had an accident?"

"He was murdered," I said. "You should call the police immediately."

"That is for Her Grace to decide," he said. "She must be notified first. Oh, dear. The poor lady. She's with the doctor, trying to save the life of Lady Irene. Both of her children in one morning—it is too much. Too much." He fought to keep his own voice steady then regained his composure as we entered the foyer and stood, dripping onto the marble floor. "If you will, please wait here. I will go up to inform Her Grace immediately."

"It had to be some kind of deranged tramp," Mr. Smedley said. "So many men have gone funny since the war. Gassed, you know, or shell-shocked. And now there is no work for them—well, I suppose one can understand. He probably asked the duke for money or food or even a light, and the duke ordered him off his property and something snapped."

I decided to stay silent. A deranged tramp would suit the family perfectly, I thought. And of course it was possible. Jack's knife might well have been lying around quite visible in the tack room. Maybe a tramp had managed to sneak in and spend the night in the stables, and had taken the knife. That explanation rather pleased me.

Because of the luxuriously thick carpets at Kingsdowne, we didn't hear Edwina coming until she was halfway down the stairs. "Oh, Georgiana, my dear," she said, holding out her hands to me as if she was graciously greeting a new visitor. "I'm so sorry you had to witness . . . It's true what Huxstep says then? You found my son's body?"

I nodded. "Yes, I'm afraid I did."

"It was definitely he?"

"It was. And I can't tell you how sorry I am."

She pressed her hand to her mouth for a moment before she composed herself. "What an awful shock for you, my dear. Some brandy, do you think?" For a moment I thought she was about to embrace me, but she stopped short when she saw my sodden outer garments.

"I'm really quite all right, thank you," I said.

"Where is he?" she asked. "I must go to him. Do you think you could take me to him, please?"

"He's in the glen," I said.

"That stupid theater project of his. I knew it would lead to disaster, but I never imagined anything like this. Huxstep said he was murdered, but that can't be right. Not on our own grounds. Perhaps he had a heart attack?"

"I'm afraid there's no doubt. He was stabbed," I said. "May I suggest you summon the police at once?"

"Huxstep is already doing so," she said. "Although who knows how long before they'll get here. I expect it will only be Constable Barber on his bike, but no doubt he can put through a telephone call to Sevenoaks for someone a little more senior."

As she spoke, Huxstep came to join us. "The police are on their way, Your Grace, and I suggested that they send their most senior man. Is there anything I can do for you until they come?"

"Lady Georgiana is going to take me to see my son's body," she said. "Please have somebody bring me my raincoat and my brogues."

"Your Grace, I think, given the inclement nature of the weather . . ."

"Your job is not to think, Huxstep," she said curtly. "Your job is to bring me my raincoat."

"Yes, Your Grace," he said. "I only wanted to spare Your Grace the distress of seeing your son's body."

"I thank you for your concern, but I am not a child, Huxstep. Nor am I a frail old woman. My coat, please. And an umbrella."

While we waited I asked, "Is there any news of Irene?"

"The doctor is administering a stomach pump," she said. "He thinks he will be able to save her. Two children in one fell swoop. It was bad enough when I got the news about Johnnie. I don't think I could bear it if the others were both taken from me. Where is my grandson? Where is John?"

"I don't know, Your Grace. I haven't seen him at all this morning."

"He should be informed that he is now Duke of Eynsford," she said with great dignity. "This is his house now. I realize that he is not yet twenty-one; thus, he will need a guardian to administer it for him until he reaches majority. I hope he will have the sense to allow me to guide him." Her hand was at her throat again, clutching the jet-and-diamond brooch. "Your friend Lord Kilhenny's son. Do you think he could be persuaded to come down again? A young man like John will need the strength and example of someone nearer his own age."

I didn't like to say I had no idea where Darcy could be found in London. He had no fixed address in town, but usually managed to live rather nicely in the houses of those who were wintering on the Med or were off at their country seats.

"He said he would come down as soon as he was able." I felt overwhelmed with great longing to have him here with me, to feel those strong arms around me. "I will see if I can contact him."

Huxstep returned, and produced the raincoat; an elderly maid carried the duchess's shoes. The latter sat on a chair while her maid knelt to remove her footwear.

When she had put on the brogues, she turned to me. "In the glen, you say?" and she started toward the front door.

"You can't go alone, Your Grace." Huxstep stepped forward to block her path. "One of the staff should accompany you. Let me summon Frederick."

"It's all right. I'm going with Her Grace," I said.

"But should you not have a man to escort you?" Huxstep asked. "There is a murderer on the loose. I will be happy to come myself, or maybe the gentleman from London . . ." He looked at Mr. Smedley, who had been standing off to one side, looking extremely miserable.

Smedley shook his head violently. "Oh, no. Dear me, no. I do not wish to see that sight again. In fact, I think I should return to London."

"You can't go yet. You'll be needed to make a statement to the police," I said.

"But I had nothing to do with this. I just happened to stumble upon the body."

Huxstep went over to him. "If you'd care to let me take your overcoat, sir, I will have some coffee sent through to the morning room until we ascertain what is to happen next."

"Most kind," Mr. Smedley said, relieved.

"And I will send Frederick with you, Your Grace," Huxstep said firmly. "He can hold your umbrella."

I saw how extremely tactful butlers can be. He was not suggesting that she needed protection, merely an extra hand to hold an umbrella. I didn't give much for the umbrella's chances against this wind, but I was glad to have a footman with us. After all, as Huxstep had pointed out, there was a murderer on the loose.

We stepped out into the full force of the gale again. Frederick struggled to hold the umbrella over us, but it wasn't much use. The rain was being driven horizontally. The dowager duchess moved closer to me, and I offered her my arm. She took it gratefully.

"Were those young men of his not with him?" she said. "Usually they follow him everywhere like ducklings. If only they had been with him, this would not have happened."

"I haven't seen them at all this morning," I said. "Your son's valet said that his master was going to take another look at the site for his project before the architect came and also to post a letter."

"Post a letter?" She looked surprised. "One of the staff could have done that for him."

"He wanted to make sure it caught the early post, I understand."

"I wonder what was in it that was so important?"

We walked on, each digesting this silently. I don't know what she was thinking, but I was wondering whether somebody wanted to make sure that the letter was never posted.

Chapter 16

Cedric's body was lying exactly as I had found it, its upper half hidden under his jacket.

"Don't come any closer, Your Grace." Frederick handed me the umbrella, then went forward to lift the jacket from the body. The duchess gave a small gasp of horror when she saw him.

"Cedric," she whispered. "My son. This is an outrage. Nobody should have to end up like this." She took a step closer to the body. Then she said, "But surely that is John's knife."

"Yes," I said. "It certainly looks like it."

She stared at me in horror. "You don't think . . . Do you?"

But that was exactly what I was thinking. I was also thinking that something wasn't right about that body. Something I was seeing did not make sense. I tried to work out what it was.

"Why on earth would he have removed his jacket in this weather?" the duchess asked.

That was something else that had troubled me. It did cross my mind that he might have been killed elsewhere—inside a building warm enough to make him remove his outer garment—and then his body dumped here. But it would have taken strong men to carry him this far, and there was no sign of any wheeled conveyance. Besides, with this amount of rain any cart or wheelbarrow would have become bogged down in mud.

It wasn't my problem, I told myself. The police would no doubt get to the bottom of things as soon as they got here.

"Beg pardon, Your Grace," a voice called, and we saw a police constable hurrying toward us. "They were saying that there's been a murder, and . . ." He broke off as he came in sight of the body with the knife still sticking from its back. "Ooh, heck," he said. "It really is a murder." From his face it was clear he had never seen a dead body before. He looked quite green. "Do you happen to recognize the deceased?"

"Of course I recognize him," the dowager duchess snapped. "It's my son the Duke of Eynsford."

I think he murmured "bloody hell," under his breath but he said out loud, "Nobody is to touch anything until my superiors get here."

"And when will that be?" the duchess asked. "I do not like to think of my son lying here in the mud. It is not seemly."

"It's a crime scene now, Your Grace. The detective inspector who comes will want to see exactly how the body was lying and to see if there were any suspicious footprints around it." He gave us a look, and I realized that both Frederick and I had gone up to the body.

"His coat was covering his head," I said. "We had to remove it to see who it was and whether he was dead. So our footprints will be there."

"Never mind, miss," he said. "I don't suppose your little footprints will have done too much harm."

"We need to cover him with something," the duchess said. "I hate to see him lying there with the water splashing all over him." She looked at the constable. "You should stay here and guard the body until your inspector arrives."

"I have to stay here?" His face fell.

"Of course. The murderer might return and try to dispose of the body."

I could tell this didn't cheer him up, but he managed to say, "Very well, Your Grace. I shouldn't think our detective inspector will be too long."

"We should go back to the house," I said to Edwina. "It won't do any good if you catch cold as well as everything else, and Irene will need you when she regains consciousness."

She nodded. "Yes. And I'll have to inform the family immediately, especially John."

We trudged up the hill in our sodden clothes with Frederick trying to control the lurching umbrella. Huxstep was waiting for us anxiously.

"I have coffee and brandy waiting for you in the Long Gallery, Your Grace," he said. "Let me take your coat."

"I would like the grounds staff to take a tarpaulin down to the police constable and make sure that my son's body is properly covered until the inspector gets here," Edwina said as her coat was being removed. "And please inform me the moment the inspector arrives."

"Very good, Your Grace," Huxstep said.

Our coats having been removed, we went through to the Long Gallery, where a giant log was burning in the hearth. "I think we both need some brandy in our coffee," Her Grace said, and poured a generous amount into both cups. I felt the warmth of the alcohol flood through my body, and realized that the cold I had felt was not just from the rain, it was from shock. Huxstep came back to join us. "Your Grace, what are your instructions concerning the servants? I have told Frederick and the groundsmen that they are to say nothing until you inform the whole staff."

"Thank you, Huxstep. Yes, I shall want to address them all, but first I must see my daughter. Then I'll talk to the family. Please let the family and guests know that I wish to speak to them, then have all the staff assembled in the servants' hall in half an hour."

"May I suggest you assemble the family in the library, Your Grace? It has the right air of solemnity."

"Spot on as usual, Huxstep." She nodded with almost a smile. "Please summon everyone to the library."

"Everyone, Your Grace? Does that include the children?"

"I think it should, since it concerns them," she said.

"And what about those young men who were the duke's guests?"

Edwina frowned. "Yes, I suppose they'll have to know, and then they can go home, thank goodness."

"And the visitor in the morning room, Your Grace?" Huxstep asked with no trace of expression on his bland face. "Should he be included?"

"I see no reason to include him in family business. His visit here was incidental. Leave him where he is."

I put down my coffee cup. "I have to go up and change my wet shoes and stockings. Would you like me to bring down the children when I come?"

"How kind." She touched my arm gently. "You have been such a help to me, Georgiana. I see now why the queen spoke so highly of you."

"What about Sissy?" I asked. "She shouldn't be left out."

"Of course not. Huxstep," she called after him, "send up two of the staff to have Miss Elisabeth carried down to the library."

"And about their mother . . ." I began. "I presume you'll want to break this news to them yourself?"

"If my daughter has made a good recovery, I see no reason why they should need to know," she said. "Especially if it transpires that she tried to take her own life. They have had enough upset in their young lives. They must see their mother as their rock."

I went upstairs thinking that actually I'd been no help at all. Jack had arrived, and I hadn't managed to stop him from picking up his chicken, ruining a hunt or, apparently, from killing his uncle. In my eyes, my visit so far had been a hopeless failure. I paused at the top of the stairs. Could Jack have crept down that path behind his uncle and stabbed him to death? It seemed so unlike the glimpses I had had of his character. He had been angry with Cedric yesterday. He'd even challenged him to step outside and fight. But that was man to man, not sneaking up behind someone's back. The Jack I had seen was a simple sort of chap. He'd punch someone if they insulted him. But kill him? I shook my head. Nothing about that body on the path made sense to me. I wished the inspector would hurry up and get here.

There was no sign of Queenie—probably down in the kitchen having elevenses, knowing her. She had an absolute fondness for cakes and biscuits. So I changed my shoes, draped my wet stockings over a chair by the fire, took off my wet skirt and rubbed my hair with a towel before I went upstairs to the nursery. I was nearing the head of the stairs when I heard voices, and saw the three Starlings coming toward me.

"You're wanted in the library, I believe," I said.

"Oh, so that's where Ceddy's been hiding out," Julian said. "We wondered where he'd got to."

"Of course we didn't exactly go looking for him this morning, after last night," Adrian said. "We were seriously put out, weren't we, boys?"

"Absolutely shattered. We simply couldn't believe he'd do a thing like that," Simon agreed. "Then this morning, after a good breakfast, we came to the conclusion that he was just teasing, just pushing buttons. You know Ceddy—he loves to push buttons. So we decided to forgive him after all, and we were going to give him moral support with his architect, but then we couldn't find him and it was blowing a gale."

"So we went to work on the play in the ballroom instead," Julian said. "We thought we'd get that problem scene all smoothed out and surprise him."

I tried not to let my face show what I was thinking.

"We'd better not keep him waiting a second longer," Simon said. "You know how he hates to be kept waiting. Off we go then. Fly like Peter Pan."

And they ran down the stairs. In spite of everything, I had to smile as I climbed the last flight to the nursery. All three of the men were remarkably like Peter Pan, living in a pretend world. But as they said, they had been seriously put out when Cedric announced that he was planning to adopt his valet rather than one of them. Had they really not taken him seriously, or had they decided to stop him?

I tapped on the schoolroom door and went in. The twins were standing beside the table, with Mr. Carter behind them.

"Carefully," he was saying. "Pour it steadily."

They looked up in surprise when they saw me.

"I'm sorry to disturb you," I said, "But Her Grace has requested the presence of the children in the library at once."

"Oh, crikey." Nicholas glanced at Katherine. "What do you suppose we have done this time?"

"Nothing that I can think of," she said. "We've been silent and invisible, as far as I know."

"That's when I'm most suspicious about you," Mr. Carter said. "So off you go then. You shouldn't keep your grandmother waiting."

"But what about our experiment?" Nicholas complained. "Now we'll never get a chance to finish it."

"There's always tomorrow. It can wait," Mr. Carter said.

"Do you know what this is about, Georgie?" Nick asked. "Are we both in trouble?"

"Nobody's in trouble, as far as I know," I said. "Your grandmother wants to talk to the whole family."

"At least it's Grandmama and not Uncle Cedric," Katherine said. "If it was him, we'd know we were in real trouble."

"By the way," Nick said, "speaking of trouble, we saw that funny local bobby cycling up the hill toward the house. He was having such a hard time riding in the rain and against the wind. When he was halfway up, his helmet blew off. We had a good laugh, didn't we, Kat?"

"We did," she said. "So what was up this time? Somebody tried to poach a deer again?"

"I really don't know," I said. "You'd better get downstairs. And someone is coming up for your sister. Is she in her room?"

"Yes, she's reading Dickens." Nick made a face. "She actually likes Dickens. Can you imagine? I mean, Sherlock Holmes I can understand. That is fun. But Dickens? So boring. Come on, Kat," Nicholas said. "We'd better bugger off."

"Nicholas. Where did you hear such language?" Mr. Carter demanded.

Katherine grinned. "From Uncle Cedric's strange followers. We've increased our vocabulary by leaps and bounds."

"And you'd be amazed what we've learned of anatomy from the pictures drying in Uncle Cedric's darkroom," Nick said.

"Shut up, Nick." Kat gave him a dig in the ribs. "You'll get us in trouble. You know it's off-limits."

"So are lots of places, but that hasn't stopped us yet." He gave a final wicked grin as they ran off.

Mr. Carter gave me an apologetic smile and shook his head. "Those children have too much time on their hands and no real direction. It's not healthy."

"I think they just delight in shocking adults," I said. "They seem rather fun to me."

"But not what their grandmother wants. Has she heard them using language like that? Is this what the summons is about? In which case, I'll probably be on the carpet too."

"No, it's nothing like that," I said. "But Her Grace wishes to address the staff in half an hour or so. I know you don't count as staff but I suspect you should hear what she says as well."

"I see." He was frowning. "You really don't know what this is about?"

"I'm not at liberty to say, Mr. Carter, only that it shouldn't affect you in any way."

"That's a relief." He paused. "I heard there was a rumpus last night, and that the children's mother was threatening to walk out or be kicked out. I thought I might be out of a job."

"It's nothing to do with that. I can reassure you there."

He managed a smile. "Thank you. I'll go down in a little while then, shall I?"

"In half an hour, so I understand."

I went across and tapped on Sissy's door. Two people looked up as I entered. I was surprised to see Jack sitting beside Sissy, their heads close together over a book.

"Oh, there you are, Jack," I said. "They've been looking for you."

"Sissy is helping me with my reading," Jack said guiltily. "I'm not so hot at big words."

"How very nice of her," I said and watched her blush. "You're going to be taken downstairs, Sissy," I said. "Your grandmother wants to speak to the family, including you."

"How exciting." Sissy's face lit up. "I haven't been down for ages. Are they sending servants up for me?"

"No worries," Jack said. "I can push the chair to the end of the hall and then carry her down the stairs."

"Jack, I think it takes two people," I began, but he reached into Sissy's chair and lifted her as easily as if she was no weight at all.

"There you are. Like I said, no worries." He had a big grin on his face. He put her back in the bath chair, opened the door and set off at a great pace down the hall. Oh, dear, I thought as I watched them go. I do hope she's not falling for someone who might have killed her uncle and tried to kill her mother.

Chapter 17

The tableau assembled in the library looked like the set from a period stage drama. The old sisters in their outmoded fashions were sitting in high-backed, leather armchairs. The twins sat cross-legged on the floor. The three Starlings stood uncomfortably by the bookcase on the wall. There was no sign of Edwina.

Everyone looked up expectantly as the door opened, but it was Jack carrying Sissy. One of the servants followed with the bath chair. They settled her off to one side, by the fire.

"Isn't this exciting?" Simon said in a stage whisper. "I keep expecting a detective in a deerstalker to appear at any moment saying, 'I've called you all together to name the murderer.' "

"As long as it's not 'I've called you all together to tell you to leave my house this instant,' " Nick replied.

"Do you think Ceddy's waiting to make a grand entrance?" Simon whispered.

"With his mother. What a fearsome duo. And where is Lady Irene? The main players are not here yet. Only us bit parts."

As if on cue, the door opened and the dowager duchess came in. Her gaze scanned the room. "Good. You're all here," she said. She noticed Jack. "There you are, John." Her voice sounded breathless.

"We hadn't seen you all morning. We thought you might have gone out."

"What, in this weather?" Jack grinned. "Not me. I'm not used to rain. We only get six inches a year where I come from."

"You're here now. That's the important thing," she said, "because this concerns you more than anyone else."

She looked around the room. "I should first tell you that my daughter, Lady Irene, is awake and drinking some black coffee. That is wonderful news, is it not?"

"What happened to Mummy?" Sissy asked. "Is something wrong with her?"

"She was a little under the weather. She's quite all right now, and that's all that matters," Edwina said smoothly.

"What happened to Lady Irene?" Adrian whispered to me.

"Took a sleeping draft and they couldn't wake her."

"Tried to kill herself, you mean?" Adrian whispered back then turned red when he realized that Edwina was frowning at him and clearing her throat.

"I have more news to impart," she said. "News that is almost too horrible to express out loud. I am afraid to tell you that my son Cedric, Duke of Eynsford, is dead."

There was a little yelp of horror from one of the Starlings.

"Not Ceddy!" one of them exclaimed.

"Poor Cedric," Princess Charlotte said. "I told you the Ouija board spelled out 'death,' didn't I? The spirits never lie."

"Damn your spirits, Charlotte," Edwina snapped. "My son was murdered."

There was a stunned silence during which all one could hear was the crackle of the fire, the drumming of the rain on the window and the constant *drip, drip, drip* from a nearby drainpipe.

"Where did this happen?" Virginia asked at last.

"In the glen, on the estate. Lady Georgiana found him when she took the architect to meet Cedric."

"And he was definitely murdered?" Charlotte asked.

"Very definitely," Edwina said. "There can be no doubt that somebody killed him in cold blood."

"On the estate." Virginia looked around nervously. "One doesn't expect the criminal classes to have infiltrated our safe and secure little world. I wonder what it was—had he fallen foul of criminal types, perhaps? Did he have gambling debts? Or did he just surprise a burglar making off with some of our silver?"

"We must wait for the police to find out the truth," Edwina said. "An inspector is on his way now."

"How was he killed, Grandmama?" Kat asked.

"Such matters are not suitable for children, Katherine," Edwina said.

"I only wanted to know whether you took one look at him and could see he had been murdered," Kat insisted. "We like reading detective novels, you know, so we're interested. I don't need to know the details if they are not suitable for my ears."

"If you wish this morbid curiosity satisfied, then I can tell you that your uncle was killed with some violence."

I saw Katherine give her brother a satisfied grin, and I wondered whether they might have had some kind of bet on this.

Edwina cleared her throat again and went on. "The important point at this moment is that there is a new duke of Eynsford. John, you have now taken your uncle's place. This is now your house, your estate."

"Stone the flaming crows," Jack said. He gave me a look that was half panic, half amusement.

"The duke's suite of rooms will be prepared for you as soon as the police have finished their investigation and your uncle's belongings can be removed. As of now they will be untouched, in case the police find any kind of clue in there."

"But I thought you said he was killed in the glen?" Virginia asked. "Are you trying to say that he was not murdered by an outsider?"

"I have no idea, Virginia," Edwina said. "I just wish nothing to be touched until the police have made a thorough investigation." She looked around the company. "Now, if you will excuse me, I have to address the servants and apprise them of the situation. John, you will come with me. It is right and fitting that they are formally introduced to you. They are your staff now."

She took his arm. He looked absolutely stunned as she started to lead him off. She paused in the doorway and looked back at us, all frozen in place with shock. "I suggest that we all stay reasonably close by, as I'm sure the police will want a statement from each of us. And it goes without saying that nobody should attempt to go anywhere near the glen." She paused and glared at Nick and Katherine. "Out of morbid curiosity," she added. "Because you'll find a policeman guarding the site, and there will be serious repercussions from me." Then she gave a little jerking nod of the head and went out the door with Jack in tow.

Nick and Katherine rushed over to me. "Isn't it thrilling, Georgie?" Nick said, his eyes sparkling. "A real murder, and awful Uncle Cedric at that. If anyone had to be murdered, I'm glad it's him."

"It's 'he,' Nicholas," I said, "and I don't think you should say things like that out loud. It will get back to your grandmother."

He nodded. "I only meant . . . well, there are some people one likes and others one doesn't. I'm going to take another look at Sissy's Sherlock Holmes book and see what he would have done to find clues. What's the betting there are tiny clues all over the place that the police will overlook, eh, Kat? You know, the match from a certain matchbox that showed the murderer was left-handed and came from Austria?"

"I think you two should stay well out of the way of the police," I said. "Real-life murders are not like Sherlock Holmes. Besides, it's your uncle who died. You should be in mourning."

"It's hard to be in mourning for someone so nasty," Nick said as we came out of the room into the hallway. "He made it horribly clear that he never wanted us here. He was stinking rich and yet he wouldn't pay for school for me and Kat."

"Kat and me," I corrected.

"You see how desperately we need schooling, don't you?" Katherine said. "Utterly hopeless, that's what Mr. Carter says."

"I think you are lucky to have such a fine tutor. You should make the most of his brilliant brain."

"Anyway, everything will change now, won't it?" Katherine said happily. "Jack is now lord of the manor, and he'll want to help his poor relatives."

"I wouldn't count on it," I said.

"Why not?" Kat looked puzzled.

"Because one never knows everything about people. Jack might decide to take his money and go back to Australia and convert this house into a hotel."

"Surely not. Jack's a good fellow," Nick said.

"One never knows," I repeated.

"Do you think there are elevenses in the morning room or the Long Gallery?" Nick asked, his mind turning to more important matters for eleven-year-old boys.

"You will tell us when the police arrive, won't you, Georgiana?" Kat said. "Me and Nick want to follow them around and observe their every move. We might want to be detectives when we grow up."

"I don't think the police will take too kindly to being followed by you," I said, smiling at her eager face. "If I were you . . ."

This was interrupted by Nick's call. "Kat, come in here and see. Sandwiches, cakes, the lot!"

And she ran after him. How simple life was for children, I thought.

I had just reached the foyer and was debating whether to follow the children in the direction of food in the Long Gallery or to do the more charitable thing and join poor Mr. Smedley in the morning room when there was a loud rap on the front door. The police had got here really quickly, which was good. The way the rain was coming down, any kind of clue from the crime scene would soon be washed away. I lingered in the hallway, curious to see the inspector who was going to take over the case, as Huxstep came hurrying from the rear of the house, brushing down an invisible fleck from his black coat.

I watched him open the door and start in surprise. "Oh, good morning, sir. We had no idea that you were coming. You've caught us off guard. Please do come in. Most inclement weather for a drive, isn't it?"

Then the door opened wider and into the hall came Darcy, followed by an elegant creature hidden under a black, hooded cape. Huxstep shut the door behind them.

"I will inform Their Graces that you are here," he said and hurried off again.

I was about to go to Darcy, then hesitated at the thought that he'd brought a woman with him—an elegant woman at that. Who on earth could she be? Not one of his sisters. They weren't tall, dark or sophisticated like that. Then the woman said, "If I'd known it was going to bucket down like this in the country I'd never have left town." The hood was thrown back and beneath it was Belinda.

I rushed over to them. "You came. It's amazing. How did you find out? Who called you?"

Darcy held out his hands to me. "Hello, old thing. I won't hug you—I'd get you rather wet. Hold on." And he removed his overcoat, looking around in vain for a servant to take it. "But why do you seem so surprised to see me? Didn't I tell you I'd come down as soon as I could? And do you see who I brought with me? I met her at Crockfords last night, and she said she was pining for you and had something she was about to post to you, so why didn't she come with me and deliver it in person?"

"Your shoe, darling," Belinda said, beaming at me. "Your lost evening slipper? I retrieved it from the terrible Mrs. Tombs. I think I deserve a medal for braving that dragon. And when Darcy said he was coming down to help the heir to the Eynsford estate, I was curious to see the backwoods boy for myself."

Darcy gave me a wink. "I might hand over the job. If anyone can educate a backwoods Australian, it is Belinda."

"I don't think the dowager duchess meant that kind of education," I said as I stepped forward to kiss Belinda's cheek. "But it's lovely to see you both. So you just decided to come down today. Nobody telephoned you? You haven't heard the news?"

"What news?"

"Terrible things have been happening. The duke has been murdered. Lady Irene was drugged and nearly died, and the police are on their way."

"Good God," Darcy muttered. "Any idea what was behind this? Are there any crazy members of the family locked away in a tower?"

"It's not funny, Darcy," I said. "It's rather alarming, actually. I was the one who found the body, and he'd been stabbed with . . ." I went to say, "with Jack's knife," but I couldn't bring myself to do so. Obviously it would come out in the police investigation. Until then, I was going to keep quiet.

"The duke has been murdered?" Belinda said quietly. "You mean Cedric? Poor Cedric has been murdered? But that's too, too awful."

I looked at her in surprise. "You know Cedric Altringham?"

She put her hand to her heart. "Cedric and I—thick as thieves, darling. That was another reason for coming down here—to surprise dear Cedric."

"I'm more than amazed," I said. "I thought Cedric didn't like anybody."

"That was only the front he put up to keep people at bay. Underneath—what a sweetie pie."

I shook my head, trying to come to terms with Cedric Altringham being a sweetie pie. "My impression was that he couldn't stand women," I said. "He always had a bevy of young men around him, and absolutely refused to marry, which was why Darcy had to go in search of Jack."

Belinda paused as if thinking. "Jack—he's the young Australian?"

"He is."

"Darcy said he's a lot of fun. I gather they got up to high jinks together on the ship home."

"I can believe it." I glanced at Darcy, who grinned.

Belinda shifted uneasily. "Where is everybody?" she asked. "Usually these houses keep a pack of servants, and nobody has come to take our coats yet. I'm freezing out here. And we've luggage in the motor."

"The dowager duchess is breaking the news to the servants at this moment," I said. "And introducing them to the new duke."

"So she's acknowledged that Jack is the rightful heir, has she?" Darcy asked.

"Oh yes. Fawning all over him. He looks just like his father, you see."

"Well, that's good, at least," Darcy said. "My journey to Australia was not in vain. Poor old Jack. Talk about being thrown in at the deep end."

"Her Grace was hoping you'd come down and guide him along for a bit, and now here you are." I slipped my hand through his. "Goodness, you're freezing."

"Yes, well the motor I borrowed had a rag top that leaked and no heating," he said.

"Leave your coats on the floor and come through to the Long Gallery. I gather there is food and coffee there."

"Thank God," Belinda said. "I should have worn my mink and fur boots."

As we walked, something struck me. "Belinda, you said you've brought luggage. Are you planning to stay too? I'm not sure about that. The dowager duchess is a stickler for protocol."

"You think she'd turn away a good chum of poor old Cedric?" she said. "I just flung a few things into a bag just in case I decided to stay. I don't have to. But on the drive down, it occurred to me that I might be some help. You know, give the young chap some pointers," she said. "He'll have to know how to handle sophisticated women, and he'll find himself the most eligible bachelor in England, won't he?"

She stalked on ahead. I looked across at Darcy, and he raised an eyebrow, making me smile. We entered the Long Gallery. Belinda was already bearing down on the cake dishes with their tiers of good things to eat and the silver coffeepot on a tray and the roaring fire.

Darcy drew near to me. "Don't worry," he said. "I've got a feeling that Jack can take care of himself."

"I hope so," I replied. "Because I have a feeling he's going to need a bit of help in the days to come. He's going to need someone on his side." I drew closer to Darcy, my hand brushing against his. "I'm so glad you're here," I added, and kissed his cold cheek. "This beastly business. I wish I weren't mixed up in it."

"I presume you're only an innocent bystander," he said.

"Witness," I said. "I found him, Darcy. I'm going to have to face the police and probably the press. I just wish I hadn't been the one who found him. And there's a murderer at large too. Probably someone in this house."

He slipped his hand through mine. "Don't worry. I'm here now," he said. "I won't let anything bad happen to you."

"I'm also glad you're here, because . . ." I began. I was going to add my suspicion that something wasn't right about that crime scene. But as I pictured it in my mind, I couldn't think exactly what. I could see Cedric lying there with Jack's knife sticking out of his back, his coat over him and water splashing over his arm and head. Exactly what was bothering me? I shook my head and went into the Long Gallery alongside Darcy.

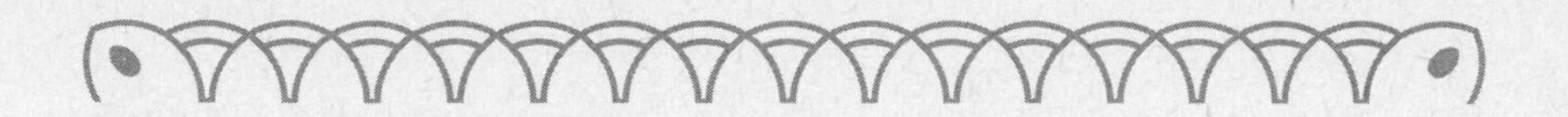

Chapter 18

The rest of the family was already seated around the food and near the fire. The old sisters were munching away merrily as if this was any other morning and they hadn't just lost their nephew.

The twins were working their way through a plate of biscuits. Sissy sat by the fire, watching, hoping that someone would pass her something, I suspect, but too polite to ask. There was no sign of the Starlings.

Virginia was the first to notice us. "Why, it's my favorite handsome man come back to see me," she said, holding out her hand to Darcy. "How good of you to come in our hour of need."

Darcy did as expected and went over to kiss the extended hand. Then he kissed that of Princess Charlotte with an attractive little Continental bow. "Your Highness," he murmured.

"Such perfect manners," she murmured, fluttering eyelashes at him. It's that Irish blarney coming out, I thought. I was just pouring coffee for the new arrivals when Edwina entered the room.

"Mr. O'Mara—you've come. I can't tell you how glad I am to see you. You've heard our terrible news, of course. My grandson will need your guidance in the coming days." She stopped, having just noticed Belinda, and raised her lorgnette up to examine her.

"And who have we here?" she asked.

"Your Grace, this is my friend Belinda Warburton-Stoke," I said. "She motored down with Mr. O'Mara, and brought me some things I'd left behind in London."

"Warburton-Stoke?" Edwina asked. "Hampshire family?"

"Yes, Your Grace," Belinda said.

"I believe we have a cousin who married a Warburton-Stoke, don't we, Charlotte?"

"Primrose Haversham, wasn't it?" Charlotte and Virginia looked at each other for confirmation.

"I have a great-aunt Primrose," Belinda said.

They smiled and nodded. "Then we must be related. How delightful. How I wish that you had arrived at a happier moment." Belinda had undergone the usual ordeal by fire of the aristocracy. Those time-honored questions. Who are your family? Do we know them? Are we related to them? In other words, is she one of us and does she belong here? Now that a relationship had been proven, she was accepted.

"I can't tell you how sorry I am to hear the news about your son," Belinda said.

"Belinda was a friend of Cedric," I said.

Belinda blushed but said nothing.

"My son, friends with a young woman? How extraordinary," Edwina said. "I wish he'd brought you down here, my dear. Rather than those dubious young men."

"Belinda's a fashion designer," I explained. "She has worked with Chanel."

"Ah, so that explains it." Edwina nodded. "Cedric mentioned he had found a brilliant costume designer for his new play. So that was you, was it?"

"I'm not sure which play he was talking about," Belinda said modestly, eyes focused on the pile of sandwiches. "He had irons in so many fires, didn't he?"

"He did. And none of them in the right fires, if you want my opinion," Edwina said. "But you are more than welcome here, and I'm sure Cedric's death has shocked you as much as the rest of us."

"Devastated," Belinda said. "I feel utterly hollow." She looked around. "That poor boy, suddenly finding himself Duke of Eynsford. Where is he?"

"My grandson needed some time to be alone to digest this news," Edwina said. "I can't say that I blame him. He'll be down when the inspector gets here." She stopped and stared out of the window. "Ah, here comes what looks like a police motorcar now. They made good time from Sevenoaks."

A black motorcar came up the driveway, stopping outside the front door. A large man with a red face and an impressive paunch extricated himself from the backseat and stood staring up at the front of the house as if he couldn't believe what he was seeing. A younger, plain-clothes officer exited from the other side of the car while two bobbies in uniform emerged from the front seats. The large man must have said something to the others because they all grinned. I noticed that the rain had slowed to a drizzle

At this point Mr. Huxstep, with his impeccable timing, appeared at the front door with a large umbrella.

"Are you the duke?" a rather loud voice demanded, as the big man strode up the front steps and in through the door while Huxstep tried to keep up with him.

"No sir, I am His Grace's butler," Huxstep replied with great dignity. "The dowager duchess is expecting you. Whom shall I say is calling?"

"Detective Chief Inspector Fairbotham, Royal Kent Constabulary," the big man's voice boomed as they entered the entrance hall. "This young chap is Stubbins, my sergeant. I'm told there's been a murder on this estate. Someone's not having me on, are they? It's not the bright young things' way of livening up a rainy day by calling out the police on false pretenses?"

Huxstep chose not to answer that. "If you'd like to follow me to the library, I will inform Her Grace that you are here."

And the voices died away down the hall.

"What an uncouth-looking man," Edwina said. "And with a northern accent too. I wonder why the Royal Kent Constabulary had to go looking for an inspector from northern climes. I've always felt that civilization, as we know it, ended at a line drawn between Oxford and Cambridge."

Huxstep now appeared in the doorway. "I've shown Detective Chief Inspector Fairbotham into the library, Your Grace."

Nick and Katherine nudged one another. "He did have more than a fair botham, wouldn't you say, Kat? His name should be changed to Large-botham."

"That is enough, children." Edwina frowned. "One does not mock those who are socially beneath us. It simply isn't done." She turned to Huxstep. "Please make sure that His Grace and Cedric's young men know that they will be wanted downstairs shortly. I'm glad you put the inspector in the library. Most suitable. One does not want the man to be overawed by his surroundings in a room that is too large. It makes them so defensive."

She held out her hand to me. "Georgiana, I am going to speak with him first, to make sure he gets his facts right and doesn't come up with any strange ideas. Since you were the one who discovered my son's body, maybe you should come with me."

"If you wish, Your Grace," I said, trying to think of a way that I could bring Darcy along with me. Frankly, I wasn't looking forward to coming face-to-face with that large, loud police inspector. I'd had my share of encounters with the police during the past few years and not many of them had been pleasant. It had been my experience that most of them had a chip on the shoulder toward the aristocracy.

The walk down the hall seemed to take forever. Huxstep went ahead, opening the door for us and announcing, "Her Grace, the dowager duchess of Eynsford, and Lady Georgiana Rannoch."

Inspector Fairbotham rose to his feet, looking uncomfortable. "I'm sorry you ladies have had to get involved with this, but I understand there has been a murder on your property. Do you happen to know the name of the deceased?"

"Of course I know his name. It's my son the Duke of Eynsford," Edwina said testily.

"The duke? You saw his body yourself, did you? You identified him?"

"I did."

The inspector looked surprised and a little impressed. "And where was he found?"

"We have a little glen leading down from the lake," Edwina said. "He was lying beside the path."

"Who found him initially?"

"Chief Inspector, may I suggest that we all take a seat, if this is to be a long conversation?" Edwina said. "I find conversing while still standing most uncivilized." She motioned the inspector to an armchair and took the other armchair herself, leaving the upright chairs to the sergeant and me.

"Right, let's begin again, shall we?" he said. "Who found him?"

"I did," I said. "He had arranged to meet with an architect this morning to look at the designs for an amphitheater he was planning to build on the property. It seems that he left the house quite early this morning to have another look at the site. When the architect arrived, I volunteered to escort him to meet the duke. We came upon his body in the glen, and rushed straight back to the house to call the police."

"And where is the body now?"

"Still lying exactly as it was," I said. "We knew you'd want to take a look at the crime scene. Her Grace had it covered with a tarpaulin so that the rain didn't wash away all the clues."

The inspector nodded. "That was thoughtful of you. So the body is still lying where it was found, under a tarpaulin, in what you describe as a glen, which I thought only existed up in my part of the world." He had attempted to make a joke, I suspect, but Edwina was not amused.

"My husband's grandfather enjoyed his fishing expeditions to Scotland so much that he re-created a glen on the property," she said stiffly.

The big man grinned. "What you aristocrats will do to amuse yourselves!"

"I don't think it is any concern of yours how we choose to landscape our property," Edwina said even more stiffly. It was clear she had taken an instant dislike to him.

"So back to you, miss." He turned back to face me.

"Chief Inspector, may I point out that Lady Georgiana is also the daughter of a duke, granddaughter of a royal princess, and thus is not a 'miss,'" Edwina said. "One addresses the daughter of a duke as 'my lady,' and one addresses the wife or widow of a duke as 'Your Grace.'"

"I think you'll find, *my lady*," he said, with great emphasis on the last two words, "that in a police investigation, I'm the person in charge. At this moment, everybody in this house is a suspect in a murder inquiry so it's your job to make sure my inquiries go as smoothly as possible, without interruptions. Now, can we get on without interruption?"

Edwina's face turned so red I thought she might explode. "I will have a word with my friend the Lord Lieutenant of Kent," she said. "He may feel that Scotland Yard should be called in. I am not sure that the Kentish constabulary is equipped to handle a case of this magnitude."

The chief inspector's face had also turned red, as if he was using all his willpower not to say something he'd regret later. "In my opinion, madam, there isn't much difference between the murder of a hooligan on the streets of London and the murder of a duke on a big estate. They all come down to the same basic human emotions—jealousy, fear, greed and revenge. So don't worry: I am more than equipped to handle your case. I will now question this young lady and then, hopefully, our police surgeon and photographer will have shown up with the van, and we can take a look at the body."

"Now, miss." He turned back to me. "Let's get the timing right on this. At what time did you discover the body?"

I chose to overlook that he'd called me "miss." I thought that Edwina had probably annoyed him enough for both of us—and a policeman who is annoyed can make life dashed unpleasant.

"I'm not sure of the exact time," I said. "It must have been around nine forty-five or maybe even ten o'clock."

"And how long before this had the duke left to go and inspect his theater site?"

"I didn't see him go, but I understand from the butler that it must have been a good while. Possibly as early as eight o'clock."

"Did nobody think that was a long time to be gone looking at the landscape in this kind of weather?"

Edwina cleared her throat. "In a household the size of this one, Inspector, one's movements are not closely observed. My son only chose to make us conversant with his activities when it suited him. He sometimes failed to mention that he was going up to town, which Cook found most irritating."

"So he was seen going out at eight o'clock, was he?"

"I believe the footman Frederick asked if he wanted an umbrella as it looked like rain," I replied. "But you should ask Frederick yourself."

The policeman nodded. "So let's get back to you. A man arrives, says he is the architect and asks to be taken down to meet the duke at the theater site. That's correct, miss?"

"Absolutely, Inspector," I said.

"It's chief inspector," he said.

"Sorry. So it is." I met his gaze, and saw that he got my point.

"And I take it that it was already raining by that time?" he asked.

"Coming down really hard. And the wind was blowing too. We

were soaked." He nodded, indicating that I should go on. "We followed the path until we came to the glen. The stream was rushing past, out of its banks, and was splashing over something beside it. Mr. Smedley, the architect, said, 'What's that?' and I went forward and saw that it was a person, with his jacket covering the top half of his body. I lifted it off and saw that it was the duke and that he was dead."

"And how did you ascertain that he was dead, miss . . . my lady?"

"I've seen dead people before," I said. "And he had a large knife sticking out of his back."

He looked at me with new respect. "I'm surprised you can tell me all this so coolly. You say you lifted the coat off him. What was Mr. Smedley doing all this time?"

"Looking rather green, actually," I said with a grin. "He kept urging me not to faint, but I thought he might faint himself. It was quite awful."

"I'm sure it was." He sucked on his lip thoughtfully. "So you came straight back to the house?"

"I replaced the coat over his upper body, as I had found it," I said. "Then we returned to the house, informed Her Grace and the police were summoned."

He glanced at his sergeant. "Got all that so far, Stubbins?"

"Yes, sir," Stubbins replied.

"And you say you went to see your son's body for yourself, Your Grace?" he asked, proving that he could get modes of address right if he wanted to. "Who accompanied you?"

"Lady Georgiana was kind enough to brave the storm for a second time to show me the body," Edwina said. "It was exactly as she described, and I was most distressed to see the rain and creek water splashing all over it. I ordered a tarpaulin to be placed over my son's body."

The chief inspector rose to his feet. "Thank you. That will be all for now. I would like to have all members of the household assembled for questioning when I return from viewing the body."

"Servants too, I presume?"

"Naturally."

"I'm afraid my daughter, the Countess Streletzki, will not be able to join us downstairs," Edwina said. "I don't think she will be well enough to answer your questions."

"Oh, no? Conveniently come down with a cold, has she?"

Edwina eyed him coldly. "She is recovering from what might have been an attempt to kill her last night with an overdose of sleeping powders."

She clearly enjoyed Chief Inspector Fairbotham's look of surprise.

Chapter 19

"So were you grilled?" Darcy asked when I returned to the Long Gallery. "Did he give you the third degree?"

"It was jolly uncomfortable, actually," I said. "I think he was attempting to be chummy and good-humored but the duchess took every remark as an insult, and kept putting him in his place. He just asked me questions and I answered them. In fact, he was impressed that I could describe a dead body without having a fit of the vapors."

Darcy grinned. "I take it you didn't mention other dead bodies you'd seen?"

"Unfortunately I did mention it. So I'm now probably his number one suspect. Especially since I already admitted that I was the one who found the body. Although I'm not sure I'd have had the strength to plunge a knife into his back with such force."

Nick looked up, a half-eaten sandwich in his hand. "So he was stabbed, was he? Kat and I were dying to know."

"Don't you think you should probably return to your schoolroom before you hear other things not meant for your ears?" I said.

"We can't," Kat said. "The inspector said we were all to be questioned."

"Poor Mr. Carter will be wondering where you have got to," I said. "And you'll spoil your lunch if you eat any more."

"I don't expect Mr. Carter will be there," Nick said. He glanced across at his sister. "We went up a few minutes ago and nobody was there, not even Nanny. That means the police are going to question everybody in the house, including servants. For all we know, Mr. Carter might have done it. He does have queer fits, you know, from the shell-shock in the war."

"Yes, he put his hands over his ears once when a car backfired," Kat chimed in. "And he shouted, 'Make it stop.' Afterward, he was really embarrassed."

"I don't think it's right to talk about your tutor like that," Princess Charlotte said. "If you were told to go to your schoolroom, you go to your schoolroom. In my day, children would not dare to answer back their elders."

"Sissy can't go back to the schoolroom unless somebody carries her," Kat said. "And we wouldn't want to leave Sissy all alone down here with the grown-ups, in case she gets grilled by the police and confesses to the crime."

"Don't be silly, Kat," Sissy said. "I'm perfectly all right, and I'm really old enough to be downstairs anyway. You're not."

Before this confrontation could continue, Edwina appeared at the entrance to the Long Gallery. "Ah, there you all are," she said, brushing an invisible strand of gray hair from her face as if the distress of the moment might have spoiled her usually immaculate appearance. "The inspector has gone to look at Cedric's body. He will then wait for the police surgeon to arrive before they move him. When he returns, he wants to speak with us in turn in the library. He will require a statement from each of us."

"A statement? What about?" Princess Charlotte asked.

"The murder, of course," Edwina said testily. "Really, Charlotte, you are annoyingly stupid sometimes."

"But none of us knows anything about the murder," Charlotte said.

"Quite right," Virginia agreed. "If Cedric chooses to go wandering the grounds at some ungodly hour and gets himself murdered by a nasty tramp, then I really don't see what point there would be in talking to us. I, for one, was enjoying a rather pleasant dream when Cedric went out. I was back in Vienna, and a certain Hungarian captain was . . ."

"All the same," Edwina interrupted curtly, "the inspector has summoned us and we will do our best to help him solve my son's murder. Between ourselves, I don't think he is the brightest man in the world, and I will be calling my friend Sir John Bellingham, the lord lieutenant, to see if the Kentish constabulary might have someone more suitable for the job at their headquarters in Maidstone. Or whether he thinks we should call in Scotland Yard."

"I have contacts at Scotland Yard," Darcy said. "Do you want me to put out some feelers there?"

"Put out some feelers? What an extraordinary expression, Mr. O'Mara. Have you turned into an octopus? Or a butterfly, maybe?"

Darcy grinned. "Let me rephrase, Your Grace. Would you like me to make some discreet inquiries about Scotland Yard's possibility of their taking over this case?"

"Let us see what my friend the lord lieutenant says first. One must be careful not to tread on toes." She looked down at Darcy. "I take it you will be staying with us for a while, Mr. O'Mara?"

"In the circumstances, I think I should," Darcy said.

"Much appreciated." She nodded at him with satisfaction. "I think your old room is still ready for you, if you'd like to refresh yourself after your journey. I'll ring for Frederick to fetch your bags."

"Thank you, Your Grace," Darcy said.

Edwina now turned her gaze on Belinda. "And Miss Warburton-Stoke, I gather you only came to bring Lady Georgiana some of her belongings. Most kind of you."

I tried not to smile, interested to see how Belinda was going to take not being invited to stay. She was usually good at inveigling invitations.

"I confess I was curious to see Kingsdowne for myself," Belinda said, "after Cedric had told me so much about it. But given the circumstances, I couldn't possibly intrude on the privacy of a family in mourning. I'll ask Mr. O'Mara if he'd be kind enough to drive me to the station."

I was surprised at this, and wondered if it was because she didn't want to get mixed up in a murder investigation.

"Unfortunately, the inspector made it clear that nobody is allowed to leave until he has a statement from each of us," Edwina said. "And I'm afraid that includes you, as you were in the house when the inspector arrived. Perhaps you should at least stay for the night, since you have taken so much trouble for your friend. I'll have Elsie make up the room next to Lady Georgiana's, and perhaps your maid"—she gave me a knowing look—"could look after Miss Warburton-Stoke as well, since she has not brought one of her own."

"Thank you, Your Grace. Most kind," Belinda said. "I do have a small traveling bag in the car, if your footman would be kind enough to bring it up to me. I'd like to spruce myself up after that journey in a leaky sports car."

"I'll take you up to my room until yours is ready," I said. "Come on. Follow me."

We started up the stairs.

"Ye gods, look at those murals," she said with a grin. "Those nymphs and satyrs are certainly having a good time, aren't they? Look where that satyr's hand is! It's a wonder that virginal visitors to the house don't swoon."

"I don't think they study the mural as carefully as you're doing," I said, having not noticed the hand myself until now.

"You'd have thought they might have given poor old Cedric a few more ideas, wouldn't you?" she muttered as we swung into the long hallway.

I moved into step beside her. "Belinda, did you really know Cedric Altringham?"

She shot me one of her wicked, quizzical smiles. "I could have met him, possibly. I understand he frequented Crockfords. And I am a designer of sorts, and one meets a lot of chaps in the arts world."

"In other words, you never met him." I opened the door and let her into my bedroom. "Belinda, you are incorrigible," I said, laughing. "What are you really doing here?"

"If you must know, I met Darcy at Crockfords last night and he was telling some other chaps about being assigned to educate the heir to the Duke of Eynsford. And I remembered that was where you had gone and something to do with educating a young Australian. Then one of the chaps at Crockfords said, 'That family is rolling in dough isn't it? Isn't the current duke one of the wealthiest men in the country?' And then someone else said, 'And unmarried too. Lucky Australian heir, that's what I say. Maybe I could claim to be another long-lost cousin or something.' You know, I'd been about to ask Darcy to deliver your slipper to you, but then I thought, the current duke and the heir, both stinking rich and unmarried. How can a girl go wrong? So I hitched a ride with dear Darcy, and here I am."

"I suppose it's preferable to your car conveniently breaking down outside someone's gate," I said, mentioning a trick she had tried with great success more than once.

"Yes, here I am. Too bad that one of my options chose today to be murdered."

"Cedric wouldn't have looked at you twice. He likes young men," I said. "I mean, liked. You know, he was rather an unpleasant man but I still feel sorry for him. Nobody deserves to end up that way."

She nodded. "And now the poor, dear, Australian lad will need guidance and companionship more than ever. I do hope they'll let me stay for a while. I may have to hint to the police that I know more than I actually do, just so that they forbid me to leave."

I looked up. Belinda had never struck me as the altruistic sort. "Belinda—you weren't thinking. . . ."

Belinda grinned.

"He's a boy, Belinda. A mere boy."

"He's twenty. That's only four years younger than me. Hardly any age difference at all. And he'll need an older and more experienced wife to guide him and introduce him to the ways of . . . society."

"And to help him spend his money, if I know you."

"Darling, one does need to be financially secure. I'm sick of never knowing where the next penny is coming from."

"Well, so am I. But I wouldn't dream of seducing poor Jack Altringham, especially while he's in a state of shock over losing his uncle and becoming the duke within a week of coming halfway around the world."

"All the more reason to let him know he has a friend in a strange country who will guide him through his shock and confusion. And I'd forgotten that he's now the duke." She went over to my mirror, and took out her lipstick case from her purse, carefully shaping her lips in bright red. "A rich duke, young and virile too. What more could a girl want?"

A picture of Cedric lying there with that knife in his back floated before my eyes. I wanted to warn Belinda that she might be wasting her time on someone who would inherit neither the title nor the money and might end up on the end of a rope—a silken cord, of course, now that he was a duke, but a cord nonetheless. I hoped the police would discover the clue that led to another likely candidate because I liked Jack. I didn't want to find that he was the one who plunged his knife into Cedric's back.

Belinda put the finishing touches to an already perfect face and smoothed down her dress over her perfect figure. I found myself watching her as if I was noticing a stranger for the first time and not someone I'd known for many years.

"Belinda, I'm amazed you're not married yet. You really are quite stunning," I blurted out.

She smiled at me, still looking past her own image in the mirror. "Thanks, old bean. But I can now tell you why I'm not married—to the right sort of chap, I mean: damaged goods. Nobody is going to let their son marry a girl who isn't a virgin, and I'm afraid the word is out that I do enjoy a good roll in the hay." She snapped her purse shut. "I fear I am doomed to be the perpetual mistress rather than the wife, like your mother."

"Mummy married several of hers," I pointed out. "She still is married to a Texas oil millionaire, so I believe."

"Not that I mind being the mistress rather than the wife, as long as the chap has the means to keep me in the style to which I'd like to be accustomed."

"But don't you want the security of your own home and family?" I thought of myself and Darcy, and a brood of adorable, little, dark-haired babies.

"Heavens, no. Can't abide children. Don't know how to talk to them the way you do. You're a natural, which is lucky if you marry Darcy."

"Why if I marry Darcy?"

"Catholic, my dear. No birth control allowed. You'll be popping them out like rabbits." She laughed at my blank face. "Goodness, you are an innocent, aren't you? How do you think the rest of us manage not to get pregnant all the time? Come on, let's go down to Auntie Duchess and see how the investigation is progressing."

"It was lucky that you were related to them, wasn't it?" I said as we walked to my door. "Otherwise Edwina would have bid you a polite good-bye, given the circumstances."

Belinda looked back and smiled. "It's quite possible that we are related, I suppose, but . . ."

"But what?"

"I don't actually have a great-aunt Primrose."

With that, she swept out of the room ahead of me.

Chapter 20

I came down the grand staircase thoughtfully. Belinda had been my best pal at school. She'd already been worldly wise and had helped me navigate the shark-infested waters of finishing school and being away from the nursery for the first time. In many ways she was a good friend—but in other ways, she was just like my mother. To her, other people were put on this planet for her personal use. I thought of the way she'd dismissed Cedric's death as an inconvenience to her rather than as the terrible tragedy that it was. It doesn't matter who is the victim—murder is still the most terrible of crimes.

We came down to the central hall just as the inspector was entering the front door. The rain had obviously picked up again, and his thinning hair was plastered to his head. His face was bright red from the exertion of walking up the hill. It was not a pretty sight. He paused in the doorway to catch his breath, dripping water onto the marble floor.

"Ah, there you are, Lady Georgiana. I'm glad to see you. I'd like a little word, if you don't mind."

I shot Belinda a look of apprehension. "I'll go and see how Darcy and the others are getting along," she said. "Maybe Jack has put in an appearance."

Left alone with Chief Inspector Fairbotham, I waited to find out what he wanted, and hoped it wasn't to go back to the glen and view the body again. He eased that fear by saying, "The police surgeon has just arrived and is with the body now. So is our photographer. Not a pleasant thing for a young girl like you to have witnessed."

"No, not very pleasant," I agreed.

"Lady Georgiana," he said. "I wonder if I might have a word with you in private?"

"I believe Her Grace has put the library at your disposal," I said. "Perhaps you'd like to make that your headquarters, so to speak."

"Good idea," he said. "At least it's nice and warm in there. Miserable old day outside, isn't it?"

I agreed that it was as I led him down the hall to the library.

"I'm not sure that I can be of any help, Chief Inspector," I said tentatively. "I've already given you my account of how I found the body."

"What I really want from you is some background," he said. "So that I don't start out at a disadvantage, you know." He looked at me and nodded. "You seem like a sensible, levelheaded kind of girl. Didn't have hysterics on finding a body. Had the presence not to touch anything at the murder scene. And I understand that you're not related to anyone here?"

"No, I'm just a visitor," I said. "I was invited to stay by the dowager duchess. She wanted some young people in the house when the heir to the dukedom arrived from Australia."

"I read about that," he said. "Rum business, wasn't it—finding a long-lost heir on a sheep station in the middle of nowhere. Almost too good to be true."

"I believe a lot of background checking was done before he was brought here. He has a valid birth certificate, and his mother had a valid marriage license."

"But until recently the family didn't even know of his existence?"

"That's correct. His father, who was the younger son of the old duke, went to Australia before the war, but returned home to serve his country as soon as war was declared. He was killed in action almost immediately and never had a chance to tell his family that he had married. And he never had a chance to see his son either."

"Sounds rather fishy to me," the inspector said.

"Well, the dowager duchess accepted Jack immediately. Apparently the resemblance to her dead son is very strong."

"All the same, I think we'll get in touch with the police in Australia, just in case. It wouldn't be the first time that someone has shown up out of the blue claiming to be the heir to a fortune."

"Except that he was reluctant to come and feels clearly out of place here. I think he can't wait to get back to Australia."

"With the money in his pocket now, eh? I understand that the dukedom comes with a serious fortune."

"I didn't get the impression that money was all that important to Jack."

"Money's important to everyone, my dear young lady," he said. "Trust me. Wave enough pound notes in front of someone and they'll be willing to commit all sorts of crimes." He motioned me to sit in one of the armchairs beside the fire, and took the other one himself. "Now as I said, you seem like a sensible type of girl, so I wanted to get your take on this family before I start to interview them. Is there anything I should know? Any arguments or hostilities going on behind the scenes?"

"Look, Chief Inspector, I don't feel comfortable in the role of the telltale," I said. "As you said, I'm an outsider and I've only been here for a week or so. That's only long enough for superficial impressions."

He was looking at me half amused, half suspicious. "You lot always stick together, no matter what, don't you? It's always us versus them. All right. Give me those superficial impressions then. Let's start with the man who has been murdered: Duke Cedric. Tell me about him?"

"Well," I said, trying to collect my thoughts. "I'd say he was a selfish man, brought up to have his own way and to get what he wanted. He had little regard for the feelings of others."

"Give me an example."

"Well, his niece Elisabeth was crippled in a horse riding accident. Apparently there is a clinic in Switzerland that might be able to cure her, but Cedric refused to pay for her to go there for spinal treatments. On the other hand, he wasn't hesitating at all to shell out loads of money to build a big theater on the property. And he made it clear to the rest of his family that he found them a nuisance and wanted them out of his house—even though it has hundreds of rooms."

"And who are the other members of his family that he finds such a nuisance?"

"Well, his mother, the dowager duchess. You've met her."

"Oh yes," he said. "I've definitely met her."

"As you saw, she's very much an aristocrat of the old school. She used to be my grandmother's lady-in-waiting."

"And your grandmother was?"

"Queen Victoria's daughter."

"Blimey," he muttered. "Do go on."

"She is very hot on everything being done correctly. And a terrific defender of the dukedom."

"I don't suppose she was too thrilled when a young lad from the outback arrived then?"

"Actually, it was she who sought him out. The survival of the title and property are all-important to her. She was furious with Cedric for refusing to marry and produce an heir."

"Yes, why didn't he ever marry?"

"He wasn't much interested in girls, Chief Inspector, as you'll soon discover when you interview the other people in this house."

"I see. Had a male companion, did he?"

"Several."

"Hmmm." He stroked his chins. "Several male companions. Any idea where I might find them?"

"In the house somewhere," I said. "They've been staying here. They are supposed to be working on a play that was going to be part of Cedric's theater festival this autumn."

"Right." He took out a notebook and scribbled down some words. "Any other non-family members live in the house?"

"Well, I'm here at the moment and so are two friends of mine, the Honorable Darcy O'Mara, son of Lord Kilhenny from Ireland, and my school friend Belinda Warburton-Stoke. Mr. O'Mara was the one who was sent to fetch the heir from Australia."

"And Miss Warburton-whatsit?"

"She only came to deliver a lost evening slipper to me that I'd left in London. She arrived right before you did."

"Convenient of her," he said. "Now, let's get back to the rest of the family. A whole pack of 'em, by the looks of things."

"Well, there are the dowager duchess's two sisters," I said. "Princess Charlotte is the widow of a Russian prince who was murdered in the Bolshevik uprising. She fled to Paris and then came here. The other sister is the widow of an Austrian count, and I'm not sure how long she has been living here."

"Blimey," he said. "You nobs don't exactly marry the boy next door, do you?"

"Actually, their father was ambassador to Vienna so she did marry the boy next door," I said.

"And these old women," he went on. "What are they like? A bit dotty? I know there's a lot of inbreeding among your sort."

I could feel my hackles rising. "You know, Chief Inspector," I said coldly, "you'd get a lot more cooperation from the occupants of this house if you didn't start out by insulting them. You put our backs up. We clam up. Simple as that."

"Good point," he said. "I was just trying to lighten things up, you know." He paused. "And between you and me, I'm a bit nervous myself. I've never been in a house like this before. Nor have I ever had dealings with the family of a duke."

"Let me give you a hint then," I said. "Noble families take their ancestry very seriously. It doesn't do to poke fun at it."

"Point taken," he said. "I'll be suitably reverential from now on. I may even tug my forelock and grovel, if it will help."

I had to smile at this. "No groveling needed, but it does help if you give them due deference."

"Right you are. So we've got the duchess, the lad from Australia, two widowed sisters and the hangers-on of the dead duke living here. Anyone else?"

"Lady Irene and her family," I said.

"Oh, Lord, yes. The one who took the overdose of sleeping mixture last night. Tell me about her."

"She is the dowager duchess's only living child now," I said. "She married a Russian count she met in Paris. They have three children—a girl of fifteen—the one I told you about, who damaged her spine; and twins, who are eleven, I believe."

"Ah yes, I met the kiddies already. Too ghoulish for their own good, I'd say, but then, when you're eleven you've no real concept of death, have you? They clearly think it's a lark. So Irene and her family live here full-time, do they?"

I tried not to wince at the use of the word "kiddies." "For the past two years."

"And the Russian count?"

"Not a happy memory for the family. I gather he got through Lady Irene's fortune and then ran off with a South American dancer."

"So she had to come back home to Mum?"

"Exactly, and isn't enjoying it too much being dependent on others."

He stroked his chin again, staring into the fire. "So this overdose of sleeping powder last night—was she the type of woman who might get despondent enough to take her own life, would you say, or was it just an accident?"

"I really don't know her well enough to comment on that," I said, and decided to stay silent about the row with her brother and the way she had stormed out of his rooms the week before. No doubt that would all come out when he spoke to the others. "And there is a third possibility you haven't yet mentioned, Chief Inspector," I added. "That someone attempted to murder Lady Irene as well."

"Yes, the old duchess mentioned that, didn't she? All right. Let's take this one step further, Lady Georgiana. Any idea who?"

"I've no idea at all," I said. "As I said, I'm a recently arrived guest myself. I wasn't personally acquainted with the family until now."

"Ah." He gave a self-satisfied grin. "So you are thinking along the lines of it being one of the family then—not an outsider?"

"I haven't really given it much thought, Chief Inspector," I said, trying to keep my face a serene mask. "I suppose it's entirely possible that an outsider was lying in wait for the duke on that footpath. Since I know nothing of his lifestyle, I couldn't even begin to suggest whether he had enemies elsewhere." I remembered what Virginia had said. "Or if he bumped into a tramp who wasn't right in the head. You do see them wandering about these days, now that there's no work to be had, don't you?"

He looked hard at me. "Now, that would be convenient for all concerned, wouldn't it? Blaming it on the mysterious tramp who just happens to vanish afterward. I've read it in a dozen books."

"I'm just throwing out all possibilities since you asked for my opinion, Chief Inspector. I suppose a family member could just as easily have bumped off the duke in the house whenever they chose. A good shove down one of those long flights of stairs might have done it."

He looked at me with an expression of amusement mixed with amazement. "You certainly are a modern young woman, aren't you? Cool as a cucumber."

"I don't feel cool," I said. "Actually, this whole thing has made me feel rather sick. But I do want to help if I can, and there's one thing that may be relevant. The duke went out to post a letter, so one is told.

When I came across him though, there was no letter in his hand. Did you perhaps find one in his pockets?"

"No," he said. "There was no letter. Any idea what was in this letter?"

I paused then shook my head. "As I said before, I really didn't know the Duke of Eynsford."

He frowned as he stared at me. "And where might the duke have written this letter—do you know that?"

"In his study. I heard his valet saying that his master had risen early and asked for a cup of coffee to be sent to his study. Then he told the footman Frederick that he wanted to catch the early post."

Chief Inspector Fairbotham was looking at me with interest now. "And can you take me to this study? I'd like to take a look around for myself."

"All right," I said. "It's just down this hallway."

I took him out of the library and tried to remember which door they had opened to look into Cedric's study. I was glad when I found the right one. The room was stuffy and smelled of cigarette smoke and old books. In its center was a large mahogany desk, and papers were untidily heaped on top of it. Among them I spotted rough designs for what looked like his amphitheater, and I remembered that a footman had been given the sack because he had touched the papers—the same footman who had stormed up to the front door when he discovered that Cedric was planning to tear down his parents' cottage. A half-full coffee cup sat beside the blotter with a half-smoked cigarette resting on the ashtray.

"There's a possibility he might have blotted the letter and left us a hint on the blotting paper as to what all this might be about," the chief inspector said, peering down at the desk. But the blotting pad was pristine.

I pointed at the pen that lay beside the pad. "These latest fountain pens don't really need blotting, do they?" I said.

"I'll need time to go through all this stuff," he said. "There may be lots of things you don't know about him—you say he liked young men. Maybe he was being blackmailed and refused to pay up."

"Do blackmailers usually kill the goose that lays the golden egg?" I asked.

He looked up at me. "You're a sharp one, aren't you? I thought all you young society ladies would be removed from the sordid side of life. Aren't you raised in convents and finishing schools?"

"You'd be surprised what one learns in a finishing school, Chief Inspector," I said, stifling a grin. "You ask my friend Belinda when you interview her."

"He was lucky he got that letter to the post," he said. "He must have used the last envelope. There's plenty of notepaper here, but no more envelopes."

"I expect he has more in one of the drawers," I said.

The inspector pottered around a bit. "Offhand, I can't see anything here that would have a bearing on his being stabbed on the grounds," he said. "I'll get my man to go through everything with a fine-tooth comb after we've interviewed everyone. I should be getting on with that, I suppose. Can't expect people to sit around all day, can I?"

It was only when he told me I was free to go that I realized that neither of us had mentioned the knife in Cedric's back. It was the most important aspect of the murder, and yet we had both chosen to ignore it or skirt around it. I was glad because I should have had to identify it as Jack's.

Chapter 21

I heaved a sigh of relief as I watched the inspector return to the library, and I was released to go back to the others. The interview was at an end. I felt as if I'd been walking on eggshells all the time, terrified that something I said would be taken wrongly. Because when I examined it, there were so many things that could be misinterpreted at the moment—Jack's arrival to claim his position as heir to the dukedom, Princess Charlotte's séance, which spelled out "death," Lady Irene's row with her brother and his refusal to give her any money or let her use the family home in London and then Cedric's stunning announcement the night before that he planned to adopt his valet, Marcel, and make him his heir. All incidents were in their own way incriminating. All were possible motives for someone in this house. And the inspector's suggestion that the sisters might be "a bit dotty" and that insanity ran in families like theirs. They certainly were interestingly eccentric . . . And then the one salient detail that hadn't come up yet, but would: that the knife in Cedric's back belonged to Jack.

I started as a figure stepped out in front of me, pale and ghostlike in the gloom. It was Jack himself.

"Sorry," he said. "I didn't mean to startle you."

"Where have you been?" I asked. "I've hardly seen you today."

He shrugged. "I've just been wandering the halls, trying to come to terms with everything that's happened."

"I'm sure it must be a big shock to you."

"My oath, yes. I mean, it was a pretty big shock when some bloke turns up at the sheep station and tells me that I'm connected to a posh family in England and then that I'm not only connected, I'm supposedly the heir. I mean, my mum told me that my dad came from some kind of gentry, but that he'd turned his nose up at all that sort of stuff and liked Australia better, where everyone is equal. I have to say I agree with him. This sort of thing, it's all bloody rubbish, isn't it?" He laughed and ran his fingers through his blonde hair. "Your Grace." He shook his head in disbelief. "That's what one of the servants called me: Your Grace. Can you imagine? Me! I don't think I can take it, Georgie. It's too ridiculous for words."

"I expect most people in your position feel the same way," I said. "My brother certainly didn't want to be a duke, or to take over the running of the estate. And I'm sure nobody wants to be king. I know my cousin the Prince of Wales, doesn't. He told me once he'd do anything to get out of it, and he hopes his father will live to ninety-nine. But our sort of people are brought up to do our duty."

"So what's your duty supposed to be?" he asked.

"To marry well," I said. "There's no other option open to me. I'm not trained for any kind of career or profession."

"So you'll marry who they tell you to, will you?"

I had to smile. "Actually, no. I already turned down a Romanian prince. Everyone was furious with me, but I couldn't have married him."

"You turned down being a princess?"

"Possibly a queen someday," I agreed. "But he was awful, Jack. He was worse than awful. So I made up my mind that I'll only marry for love."

"So your lecture about doing your duty doesn't apply to you?" He gave me a friendly grin.

I found myself observing him. Could someone who had just stabbed his uncle be so relaxed and easy with me? He'd insisted over and over that he didn't want to be duke, or to have this lifestyle, and money didn't seem important to him. But perhaps he was just a good actor.

"I'd better go and round up everyone," I said. "The inspector is ready to talk to us in the library."

"Stone the crows," he said. "Does he have any ideas yet about who might have done it?"

"Give him a chance. He's not a miracle worker. He's only just taken a look at the crime scene, and I'm sure he won't have the police surgeon's report yet."

"My money is on one of those strange, poncy blokes who hung around Cedric," Jack said. "They were definitely emotional when he made that announcement about wanting to adopt his valet last night, weren't they?"

I decided to speak up. "You might consider that you are probably the prime suspect, Jack."

"Me?" He laughed. "Why would I want old Cedric out of the way?"

"To inherit the dukedom, of course. He got up early to write a letter then went to post it himself. There was no sign of a letter when I saw the body, so someone must have wanted to stop that letter from reaching its destination. And if the letter told his solicitor that he wanted to adopt his valet, thus cutting you out, well, then . . ."

I gave him a long, hard look. He laughed nervously. "That's a load of old cobblers. I never wanted to be a bloody duke in the first place."

"I know that," I said. "But the police might see it differently. You'd better have a good alibi for early this morning."

"Alibi?" He frowned. "I don't have any kind of alibi. I got up early, went for a walk then it looked as if it was going to rain so I came in and they were just putting out breakfast. So I helped myself then I went up to see Sissy."

"You seem to be spending a lot of time with your cousin," I said.

He blushed. "Well, I feel sorry for her, stuck up there all alone. At her age, she should be going to parties and having nice dresses and things. And she's a terrific teacher. She's helping me with my reading and writing."

"So where did your walk take you?" I went on. "Did you happen to see anyone?"

He looked sheepish. "I went to see the horses, as a matter of fact. I feel comfortable around horses, and they've told me I can ride any horse I like. Bluebird, isn't it?—he's a real cracker. Him and me get on like a house on fire."

"What time was this?"

"Early. I know it was before breakfast. Probably about seven, seven thirty."

"And did you see Cedric at all?"

He shook his head. "I told you, I don't remember seeing anybody."

"And when you came back into the house, did you see anyone then? Anyone who could vouch for your being indoors before Cedric was killed?"

He was looking at me strangely now, his eyes darting nervously. "Hey, you really do think they'll try to pin it on me, don't you?"

"Yes, I'm afraid I do."

"Do you think they'll gang up against me?"

"I don't think they'll gang up against you—least of all your grandmother, who seems thrilled to have John's son here. But it may come to a process of elimination, and you will stand out as the most likely."

"Bloody hell," he said. "The way you're talking, I've a good mind to bugger off back to Australia now."

"That would be disastrous, Jack," I said. "If you're innocent, then nobody can prove you're guilty. The one thing one can say about our justice system is that it's fair. Come on, let's go and get a cup of coffee before the grilling begins."

Before we could go into the Long Gallery, Belinda appeared as if by magic at our side.

"So this is the famous Jack Altringham at last," she said. "You've been so invisible that I began to believe you were a figment of Georgie's imagination." She held out her hand to him. "I'm Belinda, Georgie's oldest and dearest friend. I came down on a mission of mercy, to bring the evening slipper she left behind in London and found the place in an utter uproar. And now that horrid inspector says I can't leave because I'm a suspect like everyone else."

Jack took her hand and shook it. "That's too bad," he said. "I'm sure they'll rule you out very quickly. Hell, you weren't even here when poor old Cedric was killed, were you?"

"Absolutely not. Probably passing through Lewisham or one of those ghastly London suburbs—row after row of identical dirty brick." She sighed. "God, how I hate cities. I'm a country girl, born and bred."

"Are you? Then I know how you feel. I was in Sydney for a couple of days and that was enough for me. Too many people."

"I'm stuck in London at the moment," she said. "Even worse; like living in a sardine tin."

"Why are you stuck there?"

"Trying to earn a living, darling. It's not easy in these days of depression. Especially when you're like Georgie and me—not trained for anything sensible except curtsying without falling over and knowing which fork to use at the dinner table."

Jack grinned. "Yes, Georgie's been trying to drum that into my head. Load of cod's wallop, if you ask me."

"I couldn't agree more," Belinda said. "So unnecessary and so outmoded, isn't it? I mean, fish would taste just the same if one cut it with a meat knife."

"Too right," Jack said. "Look, Georgie and I were about to grab some coffee before we have to face the inspector again. Want to come along?"

"Why not?" Belinda said, as if the idea had never occurred to her. She slipped her arm through Jack's, and they went on ahead of me. I had been watching this little interchange with admiration, wishing that I'd actually taken lessons in seduction from Belinda rather than learning all the useless skills of finishing school.

"I studied fashion design with Chanel," I heard her saying. "And now I'm trying to get my own clothing line off the ground, but it's all rather depressing, since my father cut me off, having now turned twenty-one."

I almost laughed out loud. The way she phrased this had been the truth, I suppose. She had indeed turned twenty-one—only it had been three years ago. I decided not to join the group around the coffeepot, but felt it was my duty to see how Mr. Smedley was faring all alone in the morning room. I had found him an absolutely wet and spineless specimen, but I would not like to find myself a virtual prisoner in a stately home where a murder had taken place.

When I crossed the hall and opened the morning room door, Mr. Smedley jumped to his feet and stood there like a startled rabbit, ready to run. I noticed that his coffee was only half drunk and the plate of biscuits beside him untouched. What's more, he had been reading *The Lady*, which showed how distracted he must have been feeling.

"It's only me," I said. "I came to see how you were."

"How long am I to be kept here, Lady Georgiana?" he demanded. "This is an outrage. Apart from an exchange of correspondence with the late duke, I have no connection to this family at all. It's not as if I actually knew the man, so surely they could just take my statement and let me go."

"I don't see why not," I said. "I'll go and talk to the inspector if you like, to see if he'll interview you first, before he gets to the rest of us."

"Would you?" I saw relief flush over his face. "I'd be most grateful. It feels as if I've been shut away in here forever. And now that I won't be getting the contract to design the theater here—" He paused and looked up at me. "I presume the new duke will not wish to carry on with the plans?"

"I think it highly unlikely," I said.

"I feared as much. Then the sooner I am back in my office on Queen Anne Street, the better."

"Look, why don't you come with me and we'll find the inspector. I can vouch that you were with me the whole time when we found the body," I said.

"That's frightfully decent of you, my lady," he said. "Much appreciated."

He followed me like an obedient dog to the door, and we set off down the hall. No sooner were we heading in the direction of the library then we heard the clatter of running feet behind us and Nicholas and Katherine came sprinting past.

"Grandmama says the inspector wants to speak to us, one by one in the library," Nick shouted as he ran past. "He's going to grill us all and perhaps someone will break down and confess. Isn't it thrilling?"

"We thought we'd go along and see if we can be first," Kat added. "Get it over with, you know."

Mr. Smedley had gone rather green around the gills again. "In which case I think I had better retreat to the morning room until the police have dealt with the family," he said. "It would be most inappropriate if I intruded on such a difficult and embarrassing business." He attempted to turn and flee.

"If you want to escape from here in a hurry, then I suggest you get in first," I said, and marshaled him down the hall after the running twins.

He gets rattled rather easily, I thought, but then it crossed my mind that we really knew nothing about Mr. Smedley. He had shown up on the doorstep and introduced himself as the architect come to meet with the duke. What if he wasn't what he seemed? Who could say how long he had been out on the grounds before he came to the front door, or what he might have got up to there?

Chapter 22

As we approached the library, the twins went bursting in ahead of us.

"Hello," I heard the chief inspector's voice say. "And what do you two want?"

"We heard that you wanted to grill the whole family so we thought we'd be first," Nick said.

"I don't usually grill kiddies," he answered in good-natured fashion. "Unless you've come to confess to the murder—which I very much doubt."

"Oh, but we might have vital information for you," Kat said. "You never know what we might have seen. Children are very observant, you know."

"All right. So where were you when the murder took place?" the inspector asked.

"We don't know what time it took place," Nick said, "so we can't answer that."

"Early this morning. Between seven and eight. Where were you between those times?"

"We were where we always are—stuck in the nursery, getting up and having breakfast with Nanny, I suppose."

"And did you happen to look out of the window and see anything that might be important?"

"I don't think so," Nick said sadly. "Only that it was starting to rain and we thought it was beastly because we'd be stuck in the schoolroom all day."

"So I suggest you stop wasting my time and hightail it back to your schoolroom and let me get on with my work," the inspector said, no longer in such a friendly fashion. "Go on. Off you go."

He looked up as I appeared in the doorway. "Ah, Lady Georgiana. Can you take these two scamps off my hands and keep them out of trouble, do you think?"

"Of course," I said, "but first I thought you might have a word with Mr. Smedley. He's the architect who came to meet the duke this morning and was with me when we discovered the duke's body. Naturally, he's anxious to make his statement and get back to London."

"Naturally," the chief inspector reiterated. "Very well. Come on in, Mr. Smedley, and you can make a statement for us while Lady Georgiana rounds up her family members."

"Very well, although I have absolutely nothing salient to add to your investigation, I am sure," the little man said, throwing me a nervous glance as I went out.

"I don't think he'll ever find out whodunit, do you?" Nick asked. "He doesn't know the right questions to ask."

"Should he have asked you any right questions?" I asked with a grin.

"Possibly," Kat said. "We may have overheard something incriminating sometime that we didn't realize was important. We do love snooping on grown-up conversations, you know."

"You'll get yourselves into trouble one day," I said, but even as I said it I remembered the lonely time in my own nursery, and how I would creep to the staircase and hide in the shadows, listening to the adults talking down below. It's what lonely children do to feel that they are part of life.

The twins ran on ahead of me into the Long Gallery. I followed them and found the others still sitting together, not saying anything.

Nicholas and Katherine had already grabbed the last sandwiches as if they hadn't had a meal in months. I passed along the information that the inspector wanted to speak to each of us in turn. Edwina now took charge, bossing everyone and choosing the order in which they should go to be questioned.

"And there is no point in mentioning anything unnecessary to him," she said. "We have our disagreements like any other family, don't we? But I can't see what bearing those would have on my son's murder. The fact that this crime took place on a footpath that leads directly to the village and the station indicates to me that it has to have been an outsider." And she gave us a long, hard stare.

She turned to Jack. "John, dear, it is only right that you should go first, as head of the family," she said. "Nothing to worry about. A mere formality." And she attempted a bright smile as Jack shot me a worried glance and left the room.

I went to perch on the arm of Darcy's sofa. I noticed that the Starlings had now joined the group, standing nervously beside the fire.

"So was it awful?" Adrian asked me. "Do you think that brute of a policeman will try to get one of us to confess?"

"Only if he thinks you did it," I replied.

Adrian shuddered. "Don't. It's too terrifying to think about. Simon and Julian and I were absolutely shattered—still are, aren't we?" He looked at them for affirmation. "And to think that if only we'd plucked up the courage to go and talk to Ceddy this morning, we could have walked down to the theater site with him and he would still be with us now."

I wondered whether they had been told about the letter Cedric had insisted on posting himself. If it really was to his solicitor stating that he wanted to adopt Marcel, then they had as good a motive as any of the family to prevent that letter from being mailed. Was that the motive? I wondered, or was Cedric merely having a private laugh at their expense and not serious about wanting to adopt his valet?

Edwina walked across to the coffeepot, poured herself a cup then exclaimed, "This coffee is cold." She stalked across to the bell by the fireplace and gave it a bad-tempered jerk. Eventually Huxstep appeared.

"Huxstep. There is cold coffee in this pot," she said angrily. "I see no reason to let standards slip because we have a few policemen in the house. Have it replaced immediately."

"Your Grace, I must apologize," he said, "but the servants have been told they are to wait in the servants' hall until each of them has given the police a statement. I thought Your Grace knew this."

"I'm sorry. I did not know that the chief inspector now thinks he can order my servants around without my permission. I have already spoken to him once, but I will be next in line and let him know that he cannot disrupt the running of this house. Better still, would you please get me the lord lieutenant on the telephone right away? It's time someone more competent took over this case."

It was like being in a doctor's office, waiting for the next patient to be called in. We sat in near silence while Her Grace was summoned to the telephone then came back in a worse temper than before. "The lord lieutenant is off on his yacht in Monte Carlo," she snapped. "How inconsiderate of him to have deserted his post like this. I'm afraid we'll have to have Mr. O'Mara put out his feelers, as he calls them, to Scotland Yard after all."

Mr. Smedley appeared in the doorway, announcing that the chief inspector had given him permission to leave, so he was heading back to London. He could not have looked more relieved. Then Jack returned, and Edwina went in his place, presumably to give the chief inspector a piece of her mind. I didn't envy him.

"How was it?" I asked Jack when he took a seat on the sofa opposite.

Jack shrugged. "He didn't really ask me much."

Edwina came back shortly afterward, her mouth still pursed in annoyance. "Really, that man has no manners at all," she said. "I suppose it was to be expected, coming from the north like that. One doesn't associate dark, satanic mills with good manners, does one? Do go and put out your feelers, Mr. O'Mara. The sooner a competent man from Scotland Yard comes to take over here, the better."

Huxstep appeared again to say that the sergeant was still taking statements from the servants, and Mrs. Broad wanted to inform Her Grace that luncheon might be a little delayed.

"As if the servants would know anything useful," Edwina said. "What does he think we do—hire a pack of ex-convicts to work in the house? Almost all of them have been with us for years, and their parents before them. Until recently, it was considered a great honor to serve the Dukes of Eynsford. Alas, the Great War turned the world all topsy-turvy, and too many young people now believe that domestic service is beneath them. Though why they should think a noisy office or a dirty factory is preferable, I don't know."

I watched her talking, noticing how she seemed to be the only one who wanted to chat. Was it to hide her nerves? I wondered. To stop herself from thinking about her dead son? To give the appearance that nothing was wrong and life would go on smoothly at Kingsdowne?

One by one, the inhabitants of the house went to the library and returned. I could read relief in each of their faces, especially in those of the three Starlings.

"He wasn't brutal at all," Justin said as he joined Adrian and Simon. "Quite pleasant, actually. Asked if anyone had a grudge against Cedric and I said all sorts of people."

"Justin, you didn't!" A yelp of horror from Adrian.

"Well, it was true, wasn't it? I told him that Cedric wasn't the easiest person to get along with and probably put everyone's back up at the theater when they were rehearsing for that new play. Just because he was backing it, he thought it gave him carte blanche to change everything—and of course he knows nothing about the theater, really. I mean, knew. He knew nothing. I still can't believe that he's gone."

"Do you think that someone from the theater would come all the way down here to kill Cedric then?" I asked.

"Don't be silly. People in the theater learn to cope with difficult types all the time. Temperamental leading ladies, harsh critics, crabby wardrobe mistresses . . . but they don't go around killing each other. They get out their frustrations on stage. If only Cedric . . ."

He broke off as heavy footsteps could be heard in the hall, and the chief inspector appeared. "Ah, there you are," he said. "Everyone here? Good, because I've a couple of questions to put to all of you."

He stood in front of the fire, facing us. "Now then. According to your statements, nobody saw anything unusual this morning. Nobody even saw the duke get up or go out. Nobody knows any reason why someone would want to murder the duke. In fact, you are all a big, happy family with not a care in the world." He paused and looked from one face to the next. "Right, let's take another approach, shall we?" He glanced across at the entrance to the Long Gallery, and beckoned. A police constable came toward us, carrying something wrapped in a cloth. The inspector took it carefully and unwrapped it.

"Now look carefully. Have any of you seen this object before?" he asked, and held it out to us. I heard a gasp from some people and Nicholas called out excitedly, "I've seen it before. It's cousin Jack's knife."

Chapter 23

"Cousin Jack's knife?" The chief inspector stared hard at Jack. "I take it he means you, young man?"

"It's my knife, right enough," Jack said. "The duchess—I mean, my grandmother—made me go and put it in the tack room. She said she didn't want it in the house, and she was cross with me for showing the nippers how I could throw it."

"He threw it into the tree above my head," Kat said.

"It was brilliant," Nick added. "Just like William Tell."

"I see." The inspector paused. "So when did you see this knife last, sir?"

"When my grandmother told me to put it in the tack room—several days ago now."

"Did anyone else know the knife was going to be left in this tack room?" He pronounced the words as if they were both unfamiliar and amusing to him.

"I believe we were all out on the lawn when the incident occurred," Edwina said. "So I suspect that everyone overheard my telling John where he was to put his knife for safekeeping."

"And is this tack room left unlocked?"

"Of course," Edwina said. "The grooms come in and out all the time to saddle up the horses. Really, Chief Inspector—we live on a big estate, cocooned from the rest of the world. We don't need to keep things locked. We have servants looking after us and our property. The grooms actually sleep above the stables."

"So in theory anyone could have crept into this tack room, removed the knife, followed the duke and killed him with it."

"In theory," Edwina replied. "Although I think you'll find from our statements that nobody else was up and awake at that time."

"Except us," Nick said, and received a warning frown from his grandmother.

"Children should be seen and not heard, Nicholas. And we already know that you were safely in the nursery, where you belong."

The log on the fire crackled and shifted, making everyone jump. The tension in the room was palpable. I found that I was holding my breath.

Chief Inspector Fairbotham paused before focusing on Jack again. "So remind me again, sir, what you were doing between seven and eight this morning?"

"I can answer that for him," Sissy said quickly, before Jack could speak. "He was with me the whole time."

"With you, little lady?" The inspector turned to look at the slight girl in her bath chair. She was sitting off to one side of the group, and had been ignored until now, a rug over her knees.

"That's right." Sissy tossed her head defiantly. "I've been helping Jack with his schoolwork. He hardly had any schooling, you know. And he didn't want to look stupid, now that he's the heir to a dukedom. So I was giving him extra reading practice."

"Young lady, do you realize that perjury is a serious offense? You understand what perjury is, do you?"

Sissy shook her head.

"It is deliberately lying before a court of law, and it is punishable by a term in prison. Is that what you want? Or would you like to change your statement?"

Sissy's face had turned very red but she said nothing.

"Listen, I was with Sissy early this morning but she didn't know that I'd been out for a walk before that," Jack said. He turned and gave his cousin a reassuring grin. "I already told you, Inspector, that I went out early, walked around a bit, went over to the stables and then came back inside because it was about to rain. Then I grabbed a quick breakfast and went up to see if Sissy was awake, as we'd agreed to do some more reading practice."

"So you admit that you were at the stables, at the very place where the knife was stored in the unlocked tack room, early this morning?"

"Yes, but I didn't go into the tack room. I went to see the horses. I feel comfortable around horses."

"But you saw nobody and nobody saw you?"

"That's right. It was early," Jack said. "At least, early for a place like this. Back at home, we'd have had our tucker and been out with the sheep hours before that."

He didn't look nervous or uncomfortable, I noticed.

"So you never saw your uncle, the duke, at all?"

"I already told you that I hadn't. I didn't see a living soul. I let myself out of the front door. I walked around by the lake. I visited the horses, and it was about to rain so I came back inside. That's the lot."

"You came over here how long ago?"

"What is it—two weeks now?" Jack still seemed calm and unconcerned, as if he didn't sense approaching danger.

"If I understand it correctly, you were brought over here as the heir to this estate," Chief Inspector Fairbotham went on. "Rather a cushy job after being up at crack of dawn and riding around after sheep, wouldn't you say?"

"Cushy, yes, but not one I would have chosen for myself," Jack answered. "I've never wanted to be a bloody duke."

There was an intake of breath from Edwina. Princess Charlotte fanned herself. The twins tittered.

"Watch your language, boy," the inspector said. "You're not in the outback now. We don't swear among ladies over here."

"Sorry," Jack muttered. "Look, I don't know what you're getting at."

"What I'm getting at is that you suddenly appear out of the blue, from the wilds of Australia, and claim you're the heir to this estate. Funnily enough, the family accepts you as the rightful heir with no fuss at all. And then, lo and behold, a few days later the duke dies with your knife in his back. Now, I may not be the brightest man in the world, but I'd say that looks pretty suspicious to me, wouldn't you?"

"You can say what you like, Inspector," Jack replied, staring at the detective defiantly. "But I'm telling you that I didn't kill the duke."

"And yet, according to what I've been told, you and the duke had a run-in only last night. He insulted your mother, didn't he? And you jumped up and challenged him to a fight."

"Yes, I did," Jack agreed.

"But that fight never took place?"

"No." Jack shook his head. "When I'd cooled down, I saw that he was a poor specimen and I'd knock the stuffing out of him. Besides, he wouldn't agree to fight with me. He got into another argument with someone else and forgot about our little tiff."

"And what was that argument about?" Chief Inspector Fairbotham asked.

Edwina looked around the group. Nobody spoke. "I don't remember," she said. "Something inconsequential, I'm sure. Cedric was a confrontational sort of person who enjoyed making inflammatory statements just to get a rise out of people."

"I will tell you what it was about," said a voice from the far doorway, and there stood Irene, looking terribly pale but fully dressed, with a shawl around her shoulders.

"Irene, what on earth are you doing out of your bed?" Edwina went over to her. "Go back immediately. You nearly died, you silly girl."

"I'm not a girl, Mother," Irene said calmly. "I'm a woman with children, and I'm quite all right. I've just heard what happened to

Cedric, and I expect to do my part to find his killer." She walked slightly unsteadily across the room. Darcy went to help her to a seat. Katherine and Nick looked up nervously at her pale appearance and Kat crawled over to sit at her feet.

"Those children should be back in the nursery," Edwina said. "This conversation is highly unsuitable for young ears."

"But the inspector might want to ask us questions," Kat said, looking at her brother. "And we want to stay with Mummy." She rested her head on her mother's knee and Irene stroked her hair.

"Presumably you are Lady Irene?" Chief Inspector Fairbotham said.

"I am the Countess Streletzki, and wish to be addressed as such," she said, her expression not wavering. "My mother refuses to acknowledge the fact that I am still married to the count, as no divorce has taken place."

"Very well, Countess." He gave something resembling a little bow. "I am Detective Chief Inspector Fairbotham of the Royal Kent Constabulary. Thank you for leaving your sickbed. Very brave of you."

"Enough of the compliments, Chief Inspector. Let's get on with it, shall we?"

The chief inspector cleared his throat. "Let's start with what happened to you. I understand that there might have been two attempts at murder in this family. That somebody wanted to kill you as well as your brother. You somehow took—or were given—an overdose of sleeping powders last night and the doctor had to be called to pump your stomach. Correct?"

"That is correct."

"Was this overdose an accident, in your opinion? Was it possible that you took more than one of these powders?"

She continued to eye him coldly. "Certainly not," she said. "After the fracas at dinner last night, I was extremely upset. I realized that one of my migraines was coming on. Unfortunately, I have always suffered from terribly debilitating migraines as my mother can tell you. The only way to stop them is to knock myself out for long enough with a good, deep sleep. My doctor in Harley Street had prescribed a strong sleeping powder for this purpose. So I took one of the powders last night and told my maid not to wake me in the morning. The next thing I knew, I was awakened to the most unpleasant . . . there was a tube down my throat, Inspector. Most humiliating."

"So as far as you know, you took the correct dose."

"Absolutely."

"But it's possible that someone might have administered a second dose to you while you were so groggy that you didn't remember?"

"I can't speculate on what might have happened while I was in a sound sleep. As I said, the powders were designed to knock me out. I fell asleep after taking one dose. I awoke to find a stomach pump being administered. If I didn't remember anything more, how can I tell you about it?"

I looked at her with admiration. She had nearly lost her life but her voice was strong and clear and she appeared to be ready for a good fight.

Chief Inspector Fairbotham cleared his throat. "Maybe when this joint interview is over you can take me to your boudoir and we can count the number of packets of sleeping medicine still remaining. And you might be able to tell me whether one is missing, and we can surmise that someone had attempted to administer an overdose."

"Who on earth would have done that?" she snapped. "The only people in the house are the ones you see here. I am penniless and homeless, Inspector. I am heir to no fortune. I pose no threat to any of them."

"Someone in your situation might well be feeling hopeless and depressed, Countess," the inspector said cautiously.

"If you are suggesting that I attempted to take my own life, Inspector, then let me tell you that my children mean everything to me. I am a mother lioness. I would fight to the death to protect my children, and I would never abandon them. Also, I am from a very old and distinguished family. I was raised to do my duty. I hope I make myself clear."

There was silence in the room, apart from the gentle patter of rain on the windows.

The chief inspector cleared his throat again. "This little tiff at the table last night—the one you wanted to tell me about, Countess. Perhaps you'd like to recount it to me."

"It was just my brother being silly and vindictive," she said. "He liked to put people's backs up. He was always like that, even as a small boy. He'd do something naughty to be the center of attention. He'd give Mama a fright then he'd laugh."

"And what naughty thing did he do last night?"

Irene was still staring straight at the inspector, her head held high and her back rigid. "He announced that he was not satisfied with the newly arrived heir from Australia and was taking matters into his own hands. He looked at my mother and said she'd always told him he had to produce an heir, and now he was going to. He planned to adopt his choice of heir. Then he went on to say that it was his French valet, Marcel. Naturally, this caused a complete uproar. My mother said that she would do anything in her power to stop him. I threatened to go up to the House of Lords and ask advice from Daddy's old friends."

"You also wanted to stop him then, Countess?"

"Of course I did. I have great family pride, Inspector. How could I stand by idly while my brother disgraced our whole family by adopting a French valet? It was unthinkable."

"If your brother had succeeded in adopting this French valet, it would have presumably cut you and your children out of any inheritance too?"

Irene gave a dry, cold laugh. "Obviously you know little about inheritance laws, Chief Inspector. This estate is entailed. That means that the title and property goes from eldest son to eldest son. And failing that, to the oldest male relative of the line. The rest of us inherit nothing. And since my brother did not think it was his job to spend any family money on me or my children, then I could hardly have been worse off with a new duke who was an ex-valet. In fact, he would probably have been a good deal more sympathetic to my current condition."

The chief inspector suddenly swung around to face Jack. "So it seems, young man, that the only person with a strong motive for getting your uncle out of the way in a hurry would be you—the very person who admits to wandering in the grounds early this morning. The very person whose knife was found sticking out of your uncle's back."

"That's a load of old cod's wallop," Jack said. "I told you, I never wanted to be a duke in the first place. I wasn't the one who contacted the family. They came looking for me. I'd have been quite happy to stay working with sheep all my life. At least I knew who I was there. At least I knew who I could trust."

"I'll need to have my men take your fingerprints, sir," the inspector said. "In fact, I'll need fingerprints from everyone in this room."

"Outrageous," the dowager duchess said. "Do we look like the sort of people who go around sticking knives into people? My sisters and I are elderly ladies. Even if we were murderously inclined, I hardly think that we possess that kind of strength."

"A matter of formality, Your Grace," Fairbotham said. "This young man has told me that you took the knife from him and then made him put it in the tack room. So one might expect to find your fingerprints on the knife handle. And if this blade is as sharp as I think it is, then it would not take a great deal of strength to stab someone—especially if you were lucky enough to penetrate between the ribs."

"Goodness me." Princess Charlotte fanned herself again. "In my young days, one did not discuss this sort of thing, especially the mention of body parts in front of ladies."

"I take it you'd like to find out who murdered your nephew, Princess," the inspector said.

"Of course I would, but surely it can't be anyone here."

"I agree with my sister," Edwina said. "You should be out asking questions of the estate workers and in the village, and if you're looking for things like fingerprints, then are you being equally diligent about finding telltale footprints?"

"That's right," Jack said. "Take a look at my boots. I bet you don't see too many like them around here. Proper Aussie stockman's boots. Go and take a look at that body and tell me if you see my footprints anywhere around."

"As to that, sir," the inspector said, "the stream has been washing over the footpath, probably spoiling any footprints we might have found. And I have already been told that you are an expert at throwing a knife—just like William Tell, I believe that young man said. You could have followed the duke and struck him down from a distance." He looked around the assembled company. "If you'll all stay exactly where you are, I'll have my constable bring in the fingerprint kit. I assure you it's quite painless and will only take a moment."

And with that, he made a grand exit from the room.

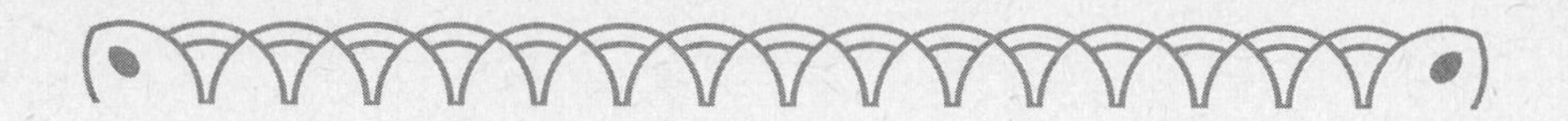

Chapter 24

Edwina was the first to speak. "If it's John's knife, of course his fingerprints will be on it. What does that silly man think he is going to prove?"

"I think he wants everyone's fingerprints to rule out those known to have touched the knife," Darcy replied.

"I touched it," Nick said, looking rather proud of himself. "Jack was showing me how to throw it. So my fingerprints will be on it, won't they?"

"I think it's high time you children were back in the nursery." Irene looked around nervously. "You've been down here long enough and this discussion is unsuitable for young ears. And you two already have too many ghoulish tendencies."

"Do you want us up in the schoolroom by ourselves?" Kat said. "We could get into all sorts of mischief with Mr. Carter's science experiments if he's not there."

"Then I will have to tell Mr. Carter that in future all your science should come from books, not experiments, if you can't be trusted," Irene said smoothly. "Is that what you want?"

"No, Mama," the twins muttered in unison.

"Then off you go, and I expect to be able to trust you not to get up to any mischief. Your grandmother and I have enough to worry about at this moment."

The twins got up and left the room, rather in shock at their mother's firmness, I thought. Sissy continued to sit unnoticed on the far side of the fireplace, staring at the rain streaking the windowpanes and occasionally glancing across at Jack, whose own gaze was fixed on the pattern on the Persian rug. A constable arrived, pulled over a side table and began taking fingerprints.

When it was Belinda's turn, she stared at her hands in disgust. "How horrid," she said. "You know, I think it was a silly mistake to have come here in the first place, and it's clearly going to be no fun with the police all over the place. I may just toddle off back to London, darling."

She thinks that Jack is guilty, I thought, but didn't say it out loud. And she did have a point. He appeared to have a perfect motive, and the opportunity and skill to carry it out.

She turned to the police constable. "Now that you have ruined my fingers with that nasty black stuff, I presume I'm free to leave. There really is no reason for my staying here any longer, you know. I only came to return a lost shoe to Lady Georgiana, and I have absolutely no connections to this family."

"What do you mean?" Edwina's voice boomed down the Long Gallery. "Have you forgotten your great-aunt Primrose? We are related, are we not, through your great-aunt? Besides, I should have thought that your friendship with Cedric might provide most valuable information to the police. The rest of us know nothing about his life in London. You may be able to shed light on who might have had a genuine motive to want Cedric dead. So please sit down again."

She was so forceful in her delivery that Belinda sat. I couldn't resist sneaking a glance and giving her a grin. It wasn't often that one saw Belinda unable to talk herself out of an awkward situation. I must say, I was rather enjoying her discomfort. She had become too used to gaining entry under false pretenses. Maybe this would teach her a lesson.

Darcy was obviously thinking along the same lines. "The rats are trying to leave the sinking ship," he muttered to me under his breath.

I nodded. Silence resumed as the police constable gathered up his fingerprint kit and left, his big boots echoing loudly across the parquet floor.

I leaned close to Darcy and whispered, "I need to talk to you. Something doesn't make sense."

"What doesn't?"

"A lot of things, but especially that knife left in Cedric's back. I suppose there's no chance that you can go and take a look at the body for yourself, is there?"

"I can hardly go out there now with the police milling around, can I? Besides, what would I see that you haven't already seen?"

"I'd just like confirmation that something wasn't right," I said. "There was something about the way he was lying that didn't add up—apart from his coat being draped over his body, I mean."

Darcy glanced out of the window. "I don't really see how I could slip away at this moment without it looking suspicious. And I expect the body has already been put into a police van by now."

"You're not being very helpful." I stood up. "I'm going to have a word with the inspector."

Darcy put his hand over mine. "Is that wise? Shouldn't we just let the police go about their business?"

"Not if they are going to get it wrong," I said. Conscious of all the eyes on me, I went over to the chief inspector, who was hovering in the background.

"Might I have a word with you?" I said, and led him out of hearing range of the others.

"Well?" he asked.

"That young man may be uncouth and naïve," I said, "but he's definitely not stupid. If he had wanted to kill his cousin, he could well have stabbed him with his knife, but would he leave the knife in Cedric's back? Especially a knife so easily identifiable as his?"

"We've already heard how skilled he is at throwing a knife. Perhaps he threw it, struck his uncle down then heard someone coming and didn't have time to retrieve it," he said.

"But the body was covered with Cedric's jacket," I said. "If he had time to do that, he'd have had time to remove the knife."

"That's true," he admitted. "That is strange, isn't it? I've wondered about that coat. Why would anyone want to cover the top half of a body but leave it there on the path in full view for anyone to see? And, as you say, leaving the knife in its back?"

"My guess would be that the person wanted the body to be found and wanted to make us think that Jack did it," I said.

"Thus getting rid of the duke and his heir at the same time?" the chief inspector said thoughtfully. "So who would be next in line if they both went?"

"Nobody. I've been told that the title would die out and that the estate would probably revert to the crown."

"You mean the king would get all this lot?"

"I believe so. I understand the title was created to include a land grant from the sovereign—which means the crown can take it back if the title no longer exists. That was the usual way things were done in the old days."

Chief Inspector Fairbotham sucked through his teeth. "So the old biddies would lose their home?"

"And Irene and her children."

He sighed. "So none of them would want to change the status quo."

"Exactly."

"Then we're back to square one," he said, "unless your boy Jack is cleverer than you think. What if he really did kill the duke but made it so obvious and blundering that we'd come to the conclusion he couldn't possibly have done it?"

"That's possible too, I suppose," I had to admit. "But I'm sure that coat is important. Why would Jack cover the body with a coat? Why would anyone? If the murderer wanted to hide the body, he could have dragged it into the nearest bushes. It was just as obvious with a coat over it."

"Unless he wasn't strong enough to move the body," the inspector said. "Or *she* wasn't strong enough."

We stared at each other, digesting this. I remembered that Edwina had said she would do anything to stop Cedric from making Marcel his heir. But surely she would never resort to killing her own son?

"There is one other thing," I said tentatively. "Remember I mentioned to you that the duke went out early to post a letter. And when I last spoke to you, the letter hadn't been found."

"That is correct," he said.

"Now I think this letter might be important," I went on. "He insisted on posting it himself, which is unusual in a house like this, where such a task could easily be handled by servants. Maybe it was important enough that someone killed him to prevent him from posting it."

"Go on," he said.

Emboldened by his apparent interest, I began to speak more freely. "Of course it's possible that he had already gone as far as the postbox and was returning when he met his killer. Might I suggest that you have your men inquire at the post office whether the postman picked up a letter from the duke this morning and to whom it was addressed? I'm sure it would have been noticed because very few letters would find their way to an out-of-the-way postbox in a small lane. And the envelope would have had the Eynsford crest on the back. Postmen notice things like that."

The chief inspector nodded. "Might be worth following up on. I thank you for your insights, my lady. But my money is still on the Australian boy. If we find a nice, clean set of his prints on the knife handle, over any other prints, then I'm making an arrest. I don't care if he is a ruddy duke."

He broke off as one of his constables approached us. "I was asked to tell you that the MO has taken the body, guv. And Phelps has finished with the fingerprinting. I suppose you want to be there when we have a go at the knife? Are we going to take the evidence back to HQ?"

"Of course I want to be there," the inspector snapped. "I'll find out where the old lady will let us set up shop and get to work. I don't fancy going all the way back to Sevenoaks."

"What about something to eat, sir?" the constable asked. "It's getting close to dinnertime. Can me and the lads pop to a pub in the village?"

"Let's see if they're going to feed us here. I'm not wasting an hour with you lot strolling to the village and having a good pub lunch. Perhaps their cook can make us some sandwiches."

"Very good, sir." The young constable looked deflated, as if sandwiches would be a poor alternative to a good meat pie or bangers and mash. I was hesitating, not sure that our conversation was at an end or what it might have achieved. When the chief inspector started back toward the group around the fireplace, I followed him.

"Well?" Edwina asked. "Are we to be kept here all day? Are my staff still prisoners of your men in the servants' hall? Our luncheon hour is rapidly approaching, and I can't expect Cook to work miracles in five minutes."

"So sorry to have kept you, Your Grace," he said. I wasn't sure whether it was meant to be sarcastic. "But I don't think I'll need you anymore—for the time being. And my sergeant should have got a statement from each of your servants by now. So you're free to go about your business—only nobody is to think of leaving the premises."

"Very well," Edwina said. "Please be kind enough to send me my butler so that we can return this house to normal. I've already had to endure cold coffee this morning."

"And given the number of rooms there are in this house, perhaps you can suggest one that I might use for my headquarters? Preferably one with a telephone in it?"

Edwina bristled. I could tell she really didn't want to have Chief Inspector Fairbotham setting up shop in her home, but given the fact that she did have many surplus rooms, she couldn't think of a good excuse for his not staying. "I suppose you might use my son's study," she said grudgingly. "There is a telephone extension in there, although of course it connects to the main telephone in the front hall, and I couldn't guarantee that your calls would necessarily be confidential."

The chief inspector chuckled. "What with old biddies listening in at the exchange, there is no such thing as a confidential telephone call," he said. "But I thank you for the offer of your son's study. It has a nice, big desk we'll find useful." He started to leave then turned back again. "And one more thing. My men will want something to eat about now. They'll obviously get things done faster if they don't have to go down to the local pub. Might there be a chance your cook can find enough to feed them with your servants?"

"The sooner you ascertain that my cook has been released from your man's questioning, the sooner we can all eat," Edwina said. "I expect there will be enough food for your men—for you too, Chief Inspector. We do not stint ourselves here at Kingsdowne." I noticed she had put him firmly in the same category as household staff. There was no indication that he should eat with us. He would have to rise to chief constable before that might happen.

"Very good of you, Your Grace," he muttered. "I'll go and find my sergeant right away."

And off he stomped. As soon as he was out of earshot, Edwina stood up and came over to me.

"What were you saying to the inspector, Georgiana?" she demanded. "If you have your suspicions, I would request that you share them with the rest of us."

"No suspicions, Your Grace," I said. "I was suggesting that the inspector put renewed efforts to tracing the missing letter. If your son thought it important enough that he wanted to post it personally, then I feel that is the key to why he was killed."

"I'm afraid we must presume that it was to our solicitor, instructing him to set up this ridiculous adoption process for his valet—absolutely absurd, as I'm sure the solicitor will tell him. I can't think what other matter would have been so pressing as to make him walk across the grounds in the rain. Cedric never was one for healthy outdoor activities." She stood staring out of the window. Then she sighed. "Well, I see no reason why we should not go in to luncheon at the usual hour, although heaven knows what Cook will have been able to prepare with policemen tramping all over the place. I rather fear we'll have to settle for something rather plain. Ring for Huxstep and tell him we wish to eat now, John."

As she went across to the bell, Jack also had risen to his feet. "How can you talk calmly of eating when your son is dead and everyone thinks I stabbed him?" he shouted, his voice echoing down the Long Gallery.

Edwina looked at him in surprise. In fact, she raised her lorgnette to him. "Such an outburst," she said. "Hardly seemly for a duke, John. Really, you will have to learn to control your emotions. Of course I'm upset at the loss of my son. I am outraged that somebody chose to murder him. But I am also aware that it is up to us to set a good example, chin up, best foot forward and all that. This household will continue as usual, except for the fact that we will be in mourning for the requisite amount of time. No gramophones to be played. No radio. No dancing. A black suit will be required, John. I should ask Mr. O'Mara to advise you as to which one is suitable."

"Bugger your mourning," Jack said. "It's all for show, isn't it? Doesn't anyone here care that a member of your family is dead? And my name is Jack, not John. I'm not your son come back to life. I'm me, and everyone better get used to me the way I am." Then he strode out of the room.

"Well, really," Princess Charlotte said, looking at Virginia for confirmation.

"A young man with spirit. I like that," Virginia said. "Reminds me of a certain cavalry officer in Budapest . . . he had the most impressive—"

"A young man sadly lacking in manners." Edwina cut her off. "But understandably upset. And given the circumstances, we should overlook it this once."

"Do you really think he stabbed Cedric?" Charlotte asked.

Edwina sighed. "We cannot rule out that possibility. He has shown himself to be a young man of quick temper. If they met in the grounds and Cedric insulted him again, who is to say he didn't turn and fling the knife in a moment of anger? Let us hope that fingerprints confirm things one way or the other, and life at Kingsdowne can return to normal."

Except for Jack, I thought. One way or the other life would never return to normal for him.

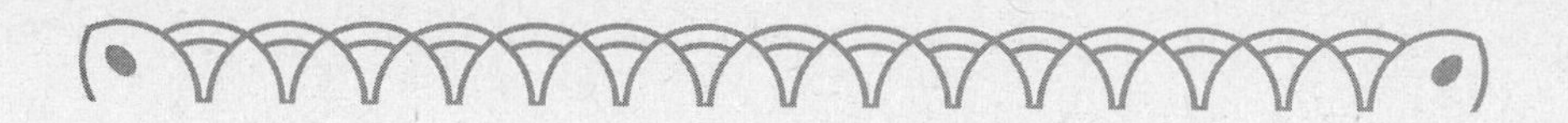

Chapter 25

Edwina came across the room to Darcy and me. "Might this be a good time for you to put out those feelers you keep talking about, Mr. O'Mara? We seem to have been left in peace at last, and the sooner a top man from Scotland Yard is on the scene, the better."

"I don't think it would be wise for me to attempt to telephone right now, Your Grace," Darcy said. "If the police have taken over your son's study with a telephone extension in it, they will be able to listen in on any call that we make."

"Surely they wouldn't have the audacity . . ." Edwina began.

Darcy smiled. "They are conducting a murder investigation. It's their job to monitor everything we do. We are all suspects, Your Grace. Surely you realize that."

"Absolute rubbish," she snapped. "So how do you propose to get in touch with people at Scotland Yard?"

"I think I'd better motor up in person, as soon as I'm given leave to go," Darcy said. "These things are better done in person anyway."

"Don't wait too long," she said. "I want my son's murder solved, and solved properly and quickly."

"I'll do my best, Your Grace. We all will. We all want the truth as much as you do," Darcy said, looking around the rest of the group for confirmation. I nodded.

"Well, I am going to see whether we are to be fed today," Edwina said. "Are you coming, Charlotte? Virginia?"

"I must say, I am a teeny bit peckish, even though in the circumstances it is not quite seemly," Princess Charlotte said, getting to her feet with difficulty from the low armchair. Her sister took her arm while Irene clung to her mother. The three Starlings waited until the family had disappeared.

"We really think that we should pack our little bags and fly," Adrian said. "We clearly are not wanted here—in fact, the old harpy will do a dance for joy when she sees the backs of us."

"And we shouldn't intrude on a family in mourning, should we, Jules?" Simon said. "It simply isn't done." And he mimicked the dowager duchess's voice to a T.

"I'm afraid we're all stuck here, whether we like it or not," I said. "At least until they determine that we couldn't have killed Cedric."

"One of us, kill poor Ceddy?" Adrian demanded. "Duckie, there is no way I could have plunged the whopping-great knife into anyone's back. I faint at the sight of blood."

"I don't see how anyone is going to be able to determine who killed Ceddy," Simon said. "I mean, a house this size . . . It would be so easy to slip in and out without being seen. Especially early in the morning, and on a day like this. When it's pouring rain, one doesn't even want to look out of the window."

"But there's only one main entrance, isn't there?" Belinda asked. She had been sitting at the back of the group by the window, remarkably silent for a while, and still had that petulant look on her face of someone thwarted. "Unless one braves the servants' quarters."

"There are French doors all the way down one side of the ballroom," I said. "And I believe I saw French doors in other rooms too."

Belinda sighed. "This is too, too tiresome. Let's hope they arrest the wretched Australian and have done with it, so I can escape back to London."

"Belinda—a few minutes ago, you were all set to marry him!" I exclaimed.

"That was before I knew that he had a violent temper and threw knives at people."

"Well, I don't think that he did it," I said. "I mean, if you were going to kill someone, would you leave your knife sticking out of his back for everyone to identify? Would you leave the body across a footpath, where it would be easily found? Jack's pretty strong. He could have dragged the body off into the shrubbery somewhere and we wouldn't have found it for days, by which time he could have worked out a perfect alibi."

"I'm going to have to keep an eye on you," Darcy said, raising an eyebrow. "You're becoming remarkably devious."

"Well, I'm hungry," Belinda said. "I believe luncheon was mentioned. Can someone please show me the way to the dining room?"

"And we'd better make the most of the last good meals we'll get in a while," Adrian said. "It will soon be back to baked beans on toast, won't it, boys?"

"I suppose it's too much to hope that Ceddy might have left us something in his will?" Julian said.

"I might have hoped until yesterday," Adrian said. "But now that nasty little minx Marcel has turned out to be his favorite all along, I think it's highly unlikely. Besides, you heard what they've said. All the money is tied up in the estate and it all goes to young Jack."

"Maybe we should start being nicer to him," Simon said with a grin. "He'll need friends in his hour of trial."

"He will," Julian agreed. "We should go and find him and let him know that we are behind him all the way."

For some reason, I heard Darcy chuckle.

"You three should not be called the Starlings, but the Vultures," I said and they laughed too.

"Starving artists and performers like us have to do what it takes to survive, duckie," Adrian said. "We thought we'd fallen on our feet here with Ceddy. I mean, a real patron of the arts who was going to build his own theater and let us write plays, act, design sets . . . it was a dream come true. Too bad of him to get himself killed." He brushed a speck from his black trousers. "Come along, boys. Let's go and find poor Jack and take him some food. He'll need to keep his strength up."

They left the room together. Belinda got up, stretched like a cat and followed them

I looked at Darcy. "Shall we?" He offered me his arm.

"Do you think we could slip away for a bit?" I asked.

He looked amused. "What have you in mind?"

"Nothing like that. I'd really like you to take a look at the crime scene for yourself," I said. "There was something seriously wrong that the inspector didn't seem to notice."

"But you don't know what it was?"

"It might come to me if I could have time to visit the place again with you."

"Chief Inspector Fairbotham did say that we were free to go about our business, didn't he? And that should include taking a stroll in the grounds. Although I'm not sure I like the way you're so eager to be involved in yet another crime investigation."

"Darcy, you spent several weeks on a ship with Jack. Do you think he's capable of such a murder?"

"Capable? Absolutely. But as to whether he actually did it—I agree with you. He's not at all stupid. He'd never leave his knife sticking out of someone's back. Come on, then. Let's slip outside while nobody is looking."

I glanced around the room, and started in surprise when I saw that Sissy was still sitting on the far side of the fireplace. I hurried over to her. "I'm so sorry. I didn't notice you were still there. Everyone has neglected you."

"It's all right. I'm used to it by now," she said, attempting a brave, little smile. "Once one is a cripple, one becomes invisible. People talk over my head as if I'm not there."

"Can I push your chair into the dining room for you?" Darcy asked.

"That would be lovely." She gave him a sweet smile. "I rarely have the chance to eat with the rest of the family because it's too much trouble to have me carried downstairs."

"Now that your cousin is here, I'm sure he'll oblige," I said, and watched her blush.

Then she reached out and touched my sleeve. "Georgie, he can't have done it, can he? Jack simply couldn't have killed Uncle Cedric."

"I hope not," I said, "but I've been involved in murders before, and it's not always easy to spot a murderer. Even the nicest people kill if they are pushed far enough, and we do know that Jack has a quick temper."

"But he was up in my room by eight thirty at the latest, and he didn't seem at all worried. Surely someone who has just committed murder minutes before couldn't sit and chat normally without giving something away."

"You wouldn't think so, would you?" I said.

Darcy had maneuvered the chair away from its niche and started to push it down the room toward the foyer.

"So you really didn't see Jack outside this morning, or were you lying to try to spare him?" I asked as I fell into step beside her.

"I really didn't." She looked up at me earnestly, shaking her head.

"I suppose it was too early for you to be sitting at your window."

"Maybe. And I might also have missed him. Nanny came in to help me dress about seven thirty as usual, and then there was a short time while I was sitting alone until my breakfast was brought up to me by Elsie at eight. I know it was eight because I've a little clock on my mantel, and it has a pretty chime. Papa bought it for me when we lived in Paris." A wistful look came over her face.

"And you didn't see your uncle Cedric at all, either before your breakfast arrived or when you were eating?"

"I didn't. If he went out about eight, as they said, then I was probably concentrating on eating my breakfast while it was still hot."

"Did you see anybody else at all?" Darcy asked

She looked up at him warily, the rather dashing and dangerous-looking stranger she didn't know. "The only person I saw was that man who came up to the house the other day and shouted at the butler—remember, Georgie?"

Darcy stopped pushing. I spun to face her.

"You saw the young man who had previously come up to the house ranting and raving, and you didn't mention it to the inspector?"

She chewed on her lip, her eyes darting from Darcy's face to mine. "I meant to. There never seemed a right moment, what with everyone talking and shouting. And I didn't think he'd believe me, after what I'd told him about Jack, and anyway it probably wasn't important because it was too early. I'd just finished dressing when he came running up the hill probably about twenty to eight. He looked as if he was out of breath and had been running hard. When he got close to the house he stopped, looked up at it, stood staring for a while, then he turned around and walked away again. Extraordinary, wasn't it? But at that time Uncle Cedric wouldn't even have left the house."

"And did he go back down the hill by way of the glen?" Darcy asked.

"No, he set off down the driveway, toward the main gate."

"You must report this to the policeman right away," I said.

"Oh, golly, do I have to?" She chewed on her lip again. "He'll cross-question me and make me flustered. And surely it isn't even relevant—because I told you, it was too early."

"Don't you see he could have set off for the main gate then changed his mind and cut across the grounds lower down, out of sight of the house, then doubled back to wait for Cedric in the glen?"

"Why would he do that?"

"Because he was William, the footman whom Cedric had sacked only recently for moving the papers on his desk."

"That's awful," she said. "Unfair."

"I wonder if there wasn't more behind that," Darcy said. "Either he wanted an excuse to get rid of this man, or there was something among those papers that Cedric didn't want anybody to see."

"Oh," I said. "I never thought of that. So maybe there is a motive for his murder that might be quite unconnected to the people in this house. He might have been involved in something underhanded—blackmail or something."

Darcy nodded.

"There's something else," I said. "William was angry because his parents live in one of the cottages that Cedric was planning to tear down to make room for his theater project. That would give him an awfully good double motive, wouldn't it?" I looked at them, quite excited now. "What if he came to confront Cedric, and as he approached the front door he heard Cedric saying he was going down to post a letter? So this man decides to cut around and confront Cedric in the glen instead—out of sight of the house."

"But how did he get Jack's knife? How would he even have known about it?" Sissy asked.

"Ah," I said. "Perhaps he'd been in the tack room before." I put my hand on her shoulder. "Look, Sissy, this evidence might just clear Jack—and that's what you want, isn't it?"

She nodded.

"Then let's go straight to Cedric's study and tell the chief inspector."

Chapter 26

Chief Inspector Fairbotham listened carefully to Sissy and then to me.

"You don't say," he said, then sucked through his teeth. "I suppose this is all true, not made up to shift our focus from the young Australian gentleman?"

"It's true," Sissy said. "I did see him, but unfortunately it was too early to have encountered the duke if he really left the house around eight."

"Unless this man then cut across the estate lower down and waited for the duke to come through the glen," I pointed out.

The inspector nodded. "And he does have a compelling motive as you say—first the duke sacks him and then wants to throw his folks out of their cottage. Any idea of his name?"

"William, I believe," I said. "The servants here will know. Also where he might be found. At least you can go to his parents' house. They'll know."

"I'm going to wait until we've found out whose prints are on that knife," he said. "And do what the young chap says and take a good look at footprints in the glen. Thank you. You've been most helpful. And if you see anything else interesting from your window, young lady . . ."

"I'll tell you straight away," Sissy said. Her cheeks were very pink, but she looked more excited than embarrassed.

We wheeled her in to luncheon. Edwina and the others were already at the table. Jack was nowhere to be seen.

"Ah, there you are," Edwina said. "We wondered where you had got to. And Elisabeth, dear. How nice to see you for a change. Do join us. Frederick, move away one of the chairs to make room for Miss Elisabeth."

We pushed Sissy into place, and took seats lower down the table.

"I must apologize for the schoolroom nature of the meal," Edwina said. "Poor Cook was quite flustered about not having enough time, so I reassured her that we'd make do."

"Making do" apparently consisted of a large meat pie, cauliflower, cheese and mashed potatoes. Compared with my usual fare it was a feast, and I helped myself generously.

"You didn't encounter John—I mean, Jack—in your travels, did you?" Edwina asked. "I'm concerned about him. I hope he won't do anything foolish like try to run away. He wasn't brought up to duty and honor as we were."

"I'm afraid we haven't seen him," I said.

Edwina summoned Frederick to her side. "Go and ask Mr. Huxstep to look for His Grace and cordially invite him to join us at luncheon," she said.

We ate in near silence then Huxstep himself came into the dining room. "Your Grace, I'm afraid the young duke is nowhere to be found. And his overcoat is missing."

"Oh, no." Edwina put her hand to her throat. "What shall we do?"

"Georgiana and I will go in search of him, if you wish," Darcy said. "I have a motor. If he's trying to catch a train, we may be in time to intercept him."

"I'd be most grateful, Mr. O'Mara. He may listen to you."

Darcy nodded to me, and we got up from the table. Darcy's sports car was housed in one of the stables. As soon as we drove it out, I saw why Belinda had complained. Spatters of rain came in through the leaky rag top.

"Not the most pleasant ride, I'm afraid," Darcy said. "God, I hope we catch him before Fairbotham realizes he's missing. Doesn't Jack realize how bad this will look for him?"

"We have to consider that he may have done it, however much we want him to be innocent," I said.

We drove down the driveway, peering to left and right through the rain-spattered windscreen. When we reached the road, Darcy turned away from the village. "Railway station first," he said, and followed the railway line until we came to a station. Both platforms were deserted, and we were told that there hadn't been a train for a half hour.

"He probably couldn't have got to the station in time for that train," I said. "I wonder if buses go from the village."

"Knowing Jack, he might have thumbed for a lift," Darcy said. He turned the motorcar around and drove into the village. The streets also had a deserted air to them, and we realized it was early closing day with the shops all shut for the afternoon. We drove for a mile or so out toward Farningham and then up toward Crockenhill, but passed nobody along the way. Reluctantly, we retraced our steps for Kingsdowne.

As we pulled up in the forecourt and got out of the car, we saw a figure coming up from the lake toward us, and recognized Jack himself.

"Where have you been?" Darcy called. "We've been looking for you. The dowager duchess was worried you'd done a bunk."

Jack grinned. "I couldn't take it any longer. I nipped down to the pub in the village for a couple of schooners."

"Schooners?" I asked.

"Australian glass of beer," Darcy said. "They don't call them pints."

"Too right," Jack said. "I needed to be somewhere normal, y'know. Nice little pub they've got down there. The barman asked me if I was the new hired hand at Drake's farm. Funny, eh? I didn't like to say I was a ruddy duke."

"It's not funny, Jack," I said. "You would have been in big trouble if the inspector had discovered you'd gone. He'd think that was proving your guilt."

Jack nodded. "Oh, struth. I suppose you're right. Didn't think about that. Just knew I had to get away or go 'round the bend. It's all too much for me to handle."

Darcy put a friendly hand on his shoulder. "Come on, my lad. Let's get you inside before anyone notices. And don't worry. This is England—finest police force in the world. It will soon be sorted out, I promise."

As Jack went up the steps to the house ahead of us, Darcy looked at me and made a face. His expression said clearly "I wish I could believe that."

We were about to go inside when I took Darcy's hand. "Come on, this is a good time for me to show you the crime scene," I said. "I don't see any policemen around."

"I don't know what you expect to show me," Darcy said, but he allowed himself to be towed along like a liner being pulled by a tugboat. "They will have taken the body away, and their boots will have messed up any evidence."

As we came close to the lake, a patch of blue sky appeared overhead. A few minutes later, the sun came out and the lake turned from iron gray to blue, with white swans reflected in its now-calm surface. Then whole scene turned from dreary to sparkling. Darcy's hand was warm and reassuring in mine, and it suddenly felt as if all would be right with the world after all. It's amazing how little I actually needed to make me happy.

We left the lake and followed the muddy footpath down the hill. Numerous footprints of big boots indicated that policemen had been and gone again. At last we came into the glen, which looked quite charming in the new sunlight. The stream had receded again, and flowed merrily over its rocks. It was hardly possible to make out where the body had lain.

"You see, I told you there was no point in our coming here," Darcy said. "Nothing worth seeing, is there?"

I studied the ground. It had been churned up by numerous feet but other than that one would never have known that a body had lain there an hour or so previously. Frankly I didn't know what I was looking for.

"Strange," Darcy said. "You'd have thought there would still be a bloodstain or two. Or perhaps the rain was hard enough to have washed them all away."

"That was it!" I exclaimed, turning to face him. "That's one of the things I thought was strange. He was stabbed with that enormous knife but there was almost no blood. He was wearing a white shirt too. When I've seen someone stabbed before, the blood completely soaked his shirts."

"Who have you seen stabbed?" Darcy asked suspiciously.

"That poor chap called Sydney when I had that visiting princess with me."

Darcy shook his head. "I wonder how many other men have future wives who mention casually the number of people they have seen stabbed. You won't be bringing that up as a topic of conversation at our future dinner parties, will you?"

"I can't help it if I've happened to come across a few dead bodies in my life. It's not as if I enjoy it, or go looking for bodies," I said. "They just seem to find me."

"We should probably warn our guests when they come to stay at our future house. I can see it now: please do come and stay, if you don't mind that people seem to die in horrible ways when they are around Georgiana."

I had to laugh and so did he. It seemed so amazing and wonderful that we could be talking about our future home together. He looked down at me tenderly, brushed a strand of hair from my face then took me into his arms and kissed me. "I've been wanting to do that all day," he said. "At last we're alone with nobody watching us."

"You never know around here," I said. "Remember, Sissy can see all sorts of things from her room."

"Let's hope she hasn't seen anything else that might put her in danger," Darcy said. "Murderers can be ruthless if they feel threatened."

"Oh, gosh, I didn't think about that," I said. "Should we suggest a guard on her to the police?"

"She has her brother and sister and their nurse up in the nursery with her, doesn't she? I presume the nurse is there at all times."

"Yes, but . . . I just wish they'd hurry up and solve this," I said. "It's horrid looking at people and wondering which of them might be a murderer. Perhaps it was that footman William, and we can all get on with our lives again."

"Perhaps," Darcy repeated thoughtfully.

"And you never answered me," I said. "Why do you think there was so little blood from that stab wound?"

"Maybe the knife being left in the wound prevented too much blood from leaking out," he said. "Or maybe he was wearing a thick, wool vest underneath that soaked up the blood."

"Don't," I said, shivering. "It's too depressing, isn't it? One day someone is alive, and the next he isn't. I don't like the thought of life being so fragile and cheap."

As I was saying this, the sun went behind a cloud again, plunging the world into gloom. I shivered. "Let's get away from here. I can still picture him lying covered with his coat, with the stream washing over him."

"Covered with his coat?" Darcy asked.

"That was another strange thing. He had taken his jacket off, and his top half was covered in it. Why?"

"He certainly wouldn't have taken it off because he was too warm," Darcy said.

"And why did his killer bother to cover him?"

"Maybe it wasn't his killer. Maybe someone else saw him and was so disturbed that they covered him?"

I shook my head. "If they were so disturbed, why didn't they call for help?"

Darcy shrugged. "I can't answer. As you say, let's get away from here. What's that building up among the rocks?"

"It's a folly," I said.

"Let's go and explore." He took my hand.

"You're not leading me there to have your wicked way with me?" I asked.

He laughed. "Too cold and damp, I suspect. I prefer my wicked ways in soft, feather beds." His grip on my hand tightened as he helped me up the rocky path to the folly.

"As I said, cold and damp," he exclaimed, looking around. It was built like a Greek temple with one circular room, surrounded by columns and with a back wall of white marble. Ivy clung to some of the columns and draped across the back wall. The view must have been enchanting on a bright, sunny day but the clouds were now gathering again, and they held the promise of rain. The place smelled of rotting leaves, mildew and decay.

"I was going to make the most of the opportunity and kiss you at leisure," Darcy said, "but now that we're here, I'm not keen to stay. Depressing sort of place, isn't it?"

I nodded. "We'll be missed anyway." I looked around, noticing the tall silhouette of the house looming above us. "We should probably get back."

"Good view from here on a nice day," Darcy said. "You can see right across the valley."

"Also the footpath down to the lane," I commented, as I toyed with this idea. "And through the glen. In fact, if someone wanted to lie in wait and watch, this would be a good spot."

"Who knew that Cedric was going to post a letter?" Darcy asked. "Surely that would have been a spur-of-the-moment decision. He went to his study, wrote the letter and then decided to post it himself. Who would have known about that? None of the family was even awake at that time."

"Except Jack," I said.

Darcy nodded. "Except Jack," he repeated. "It really doesn't look good for him, does it?"

"And also Sissy," I added. "She was already dressed at seven thirty."

"But she's hardly mobile enough to follow her uncle to the glen and stab him, having first recovered Jack's knife."

"True," I said. "Irene was drugged, and the old ladies are surely too frail to follow and stab anybody. That only leaves the Starlings."

"And they'd hardly want to stab Cedric, would they?"

"Which brings us back to the ex-footman William. He does seem the most likely suspect now, doesn't he? He could easily have made his way here through the wooded part of the estate then watched for Cedric to come into the glen."

Darcy was leaning against the wall as we spoke. Suddenly he spun around to face the wall. "Listen," he said, and knocked on the marble. "It's hollow." He examined the wall, pulled back the ivy and turned to me. "This has been pulled away recently. See how it's come off the wall here?"

"What for?" I asked.

"My hunch is that"—he felt around in the ivy— ". . . aha. See? I was right." He lifted a brass ring and pushed open a door in the wall.

I peered inside a dark opening. "Do you think it leads somewhere?"

"Maybe not," he said. "It could just be for storing deck chairs and the like, but I'll wager it hasn't been used for years."

"Oh, my goodness," I said. "The children said there were secret passages in the house and they were trying to find one, but they had never managed to. I thought it was just childish fantasy. You know—a house this size ought to have secret passages."

"What's the betting this was created so that the duke could make a hasty getaway at the time of the civil war," Darcy said. "Are you game to see where it leads?"

"It's awfully dark," I said. "We can't walk all that way in the darkness. At least, I'm not attempting it. I'll keep thinking of spiders and rats."

"I thought you were intrepid." Darcy laughed. "Actually, we're not very far from the house. The path curled around through that glen but we're only just below the stables. And I happen to have my trusty cigarette lighter with me." He produced it, and clicked it on. A tiny flame appeared. "Better than nothing," he said.

"That won't light our way very much and it probably won't last all the way up to the house."

"Oh, all right then." Darcy scooped up some dead twigs, some still with leaves on them, fashioned them into a crude torch then lit the tip. It flared into flame. "Come on, follow me."

We plunged into darkness with the flame from the impromptu torch lighting the passage with an eerie red glow. The floor and walls around us were smooth, cut into the chalk of the Downs but the ceiling was so low that we had to stoop, and unpleasant drips of water ran down inside my collar. I couldn't stop thinking about those spiders. I am normally quite brave—just not where spiders are concerned. I really wanted to go back, but I didn't want Darcy to think I was scared. The passage led steadily upward until without warning, Darcy swore and dropped the torch, whose flame sputtered and went out. We were plunged into darkness. I stifled a scream and grabbed onto Darcy.

"Damned thing burned my fingers," he said.

"Turn your lighter on again."

I heard its *click*, and he said, "Drat. I knew I should have filled it. Come on. Take my hand. Can't be far now."

We moved forward, inch by inch, until my foot kicked against solid rock.

"Steps," Darcy whispered, his voice echoing strangely. "We must be under the house now. Carefully."

Up we went, feeling our way with hands and feet until we came to a small platform and before it a solid wall.

"There must be a door somewhere." Darcy was feeling around carefully. Then he said, "Aha." Light blinded us as a door swung open. We peered out and found ourselves looking into a small, empty room. The walls were paneled in dark wood, and the only contents of the room were glass-topped cases. It was the butterfly room I had discovered in my tour of Kingsdowne when I met Adrian. Darcy helped me step through, and the door swung shut behind us, now invisible from the rest of the paneling.

"Handy," Darcy said. "Now we need to find out who might know about this, without giving away that we've found it ourselves."

"Should we tell Fairbotham?" I asked.

"Not yet. Let's wait and hear what he has found out himself first."

We came out of the butterfly room without seeing a soul. As we walked down the corridor, we heard voices coming from behind a closed door.

"It wasn't me. I didn't do it!" a man's voice was shouting.

"But you were seen, my lad." Fairbotham's voice.

"I told you what happened. I came up the path, planning to have it out with the duke and then I found him lying there, dead. I ran up to the house to report what I'd seen, but suddenly it occurred to me that someone might think that I'd done it."

Darcy and I moved closer to the door.

"And what exactly did you mean when you said 'have it out with the duke'?" Fairbotham's voice inquired.

"Tell him what I thought of him. Tell him that he couldn't throw out my parents, who had lived in that cottage all their lives. I was prepared to go to the press if necessary—let the world know how he was treating his tenants. The left-wing newspapers would love a story like that."

"So how do we know that you didn't have this little confrontation with the duke? That he didn't laugh at you and tell you to go ahead and do your worst. There was nothing you could do to stop him from doing what he liked with his land. So you were furious. You'd seen the knife before in the tack room. You went and got it and followed him, and at the right moment you stabbed him."

"I didn't. I swear!" William's voice had risen alarmingly now.

"I think you'd better come down to the station with me, my boy."

"Are you arresting me?" William asked. "You can't do that. I didn't do it. You've no evidence against me at all."

"We'll see about that. Take him to the motorcar, boys, and see what he'd like to tell us after he's been locked up in a cell for a while."

"Ah, there you are," said a peeved voice. We turned to see Belinda come up behind us. "I wondered where you'd got to. I must say, I thought it was rather mean of you to sneak off alone together, leaving me unguarded in a house full of potential murderers."

"We were sent on a commission by Edwina, Belinda," I said, wanting to laugh at her indignant face. "And anyway, why would anyone want to murder you? As you admit, you've no family connection."

"No. Let go of me. You've got the wrong man. I didn't do it!" The voice in the study had risen dramatically now.

Belinda stared at the door with interest. "Who have they got in there? Not Jack. He's sitting with Edwina, being shown the family tree, and trying not to show that he's dying of boredom." She paused, put her hand to her mouth then grinned. "Oh, dear. One has to be careful what one says in a house where people are being popped off."

Just then, the door burst open and William was pushed out, struggling as he was held by two burly Kentish coppers.

"Who was that?" Belinda asked as the young man was half dragged, half shoved out of the front door.

"An ex-footman," I said.

We walked on down the hall, and made our way to the Long Gallery.

Belinda stared after them, speculatively. "He was the one who killed poor dear Cedric then? It wasn't Jack after all?"

"Belinda, I have no idea who killed Cedric. It seems that he is another person who has a good motive."

"It's like a veritable house of horrors," Belinda said, drawing her fur-collared cardigan more closely around her. "Next thing we'll find out that it really was a batty aunt who is locked away in the garret. I can't stand it here another minute, darling. I really do have to escape back to London to keep my sanity. Can you please work your magic on the clodhopping inspector and tell him that I had nothing to do with this crime and I'm needed desperately at home."

"I should go up to London, anyway," Darcy said. "You can come with me, Belinda."

"Could I really? You're an angel, a positive angel." She reached up to stroke his cheek, and it looked as if she was about to kiss him. I felt a horrid stab of jealousy—I suspected that Darcy and Belinda had been more than friends in the past.

"Why do you have to go to London?" I asked, trying to sound unconcerned.

Darcy lowered his voice. "Why do you think? To see a pal at Scotland Yard. I can't telephone from here without being overheard, and besides, these things are best done in person."

"Then maybe I should come too," I said. "Don't you think it would be a good idea if I went to see my grandfather and enlisted his help? He's seen plenty of murders during his time on the force. Perhaps I could persuade him to come down here."

"Your grandfather is a splendid old chap," Darcy said. "But I can hardly see him dining at Kingsdowne."

"I don't mean as a guest in the house," I said. "Maybe he could pose as my chauffeur or something. Or even stay at a pub in the village."

"I think we have to be careful, Georgie," Darcy said. "I'm not even sure it's a good idea to try and bring in Scotland Yard. Your grandfather would be seen as a terrible interference. And remember, the Kentish police are officially in charge until they request help."

"But you can see that poor old Fairbotham doesn't have a clue," I said. "He's arresting people left, right and center."

"I'd say he has two reasonably good suspects," Darcy said. "Jack and William would stand out as good candidates, whoever was doing the investigation."

"I'd still like to talk it over with Granddad," I said. "Maybe he'd have an idea why Cedric's coat was put over him, and why the stab wound didn't produce much blood. I'm sure those are important clues."

"I understand perfectly, Georgie. You really want to get away from here as much as I do, don't you, darling," Belinda said. "A day in town will do you good. We could have a bite at Fortnum's."

"Now all we have to do is to persuade the chief inspector that we can leave the scene of the crime," Darcy said ominously.

"He can't possibly think that we had anything to do with Cedric's death," Belinda said.

"He clearly thinks Georgie is all right," Darcy said with a quick glance in my direction. "Those two are thick as thieves. But you, Belinda—I'm afraid you're a suspicious person to him. Someone who was chummy with Cedric in London, who is currently hard up, who arrives conveniently bringing a shoe when Cedric is killed. And you're dealing with a policeman who loves circumstantial evidence. My bet is that you'll be in the next-door cell to Jack by the end of the day."

"Don't, Darcy," Belinda said, swinging her handbag at him. "It's not funny. You're frightening me."

"He's only teasing, Belinda."

"I know. But it all sounds too plausible. I just wish they'd hurry up and find the real murderer. Let's hope there were lovely fingerprints on the knife and someone confesses."

"That's a little too easy," I said. "But I really hope they find out the truth soon. It must be horrid for Jack with everyone half believing that he did it."

"Don't you half believe he did it?" Belinda said. "The wild colonial boy. I bet they settle disputes with knives all the time in the outback."

"Well, I don't think he did it," I said firmly, perhaps trying to convince myself. "He's not stupid. Would you leave your knife sticking out of someone's back so that everything would point straight to you?"

Belinda's eyes opened wider. "So you're suggesting that someone else wanted us to believe it was Jack?"

"Precisely."

"You're very clever, Georgie," Belinda said. "Too bad you weren't born a man, or you'd have made a brilliant detective."

I caught Darcy's eye, and he winked.

Chapter 27

By tea time, the house had returned to normal. Maids delivered plates of scones and cakes then hovered behind us, ready to pour tea when required. Everyone chatted as if nothing had ever happened, and I realized that they knew William had been taken away and were relieved. The murderer was not one of them after all. An outsider—and what's more, someone of the lower classes. Cedric was dead but life would go on again at Kingsdowne as it always had.

"I have conveyed to Mrs. Broad that we will be quite content with another simple meal tonight," Edwina said as she heaped clotted cream and strawberry jam onto a scone. "Really, these policemen are so insensitive. The servants are quite upset. I caught my own maid sniveling in a corner. Says she's frightened to walk around the house in case a murderer is lurking. I told her to stop that nonsense instantly. The person who has been killed is my son, I said. It is I who should be weeping, not you. Besides, why would anyone consider a servant worth killing?"

She broke off as Chief Inspector Fairbotham came into the room.

"Any news, Chief Inspector?" she asked. "We saw our former footman William being taken away. Are we to gather that he was responsible?"

"William has been taken to the police station for questioning,"

Fairbotham said. "As yet, no arrests have been made and we are still examining the evidence." And his gaze focused on Jack. "I'm sending most of my men home for the day now, but I'll be in touch as soon as we know anything more. Enjoy your tea."

"Go on. Ask him now." Belinda dug Darcy in the side.

Darcy got to his feet and followed the inspector out of the room. Belinda followed at a distance. I didn't want to be left out and came along too. By the time I joined the conversation, Darcy had presumably asked his question. Fairbotham nodded. "I think that would be all right, Mr. O'Mara. I've no objection to your going anywhere, nor to Lady Georgiana's. And I don't suppose your young friend can give any further illumination to this case. But you'll leave your home address and phone number, young lady. And you two plan to return, do you?"

"Absolutely," I said. "Probably by the end of the day."

"Thank you so much, Chief Inspector." Belinda gave him one of her dazzling smiles usually reserved for men she planned to seduce. It worked. He blushed and gave an embarrassed little cough.

"No sense in keeping you bright young things in this gloomy place any longer than necessary," he muttered. "I expect you've got parties to attend."

As the inspector was about to head back to Cedric's study, I plucked up courage, took a deep breath and said, "One more thing I haven't yet mentioned, Chief Inspector."

"Yes, Lady Georgiana?"

"When you saw the body, did anything strike you as strange about it?"

"That coat being thrown over it, you mean?"

"That too," I said. "No, I mean that there was so little blood coming from the wound. That was a huge knife. It must have struck some kind of organ or blood vessel."

He frowned at me. "What are you suggesting?"

"I don't know," I said. "I presume some kind of autopsy will be carried out?"

"I'm sure there will be. But I don't know what you think an autopsy can show."

"I'm not sure either, but I have a funny feeling about this. We may know more when I return from London," I said.

"You never cease to surprise me, Lady Georgiana." He rubbed his chin as he stared at me. "The cool way you can talk about blood and stab wounds. I'd always thought that young ladies of quality had an attack of the vapors if the word 'blood' was mentioned."

"That was my grandmother's generation," I said. "We're all rather tough these days. We've had a world war, remember. I don't think any family came through that unscathed."

"You're right about that," he said. "We lost my younger brother at the Somme."

And he wandered off, still deep in thought. I went back to join Darcy, Belinda and the rest of the household.

"I know!" Princess Charlotte broke the silence. "It's so obvious. Why didn't I think of it before? We should have another séance after dinner tonight. Perhaps Cedric might return to name his killer."

"Really, Charlotte. Don't you think we're going through enough without bringing farce into it?" Edwina snapped. "This is no time for your strange fancies."

"My last séance prophesied death, did it not?" Charlotte said frostily. "And it would be so much nicer for all of us if Cedric's killer were found and apprehended. And who better to tell us than Cedric himself?"

"Cedric was never particularly helpful in life. I don't see his being so in death," Irene said, putting down her tea cup firmly on the table.

"Really, Irene," Edwina said. "I find it most uncharitable to speak in this way of your departed brother. You two never got along, even when you were children."

"He was always a bossy little prig," Irene said. "I'm sorry, Mother, but I can't bring myself to weep for him. And don't forget, he was prepared to cast us all out. He thought of nobody but himself."

"Nevertheless, I was brought up with the maxim that one did not speak ill of the dead," Edwina said. "And however badly he behaved, I still mourn the loss of my son."

We sat in awkward silence, each of us wishing we were somewhere else. It had begun to rain heavily again so we couldn't even escape by taking a turn around the grounds.

"Perhaps we should go up and see how the children are faring," I said. "They are no doubt dying of curiosity about what has been happening downstairs."

"Poor little things. I expect they find it all quite disturbing," Irene said. "The less they know about it, the better."

"Nonsense, Irene. They are relishing every moment of it," Edwina said. "By all means go up to them, Georgiana."

"I'll come with you," Darcy said.

"I just had to escape from that room," I said. "So much tension."

"I'd say the dowager duchess is holding up remarkably well," Darcy said as we climbed the first flight of stairs. "One would hardly think that she'd lost her only remaining son today, and almost her daughter too."

"I wonder if Fairbotham is really looking into what happened to Irene," I said, pausing to stare down the hallway toward Irene's bedroom. "His men have taken fingerprints now. They should be checking the glass that Irene used last night to see if there are any strange fingerprints on it. And I wonder if they ever did count the number of sleeping powders still remaining."

"If she has a semi-efficient maid, the glass will have been washed," Darcy said.

"Perhaps I should remind the inspector . . ." I began, turning back.

Darcy put a firm hand on my shoulder. "You're getting too worked up about this, Georgie. Too involved. Leave it be. You've got to stop this belief that all crimes are your responsibility. You are the daughter of a duke and the granddaughter of a princess, and your job is to do charitable good works, enjoy yourself and choose a suitable husband."

"I've obviously already failed at all of the above," I said as Darcy laughed.

Nursery tea was still going on in Sissy's room as we came in. Mr. Carter and Nanny were sitting with the three children. Nick and Kat jumped up excitedly when they saw us.

"What's been happening?" Nick asked. "We've been dying to know. We heard shouting and we saw the police bundling someone into a police car."

"It was William the footman," I said. "It was a good thing that you told the inspector what you'd seen, Sissy."

"But I didn't see how he could have had anything to do with Uncle Cedric's murder," she said. "I'm sure I saw him come up to the house well before eight. My clock had just chimed half past not long before."

As if on cue, the clock chimed again, striking four. We turned to look at it.

"Well, that explains one discrepancy," Darcy said. "Your clock is slow, Sissy. It's already four twenty."

"Oh dear," Sissy said. "That clock has always been unreliable. That was Papa for you. He couldn't even give me a trustworthy clock." She turned away and stared out of the window. "So I really might have seen William running up to the house after he murdered Uncle Cedric?"

"He claimed that he stumbled upon the body and that was why he was running up to the house," I said. "Then he realized that he might be implicated."

"What does 'implicated' mean?" Katherine asked.

"Involved. Possibly guilty," Mr. Carter said. "Really, Katherine, if you read a little more, you'd increase your vocabulary."

"Reading is boring. I like doing things better," Kat said. "Like our experiments. They're good. And detecting, like Sherlock Holmes. I bet we could find some good clues if you let us loose in the grounds. I bet we could solve the murder before those silly policemen."

"So now the police think William did it, and not Jack?" Nick asked.

"I don't think Chief Inspector Fairbotham has made up his mind yet," I said. "He still wants to suspect Jack."

"It sounds awful to say that I hope it was William," Sissy said, "but I really do." Her cheeks were quite pink.

We chatted a little longer then took our leave.

"You will come up again when there is any more news, won't you?" Nick asked. "We simply have to know what's going on. It's so unfair."

"We're going up to London tomorrow," I said. "So you'll have to find out from other sources."

"You're so lucky." Kat sighed. "We're stuck up here and never go anywhere."

"Let's hope it's a fine day tomorrow," Nick said. "Then we can go outside and look at the scene of the crime. Maybe there's bloodstains. Maybe we'll find clues."

"Enough of such talk," Nanny said. "Bloodstains, indeed. Since when did nicely behaved children mention such things?"

"Those children need to go away to school and lead a normal life," Darcy said to me as we came back down the stairs.

"They want to. It's a question of money. Now that Jack is Duke of Eynsford, perhaps he'll pay for their schooling."

"If it turns out. . . ." Darcy didn't finish the sentence. There were so many ifs at the moment.

"Let's hope that Scotland Yard and my grandfather can solve this quickly and everything will be all right," I said. "I hate this feeling of not knowing, of suspecting everyone."

As we came to the end of the landing, Darcy grabbed my arm.

"What's wrong?" I jumped a mile, looking around for potential danger.

"Nothing. I just thought that we might take this opportunity . . ." He drew me close to him and his arms came around me.

"Darcy, do you think we should?" I asked, looking around nervously.

He chuckled. "I say take our chances while we can."

I didn't protest as his lips came to meet mine. I suspect I was looking somewhat guilty as we came back to join the others in the Long Gallery. Belinda noticed and raised an eyebrow but nobody else paid any attention to us, as Fairbotham was addressing the assembled company.

"So I thought I should tell you that no fingerprints were found on the handle of the knife used to kill the duke," he was saying.

"No fingerprints?" Edwina demanded. "You mean no strange fingerprints."

"No, I mean absolutely no fingerprints at all. Whoever did this wiped the handle clean afterward."

"So the killer had time to wipe the handle clean but not time to move the body or to remove the knife," I muttered to Darcy. "This gets stranger and stranger."

"So we're no further ahead, unless William confesses," Irene said.

"Actually no, we are a little further ahead." A glint came into Fairbotham's eye. He turned to Jack. "Remember this morning you told us that you never went anywhere near the path in the glen, sir?" he asked. "And you even pointed at your boots and said how different your footprints would be from anyone else's?"

Jack nodded. "That's right."

"Well, it might surprise you to know that we found your footprints on that path—and nice and clear and recent they were too."

Jack blushed bright red. "I can explain that," he said. "You see, I popped down to the pub in the village for a quick one."

"The public house in the village?" Edwina actually fanned herself with a copy of *The Tattler*. "You went to a common, ordinary public house? You, a duke?"

"Well, I felt like some common, ordinary beer," Jack said defiantly. "I've been cooped up here too long. I feel like a bloody chook in a pen."

"And when was this, sir?"

"About one, I suppose," Jack said. "I can't tell you exactly."

"We can verify that he came up that path around two o'clock," Darcy said. "And told us he had been to the pub."

"I see," the chief inspector said. He was still staring at Jack. "Rather convenient, wouldn't you say?"

"What do you mean?" Jack demanded.

"Meaning that if we found your distinctive footprints on that path, you'd have a good excuse for their being there—one that had nothing to do with the murder."

"That's bloody rubbish," Jack said, standing up belligerently.

"Watch it, young man." Fairbotham wagged a finger in Jack's face. "I'm not arresting you right now, but I'm placing a police guard on the door, and you're not leaving this place again. Do I make myself clear?" When Jack didn't answer, he looked around at the rest of us. "And the same goes for all of you. I've given permission for Mr. O'Mara and Lady Georgiana to be away tomorrow, but that's it. Nobody else is to go anywhere. Is that clear?"

Nobody spoke.

"Well, I'm clearing off for the night now but I'll be back bright and early in the morning," Fairbotham said. And off he went, his large boots clattering along the hallway.

Chapter 28

We went up to change for dinner. "Maybe you should go and help Miss Warburton-Stoke," I said to Queenie. "She hasn't brought a maid with her. But please do be careful."

"Don't worry, miss. I'll be as gentle as a lamb."

"Lambs gambol around and knock things over," I said. "Luckily, there are no candles so you can't set her on fire."

"That was only once I set someone on fire," Queenie said peevishly. "It ain't fair to keep reminding me."

Then she went off with her nose in the air, looking like a respectable lady's maid.

A little while later Belinda tapped on my door, looking elegant and somber in dark green. So Queenie could do things right if she tried occasionally! I hadn't brought a black dress with me so I was stuck with the burgundy velvet. In respect of the situation, however, I had decided not to wear any jewelry and put on long, black gloves and my black-velvet stole. As we went downstairs, Belinda glanced up at the ceiling again. "They really should cover those nymphs and satyrs if this is a house in mourning," Belinda commented. "They are enjoying themselves far too much."

"The ancient Greeks seemed to go in for that sort of thing, didn't they?" I said. "Zeus was always changing into the shape of some creature or other to visit an unsuspecting lady."

"Mmmm." Belinda's face became pensive. "I wonder what sort of creature might have produced a rather nice encounter? I never thought much of the swan, did you? Too much flapping around."

I laughed. "I'm actually glad you're here, Belinda. You're so nice and normal."

She looked surprised. "You have Darcy here, darling. You should be in absolute bliss . . . creeping down the halls at night for a nice roll in the hay."

"Belinda!" I frowned. "The dowager duchess is a close friend of the queen. If word got back to her . . ."

"What could she do, darling? She can hardly send you to the tower or marry you off to a mad prince."

I had to smile. Belinda went on, "You're over twenty-one, aren't you, and your cousin the Prince of Wales misbehaves all the time."

"Yes, but not at Buckingham Palace, I'm sure."

Belinda sighed as we entered the foyer of the dining room. "You royals and your sense of duty. Quite amazing!"

Edwina and the other members of her family were all wearing black, and we apologized for not bringing black frocks with us.

"How could you possibly have known something like this would happen?" Edwina said. For the first time one could see the distress on her face. "How could anyone ever have thought that Cedric, of all people . . . that such tragedy could strike this family again. I am only glad that my husband was not alive to experience this. It would have broken his heart."

The dinner gong rang, and we went through. Jack sat beside me, looking uncomfortable in his dinner jacket. I noticed that he kept tugging at his bow tie as if it was strangling him, and wondered if he was thinking of the silken noose that is the privilege of a duke.

"You look very smart," I said, trying to ease the palpable tension in the room.

"I feel like I've fallen into a bloody nightmare," he said. "For two pins I'd run off and jump on the next boat back home."

"Don't do that, for heaven's sake," I said. "That would definitely make them think you are guilty."

He gave me a despairing look. "He's made up his mind, hasn't he, that police bloke? He's not going to find out the truth. He's determined to nail me."

"I don't think he's trying to nail anybody. He has to go on the evidence so far," I said. "It was your knife in Cedric's back. You admitted you were out in the grounds around that time, and they found your boot prints on the path. Those are pretty significant clues, Jack. If I were a police detective, I'd have to make you a suspect."

"So what hope do I have of proving them wrong?"

I leaned closer to him. "Don't mention this to anyone, but Darcy is going to have a word with some pals at Scotland Yard to see if they can send someone down to help. And I'm going to speak to my grandfather. He used to be a policeman too and he's very sensible."

"Thanks, Georgie. You're a good sheila, as we'd say at home."

I sat up again as pea soup was ladled into my bowl. The "simple" meal that Cook had been allowed to prepare for tonight turned out to be sole followed by leg of lamb, followed by apple tart with cream, and Welsh rarebit—another feast to me after Fig's austerities. Nobody spoke much. I think we were all worn out with the emotions of the day. I know I was. I hoped that Edwina would call an early night and I could go to my bed. But as Edwina stood and motioned that the ladies should leave the gentlemen to their port and cigars, Princess Charlotte announced, "If you will excuse me, I will go to prepare the room for our séance. I expect you all in fifteen minutes. Please bring the gentlemen."

"Charlotte!" Edwina gave an exasperated sigh. "I thought I made it clear that I wanted this nonsense to stop."

Charlotte drew herself up and tossed her jet-trimmed shawl over her shoulder. "I should have thought you wanted your son's murder solved, Edwina. You do not need to attend. I will consult the spirits alone if necessary, but I hope the young people at least will back me up. They'll want to hear what Cedric's spirit has to say to us."

She turned to give each of us an inquiring stare. I think I gave an embarrassed kind of nod.

"Well, I will take my coffee and then retire to my room," Edwina said. "Given the circumstances, I see no reason for us to pretend to be sociable this evening. I expect you are all as emotionally drained as I." She gave us a perfunctory nod, picked up a coffee cup and then made a stately exit.

"Fifteen minutes?" Princess Charlotte turned to us again. "You do want to know who killed poor Cedric?"

"I want to know who tried to kill me," Irene said. "I'll come."

I hesitated, not really wanting to follow, but half intrigued after what had happened last time. Belinda was standing beside me. "Are you going to this séance? I think it will be ripping fun. Do you think Cedric's spirit will really make an appearance?"

"You weren't here for the last one," I said. "It was really quite creepy. The Ouija board spelled out 'death' and we heard ghostly laughter."

Darcy gave me a sharp look. "Do you think someone was playing games with you?"

"You mean it was entirely coincidence that a real death occurred the next day?"

Darcy smiled. "Let's just say I don't believe in spirits."

"So you won't come and see for yourself?"

"I didn't say that. As Belinda said, it might be ripping fun."

It seemed that everyone else was equally curious to see whether Cedric's spirit would put in an appearance. We all made our way down the corridor to Lady Hortense's sitting room, site of the last séance. The heavy drapes were closed and the piano covered with a black drape. Chairs were arranged around a small table also draped with a black cloth. A lone, black candle stood on it, along with the Ouija board.

Princess Charlotte was already seated at the table. Her black-lace shawl was now over her head, hanging down around her face. She motioned for us to join her. We sat. I noticed that Belinda had an expectant smile on her face. Irene looked tense. I could understand that. I'm sure I would have felt equally expectant and scared if I thought that my attacker might be revealed.

"Please turn out the light," Charlotte said. Darcy got up to do so and the room was plunged into near darkness with just the one flickering candle. I hadn't noticed before but the storm had picked up again. I could hear the wind sighing through the chimney, adding to the atmosphere in the room. I could feel my heart thumping loudly.

"Hold hands," Charlotte instructed.

We did. It was comforting to feel Darcy's hand squeezing mine. On the other side of me, Belinda was trembling a little now.

"Oh spirits who have gone beyond, we call upon you now," Charlotte said in dramatic tones. "We call upon you to right a wrong, to bring us to truth." A long silence, and I could almost imagine that I heard distant whispering. "Spirits, we call upon you to find our murdered nephew, Cedric, and bring him to us." Another long silence, then she said, "I sense a presence. Cedric—are you out there? Can you hear us?"

No voice answered but a big gust of wind came down the chimney, making the candle flicker alarmingly.

"Speak to us, Cedric."

We sat in silence. Then Charlotte said, "He hasn't had time to find his spirit voice. We must use the board. Place a finger upon the planchette." We did so.

"Cedric. Can you hear us?"

The planchette moved painfully slowly over to YES.

I heard a little gasp from across the table. "He's here," one of the Starlings whispered.

"Cedric, do you know who killed you?"

YES, again, but with even more hesitation this time.

"Can you tell us?"

The planchette began to move. *C*.

Eyes went to Charlotte. Then it moved to *A*.

The planchette seemed to hover between *S* and *R*, finally settling on *S*. Then even more slowly to what seemed to be *T*. And then *O*, then *R*.

The life seemed to have gone out of the planchette. Our fingers were still touching it but it refused to move.

"Castor?" Countess Virginia broke the silence. "What does that mean?"

"Sometimes the board says funny things," Charlotte admitted.

"Castor oil? Castor bean? Castor sugar?" Adrian asked. "But he wasn't poisoned. He was stabbed."

We waited, but nothing happened. The wind seemed to have died down too and the only sound was our tense breathing.

"The spirits are no longer with us," Princess Charlotte announced.

"That was strange," Darcy muttered as we left the room. "I felt that wretched thing moving around. I know I wasn't pushing it."

"It was like that last time," I said. "Creepy."

"Creepy? Darlings, it was brilliant," Belinda said. "Now, how about finding a gramophone and . . ."

"Belinda, there's been a death in the family," I reminded her. "No music, remember?"

"Then at least let's find a cocktail cabinet," she said.

"Everyone's going up to bed." I looked around. "We probably should too."

"At ten o'clock? I haven't been to bed at ten . . . at least not alone . . . since I was in the nursery." And she grinned to us. Darcy and I exchanged a glance and I saw a question in his eyes. Just then, Huxstep appeared in that way butlers have.

"I've told Frederick that he is to help you disrobe, Mr. O'Mara, since you brought no valet of your own."

"Oh, that's quite all right, Huxstep," Darcy said. "I don't need help."

"It's no trouble, sir. It's what the servants are here for. He's waiting in your room."

And he stood at the bottom of the stairs, watching us as we went up.

"I'll say good night then," Darcy said and went off down the other hall. There was no sign of Queenie so I managed to undress myself and get into bed. I had just settled down for the night when there was a piercing scream from somewhere nearby. I leaped out of bed and rushed out into the corridor, not even stopping to put on my dressing gown. The scream had definitely come from somewhere close to me, and the only other room I knew to be occupied in this hallway was Belinda's.

My heart was in my mouth as I opened her door.

"Belinda—are you all right?" I called into the darkness.

"Only just," came the reply.

I groped for a light switch and turned on the light. Belinda was standing beside her bed, her hands on her chest as if recovering from a shock, while in her bed beside her Queenie's disheveled head poked over the eiderdown, blinding in the sudden brightness.

"What on earth?" I demanded.

"I got into bed and I touched human flesh," Belinda said, still taking deep breaths. "Not that it's the first time I've found someone unexpected in my bed, but given the circumstances, I thought it was a body."

"Queenie!" I exclaimed.

She looked sheepish as she climbed out of the bed and straightened the covers. "Sorry, miss. You know how sleepy I get late at night. You told me to help Miss Belinda with getting undressed. Well, I was all ready and waiting for her in her room, and that eiderdown looked so soft and warm, so I thought I'd just lie down for a while and next thing you know, blow me, I must have nodded off."

"Queenie," I said angrily, "if this ever happens again, you'll have to go. Do you understand?"

"Yes, my lady," she muttered, proving that she could use my proper form of address if she really put her mind to it.

Chapter 29

Up to London, thank goodness

We set off early the next morning. Fortunately the rain had passed during the night and the sky was bright and clear. The moment we were clear of the estate we started talking normally, as if a great cloud of doom was lifted from us.

"It feels as if one has just got out of prison, doesn't it?" Belinda echoed my feelings. "I can't wait to get back to London, darlings. I don't know what made me come down here in the first place."

"You were hoping to snag a rich husband," I said and watched a smile twitch on Darcy's lips.

"How brutally frank you are, Georgie. Not a good quality in a lady. Thank heavens you're stuck with Darcy, as most men can't abide frankness."

Darcy and I exchanged a smile. Belinda chatted gaily all the way up to London, trying out plans and schemes to get herself invited to a yacht on the Med or at least a good house party in the country.

"That girl will wind up in trouble if she's not careful," Darcy said after we had dropped her off at her mews cottage.

"I think she's already been in plenty of trouble. She rather enjoys it," I said.

"You know what I mean. She's going the way of your mother."

"My mother seems to have enjoyed her life," I replied. "You can drop me off at the Underground station if you like, and I can make my own way to my grandfather's house."

"Are you sure you don't want me to come with you?"

I shook my head. "He'd be embarrassed. It's better that I go alone."

He came around to open the car door for me. "Georgie, don't suggest he come to Kingsdowne. Not a good idea."

"You don't think my grandfather capable of solving a murder?"

"I just don't see . . ." he started then broke off. I knew what he was suggesting. He didn't see how I could introduce my grandfather—certainly not as a relative. Not as a servant. Not as a policeman. I did see his point. "Maybe he could stay at the inn in the village."

Darcy shook his head before giving me a kiss on the forehead. "I'll meet you at four," he said.

"Good luck," I called after him as he drove off. Then I went down the steps into the Underground station for the first leg of my journey out to Essex. My grandfather lived in a semi-detached house in an outer suburb. It was a very ordinary street of matching houses and pocket handkerchief–size front gardens, but he was well content with it (my mother having bought him the house during the time of her first success on the stage). As I opened the gate of number twenty-two and walked past the gnomes in the front garden, my heart did a little skip of anticipation. I realized that more than anything, I just wanted to see him. I knocked on the door and heard his voice growling, "'Old yer 'orses. I'm comin'."

The door opened, and a big smile spread across his old, Cockney face. "Well, strike me pink," he said. "Ain't you a sight for sore eyes! Come on in, ducks, and give yer old granddad a big hug."

I did so, feeling the comforting roughness of his cheek and the familiar smell of carbolic soap and baby powder.

"It's lovely to see you, Granddad," I said. "How are you?"

"Not too bad, my love. Chest still a little dicky, but all in all can't complain. Come on in and I'll put the kettle on." He went ahead to a tiny, neat kitchen, filled the kettle then turned back to me. "So, out with it. What brings you to my neck of the woods?"

"Do I need an excuse to visit my favorite grandfather?" I asked, smiling at him fondly.

"No, but when you come to see me, you usually want 'elp with some problem or other."

"You're quite right. I do want your advice," I said. I perched on the kitchen stool and told him the whole story while he made the tea. As he handed me a cup he looked up at me. "I don't quite know why you came to see me," he said. "It sounds like the police are doing their job."

"I'm worried that Chief Inspector Fairbotham isn't very bright," I said. "He may jump to the wrong conclusion."

"I don't know what you think I can do, ducks," he said.

"I thought you might come down to Eynsford and take a look for yourself."

He gave a chuckle, which turned into a chesty cough. "Me? Come down to a stately 'ome? Don't be daft. You couldn't introduce me as your grandfather, could you? And I'm not sneaking in pretending to be a servant. Besides, it wouldn't be right for me to poke my nose in. Nor you either. You mind your own business and stay well out of it. That's my advice."

"But it doesn't look good for poor Jack, does it? Lots of things adding up against him."

My grandfather's head cocked on one side, like a bird. "Did it cross your mind that he might have done it?"

"What for?" I demanded. "He doesn't want to be a duke. He doesn't like it here. He hardly knew Cedric, and had no reason to kill him."

Granddad was watching my face, which had changed as I said the words. "You've thought of a reason, haven't you?"

"He did insult Jack's mother, but people don't stab someone for insulting their mother."

"In Italy they do it all the time, so I've heard," he said. "So I suppose the question is who had a better reason to want this here duke dead?"

I thought. "The most likely in my opinion is William, the young man they now have in custody. He had been dismissed from his position in the household, and Cedric was going to pull down his parents' cottage. And he was seen on the grounds that morning."

"There you are then. Sounds perfect. Case solved."

"Except that the murderer used Jack's knife. How would William have found it? He wouldn't be poking around in the tack room. That sounds to me like a deliberate attempt to incriminate Jack."

"A family member, then? Someone who didn't want him to inherit the title?"

"I suppose so."

"A lot of family members, are there?"

"Not really. The dowager duchess—well, she wouldn't kill her own son, would she?"

He looked at me sharply. "Wouldn't she?"

"Granddad, surely not!" I exclaimed in horror.

"I've heard there are people to whom title and honor mean everything. You said he was threatening to adopt his French valet? And put a theater on the grounds?"

I tried to consider this: Could Edwina possibly have killed her own son to prevent him from adopting his valet and disgracing the family name? She was the one who told Jack to put the knife in the tack room, after all. She knew where to find it. But her own son? I shook my head.

"Surely not," I repeated.

"Who else then? Any other children?"

"One daughter, Irene. Only she was upstairs in a stupor at the time—it seems someone had given her an overdose of sleeping medicine."

"Tried to kill her too, you mean?"

"I'm afraid so."

"Another family member, you think?"

"There are only two old aunts, and they'd have no reason to kill Irene. She's as penniless as I am and will inherit nothing. And I can't believe either of them could have stabbed Cedric with that huge knife. Not strong enough, and they didn't even know where it was kept. Besides, he gave them a home. That's rather biting the hand that feeds you, isn't it?"

"So that's all the family? Anyone else in the house?"

"Three young men who were Cedric's followers—all artsy types."

"So they'd have no reason to want him dead?"

"They were seriously upset when they heard he was going to adopt his valet and not one of them, but one can never tell how seriously they take anything. And I don't think stabbing is their style. Too indelicate."

Granddad smiled. I took a long drink of tea. It was very strong and very sweet and went down well.

"So that's it then?" Granddad asked, refilling my cup without asking.

"Apart from some children in the nursery and their tutor and nanny. And the servants, of course. I don't know much about them but the house runs like clockwork."

"So it comes back to your boy, or the former servant who was sacked. Sounds to me like this Inspector Fairbotham is on the right track."

"Oh, dear. I wanted you to come up with something brilliant we had all overlooked. But I must say, I'd be relieved if it was William. It's rather unnerving living in a house wondering who might be a murderer."

Granddad wagged a finger at me. "That's another good reason for you to stay out of this. If someone in the house is a murderer and discovers you doing your own little investigation, then you might be next."

"Oh, no, surely not," I said, but I did see his point. Someone who has killed once has nothing to lose by killing again.

"So my advice to you would be not to go back."

"But the queen sent me there, and the dowager duchess wants me there. I can hardly do a bunk. And Darcy is driving me back tonight."

Granddad gave one of his knowing grins. "Oh, so he's at the house too, is he? You failed to mention that so far."

I blushed.

"Well, that ain't so bad if he's there to keep an eye on you. But leave the detecting to the police, my love. They may look slow and bumbling, but in my experience they get it right in the end."

I sighed. "All right. But tell me, in your experience what would give away a murderer? Would there be any small signs that he was guilty?"

He shook his head. "I've known murderers cool as a cucumber. Not so much as a flicker of an eyelid. Of course, some of 'em are so cocky that they offer to help the police with the investigation. It's sheer vanity, of course. They're having a good chuckle that the police are getting it wrong. In my experience, that's what separates criminal types from the rest of us—an exaggerated idea of their cleverness and a feeling that the world revolves around them and everyone else is put there for their benefit."

I thought then shook my head. "There's nobody I can think of at Kingsdowne who behaves like that."

"I said criminal types," Granddad said. "That wouldn't include someone who killed out of desperation. Someone who killed because it was the only way out may well be showing signs of stress."

"The only one behaving in that way is Edwina, the duchess," I said. "Oh, dear. I really don't want it to be her."

"You're showing signs of cracking up yourself, my love," he said. "You've got two nasty frown lines over your eyes. Not good for your beauty, you know!" He ruffled my hair. "Now, what say we have something to eat? I've got some nice, cold lamb and I can do some mashed potatoes and pickles. Her next door gave me some lovely pickled cabbage."

"So she's still 'her next door'?" I asked.

"She'd like to get me to the altar, but I ain't going," he said. "There was only one lady in my life, and that was your grandma. I see no sense in marrying again."

With that, he started peeling potatoes for lunch.

Chapter 30

In London and then back to Kingsdowne

It was always with regret that I left my grandfather's house. I wished he could play a bigger part in my life but there was such a huge social gulf between us. I hadn't even known he existed until I grew up. He had been kept away from me. I thought about how stupid the rules of society were as I took the train back to London.

Darcy was waiting for me at the appointed time.

"So, did your grandfather solve the case for us?" he asked as he helped me into the little sports car.

"He didn't want to get involved," I said. "He instructed me to leave it to the police."

"Very sensible."

"What about you? Any luck at Scotland Yard?"

"I came up empty too," he said. "The chap I was hoping to see is off in Yorkshire on a case, and I was told firmly that Scotland Yard will never intervene unless the local police have requested it."

"I was going to say a wasted day," I said, looking out of the motorcar window as we drove over Westminster Bridge, "but at least I saw my grandfather and I'm spending some time alone with you."

"Should we not go back to Kingsdowne but drive off together to a little hotel on the coast? Or take the boat to Paris?" he asked, his eyes teasing me.

"Both sound divine, but we are in the middle of a murder investigation. Edwina is expecting us back and we should be there."

"That famous Rannoch sense of duty again." He laughed. "But you're right. I feel I owe an obligation to Jack. I did bring the poor blighter here, and he was enough a fish out of water before this happened."

"I feel the same," I said.

"Let's hope the cook has been left in peace by the police and a splendid dinner awaits us," Darcy said. "I must say the food there is rather good, don't you think?"

"Heavenly."

A watery sun sank low in the sky as we left the city behind. Smoke curled up from cottages hidden among the trees, and we passed a ploughman leading a giant horse home for the night. The countryside seemed peaceful and serene. It was hard to think that murders happened in such a setting. I tried to follow Granddad's advice and push the whole thing from my mind.

"I wonder if the dotty aunt will want another séance tonight," Darcy said. "I must say that my experience of a Ouija board has always been that it spells out nonsense."

"But Princess Charlotte does seem to have some kind of psychic ability. She has had interesting dreams," I said. "Before Jack arrived, she dreamed about a cuckoo coming to the rooftop. That was significant, don't you think?"

I looked up as Darcy pulled the car close into the hedge. "Why are we stopping?"

"Because we'll soon be back at the house and I won't have a chance to do this," he said, and leaned across to kiss me. It was a long, wonderful kiss and was followed by another.

"I hope to God I can come up with enough money for us to marry in the foreseeable future," Darcy said. "This waiting and not being able to make love to you properly is driving me insane. My appetites are too healthy for a chaste life."

As we came up the drive and turned into the forecourt, two small figures dropped from the big, copper beech and came running toward us.

"You're back," Nicholas said as Darcy opened the motorcar door. "We thought you'd gone for good. Now perhaps we can find out what's going on. We've been dying to do some real detective work all day but that rotter Carter hasn't let us out of his sight."

"You seem to be out of his sight at this moment," I said, "or is he up the tree too?"

The twins grinned. "He was summoned to talk to the policeman. We escaped instantly," Kat said. "We wanted to listen in but Mama caught us and banished us. Nobody will tell us anything. Mama says it's too gruesome for young ears."

"Quite right," Darcy said. "There is nothing fun or exciting about a murder. Taking a life is the very worst thing that a human being can do. And your mother wants to keep you safe. If there is a murderer around, you might put yourselves in danger with your snooping."

"We'll be very careful," Kat said. "We're awfully good at snooping, aren't we, Nick? So do tell, Georgie, who do you think did it?"

"I have no idea," I said as we walked toward the house with a bouncy child on either side of us. "And if I did have an idea, I certainly wouldn't tell you."

"Spoilsport," Nick said. "We'll just have to go back to our secret snooping, Kat."

I noticed the black motorcar parked outside the garages. "So the inspector is back again, is he?"

"He arrived a little while ago. He told Grandmama he wants to speak to everyone again. And he wanted to talk to the servants first. That was when the dreaded Carter went, and we seized our chance to slip off."

"I think you'd better slip right back to your own quarters," Darcy said. "Among other things, you should keep an eye on your sister."

"On Sissy? Why? She couldn't have done it. She can't walk," Nick said scornfully.

"She looks out of the window," Darcy said. "The murderer might think that she saw something that implicates him. She may be in danger."

"Golly," Nick said. "You might be right. We'd better get back up there, Kat."

"Oh all right, I suppose." Kat sighed. "But I'd much rather be detecting. Why don't you protect Sissy and I'll try to sneak down to hear what the inspector says. I do wish we'd found that secret passage. If only it went behind the Long Gallery, we could listen in on everything."

We were met in the front hall by Huxstep. "Welcome back, my lady, Mr. O'Mara," he said. "Perfect timing. Her Grace wants everyone assembled in the Long Gallery at five thirty. And you young scamps should be back in your nursery. Nanny was worried about you. Off you go!"

"Yes, Mr. Huxstep," Nick answered meekly and off they went.

Huxstep gave me a knowing look as he took my overcoat and hat.

The family was already assembled in the Long Gallery. I took in the two sisters on the sofa, each with a glass of sherry in her hand. On the other sofa, Irene sat close to her mother. The Starlings were off to one side. They looked tense and nervous. So did Jack. He was sitting alone on a high-backed chair. Edwina greeted us. "The police inspector wishes to address us again," she said. "From the look on his face, I think he's found out something significant. Maybe our former footman has confessed. I must say I'd be surprised if it were he—always such a steady boy, I would have said. I've known him all his life." She motioned to a drinks tray. "Do have some sherry, and Mrs. Broad's cheese crisps are delicious."

Darcy poured me a glass. I had just taken a bite of a warm cheese crisp when Chief Inspector Fairbotham marched in, accompanied by his sergeant and a constable in uniform.

"Ah, good. Everyone here," he said, rubbing his big hands as he looked around us. "Splendid. Well, I've some news to impart to you . . . or perhaps one of you at least already knows what I'm going to say."

"What are you talking about?" Edwina snapped. "How can we possibly know what you're going to say? Speak up, man. Out with it."

The inspector was still rubbing his hands. It looked as though he was enjoying this moment. "Well," he said dramatically, "the medical officer has performed a preliminary autopsy and has told me something quite unexpected." He took a deep breath. "The MO is sure that Cedric Altringham was already dead when he was stabbed in the back."

"So that's why there was so little blood!" I blurted out. The others turned to look at me in surprise. "I knew that something wasn't right," I added.

"And you were spot on, Lady Georgiana," the inspector said.

"Why on earth would anyone want to stab a dead man?" Edwina demanded.

"Why indeed?" Fairbotham said.

"So what did kill my son?" Edwina asked. "Do you know that?"

"Not exactly yet, Your Grace. I can tell you that he was poisoned, but I don't yet know what poisoned him. Maybe you can shed some light for me. The night before he died—did he dine with you?"

"He did," Edwina said.

"And you all ate the same food?"

"We did. And furthermore, we were all served from the same dish," she said, "and drank wine poured from the same bottles."

"Do you know whether your son might have eaten or drunk anything after dinner, then?"

"I cannot tell you that. My son stormed out of the room in a huff, Inspector."

"Was he prone to these 'huffs,' Your Grace?"

"I don't see what my son's temperament has to do with his being poisoned."

"I would say it had everything to do with it," Fairbotham said. "Your son upset or scared or annoyed someone so much that the ultimate step was taken to silence him."

Edwina seemed to consider this for the first time. She looked around the room. "You mean one of us? Someone in this room poisoned Cedric?"

"Almost certainly someone in this house," he replied. "When we get the results from the medical chappies, we'll be able to tell more—whether it was administered to him that morning or the night before." He looked around us again. "So nobody in this room saw him the morning he was killed? Is that correct?"

There was silence. Fairbotham turned to the constable. "Would you go and fetch his valet, please?"

"That's it," I heard one of the Starlings say in a stage whisper, "talk to the valet. I've always thought he was a suspicious character. Too good to be true, if you know what I mean."

Edwina bristled. "You wish to speak with a servant in the Long Gallery? In front of us? That is most unseemly, Chief Inspector."

"Murder is an unseemly business, Your Grace," Fairbotham said, "and at this moment, everyone in this house is equally a suspect in my mind—from you down to the lowest scullery maid."

"Well, really!" Edwina muttered.

We waited and soon the constable returned with a worried-looking Marcel.

"I understand that you were the duke's valet."

"*Oui,* monsieur," Marcel replied, looking down at his feet.

"You speak English?"

"A little, monsieur."

"Your name?"

"Marcel Leclerc, monsieur."

"How long were you in the duke's service?"

"About one year, monsieur. The duke took me on when he was staying with friends in Monte Carlo last year. I was very 'appy to work for him. He treat me very well." He spoke with a heavy, French accent.

"I bet he did," came a mutter from one of the Starlings behind me.

Fairbotham paused, and I could tell he was sizing up the valet, obviously not liking what he saw. "Right, Marcel. I'm going to ask you some important questions and I want you to think very carefully. Understood?"

Marcel nodded. I noticed his Adam's apple went up and down as he swallowed hard.

"Now, Marcel. What time did your master come up to his bedroom on the evening before he died?"

Marcel frowned then said, "About ten o'clock. That was very early for him. I was surprised."

"Did he say why he'd come up early? Was he not feeling well?"

"He said, 'You're a good fellow, Marcel. You're worth ten of the others. Bloodsuckers all of them.' He was not in a happy mood, but I do not think he was feeling unwell."

"Did he ask you to bring him any kind of hot drink or medicine?"

Marcel shook his head.

"So that night, before he died, did you see him eat or drink anything?"

Marcel frowned. "He had no drink, monsieur. I did not see him take any kind of medicine, although sometimes he takes an iron tonic at night."

Fairbotham turned to his sergeant. "Get the iron tonic analyzed. And any other bottles of medicine in his bathroom." He focused on Marcel again. "So you didn't see anything pass his lips on the night before he died?"

"I did not see, no. But I do not know what he ate or drank before he retired for the night."

"And the next morning—did he have a cup of tea brought to him in bed?"

"No, monsieur. He arose early. He seemed agitated, nervous. He dressed quickly and told me he was going down to his study to write a letter. I was to bring him a cup of black coffee."

"And you did this?"

"Of course. I went to the kitchen and brought him the cup of coffee to his desk."

"You poured the coffee yourself?"

"No, monsieur. The cook poured the coffee and handed it to me. It would be quite wrong for me to help myself in her kitchen."

"Did you see the cup before she poured it?"

Marcel frowned. "The cup, monsieur? It was waiting with all the other cups, stacked on a tray."

Fairbotham frowned. "And you carried it straight to his study? You didn't leave it anywhere for someone to drop something into the coffee?"

"Monsieur—" Marcel bristled. "When the duke required his coffee, it was my job to fetch it for him immediately. I placed it on his desk beside him. He was busy writing. I went away again. I did not see him drink it."

"And then he went out?"

"I do not know this, monsieur. I was back in my master's chamber. I did not see him again. I knew nothing of his death until Frederick came and told me that Her Grace wishes to speak with all the servants. I can tell you that this news broke my heart. I had to fight to hold back my tears. My tears return now, as we speak of it again."

"Yes, well . . ." Chief Inspector Fairbotham coughed at this un-British display of emotion.

"That will be all, Marcel," Edwina said sharply. As he left the room she said, "The sooner that young man is out of this house, the better. If you want my advice, Jack, you will find yourself a reliable English valet, not some flighty foreigner."

"Ah, but Mama, my French maid is wonderful," Irene said. "She has a way with clothes that no English girl ever had."

She was silenced by Edwina's withering look.

"Is that all, Chief Inspector?" Edwina asked.

"For now, Your Grace. My men will test anything the duke might have drunk from. When we know exactly what poison killed him, then we'll be able to take the next step."

"Maybe now somebody will take the attempt on my life seriously," Irene said. "It's obvious that the same person who poisoned Cedric tried to kill me."

"I don't see what more we can do in your case, Countess," Fairbotham said, "since you didn't remember how many packets of sleeping draft you had in the first place. Of course, someone could have acquired an extra packet or two, from a doctor in London, maybe . . . but my men came up with no unidentifiable fingerprints on your glass or in your bathroom."

"Just as there were no fingerprints on that knife!" Irene said, wagging a finger at him. "You see, we're dealing with a clever killer, Chief Inspector."

"Certainly with a thorough killer," Fairbotham said. "He hasn't made any slips yet, but he will. They always do."

"I presume that this now rules out my former footman, who you are holding," Edwina said. "I see no way that anyone outside this house could have poisoned my son."

"We've already let him go," Fairbotham said.

I had a question that had suddenly occurred to me. I hesitated to ask it in front of all these people, but it had to be asked. "Chief Inspector," I said. He was about to leave but turned back to me. "Did your men manage to find the letter the duke posted that morning?"

"They did not. There was no letter from the duke in that postbox."

"That must mean that the person who found him dead on the path took the letter from him."

"It would certainly seem that way," he said. "So we must presume that the letter has been destroyed, and we'll never know what it contained. Unless anyone was foolish enough to hang on to it. But that was smart thinking of you, Lady Georgiana. I'll have my men go through the rubbish."

With that, he left.

Chapter 31

"Well, that's a turn-up for the books," Darcy muttered to me as Fairbotham left the room. "You were spot on with your observation that something wasn't right."

"I wonder who stabbed Cedric's body with Jack's knife," I said. "Such a horrid, spiteful thing to do."

We went up to change for dinner. Queenie was abnormally helpful. Clearly she had taken to heart my threat of the night before. Thank heavens there was no talk of another séance after dinner. We sat near the fire in the drawing room, making small talk but consciously avoiding the thing that was on all our minds. I expect the others were as relieved as I when we went up to bed. As we had been talking I found myself considering—now that we knew Cedric had been poisoned, that changed everything. Poison does not require strength or agility. Any of the women in the room could have easily slipped poison into something Cedric ate or drank.

The next day, we all felt we were in a sort of limbo, not sure what to do with ourselves. Edwina wanted to arrange for Cedric's funeral, but couldn't find out when his body might be released, so she was in a bad temper. It was a bright and windy day, and the twins came bursting excitedly into the morning room, where we were reading the papers.

"Mama, Jack says he'll take us out riding," Kat said. "And Mr. Carter said it will do us good to get some fresh air. That's all right with you, isn't it?"

Irene frowned then turned to me. "Do you think you could go with them, Georgiana? I'm not sure that I want them out alone with Jack."

"Why not?" Kat demanded.

"Well, after all . . ." Irene began.

Nick cut her off. "Come on, Mama. You can't think Jack is the murderer any longer. Now that we know that Uncle Cedric was poisoned it can't have been Jack. He wouldn't poison anybody."

"Besides," Kat added, "how would he know where anything poisonous was kept?"

I got to my feet. "I'll be happy to go with you," I said. "I'd love a ride." I looked at Darcy. "Coming?" I asked.

"I never say no to a good ride." Darcy followed me out of the room.

We had a terrific gallop across the Downs. Both twins were good riders and had probably never been allowed to go so fast in their lives. We were all red-cheeked and glowing as we came down the hill to the house.

"It seems hard to believe that we can be normal up here and once we get back to the house it will be back to that awful air of suspicion again," Jack said. "I can tell they'd all like to believe I did it. None of them want me here."

"Cheer up, old chap," Darcy said. "I'm sure it will all be sorted out soon."

"We want you here," Nick said. "We like you. And we know jolly well that you didn't do it."

"I just can't imagine who did," Jack said. "It had to be one of those strange little blokes who followed Cedric around."

As we came around the house to the forecourt, Nick said excitedly,

"Look, the detective's car is back again. Do you think he's found out what the poison was? Or maybe he's even found out who did it."

"I don't think so," Kat said. "He didn't seem very intelligent to me."

We handed the horses over to the grooms and made our way back to the house, the twins holding our hands and dragging us eagerly. I expected to find everyone assembled in the Long Gallery again but the house was quiet and there was no sign of any policemen. The twins looked around expectantly. "Where can the inspector be?" Kat asked. "Let's go and find out."

"You both need to change out of those clothes before you do anything else," Darcy said. "You smell of horse."

"Spoilsport," Kat muttered. "If we go upstairs, we'll be trapped in the nursery. Nanny and dreaded Carter never know anything. We *have* to find out what poisoned Uncle Cedric."

"You know you'll get into trouble if you're found down here in riding togs," I said. "Go on. Off you go."

Nick sighed, and dragged Kat up the stairs toward the nursery. I went to my room to change too.

"Pooh. You don't 'alf stink of 'orse," Queenie complained as she pulled off my riding boots. "What am I supposed to do with this lot?"

"Brush it off and air it out, I suppose," I said. "I don't know. You're the maid!"

"I ain't never had to deal with no 'orses," she muttered as she helped me off with my breeches. "The only 'orse I ever came in contact with was the rag and bone man's. Oh, and the milkman's."

I washed my face and hands, brushed my hair and went downstairs to see Chief Inspector Fairbotham standing at the bottom of the stairs, looking perplexed. "Oh, there you are, Lady Georgiana," he said. "I've been looking for the old duchess. You haven't seen her recently, have you?"

"I've just come back from a ride," I said. "I haven't seen anybody. Have you found out what killed Cedric?"

"Yes, and no," he said. "That's why I need to talk to the duchess. That butler went off to get her ages ago. I haven't got all day to stand around here."

"I'll go and see if you like," I said, but I had just started back up the stairs when Huxstep came striding out of the Long Gallery.

"I'm sorry, Chief Inspector, but I have been unable to locate Her Grace," he said. "Her maid hasn't seen her all morning, and I've had the footmen search all the rooms that are in use."

"What about the rooms that aren't in use?" Fairbotham snapped.

"I see no reason why Her Grace should want to visit a storeroom or an attic," Huxstep said. "No doubt she'll appear when she's ready."

I was experiencing a growing sense of dread. "Inspector—do you think that something might have happened to her?" I asked. "After all, one member of her family is dead, and an attempt was made on Irene's life. Could it be that someone has a grudge against the Altringham family?"

"Oh, crikey," he said. "I suppose I'd better get extra men in to do a thorough search of the grounds. And you can have the staff do a complete search of the house, if you don't mind, Mr. Huxstep."

"Of course," Huxstep said. "This is most worrying."

We all joined in a search, opening doors to rooms swathed in dust sheets and nervously peering beneath them. But an hour went by and there was no sign of the missing duchess. More policemen arrived, and I saw them searching the grounds with dogs. As I looked out of the window I saw an estate car draw up and out of it stepped the dowager duchess herself. I rushed downstairs and was just in time to see her enter the foyer as Fairbotham came striding down the hall toward her.

"Where the devil have you been?" he snapped. "We've had the whole household looking for you."

"Looking for me?"

"We were worried something had happened to you," I said.

"My dear, I just drove myself down to the vicarage to talk to the vicar about Cedric's funeral," she said. "You know it's been on my mind. The vicar was most understanding. Most. Such a kind little man."

"I thought I said nobody was to leave the property," Fairbotham grumbled.

"The village church is on land formerly belonging to the Altringham family, thus one might say that I have not left our property," Edwina said frostily. "And you should realize that a member of a family such as ours would never dream of running away." She glared at him as Huxstep arrived to take off her overcoat and hat. "Now, what was it you wanted, Chief Inspector?"

"I'd like to speak to everyone again, if you could assemble them for me."

"You've discovered what poisoned my son? What was it?"

"I'd prefer to give this information to everyone at once. I'd hate to think I gave anyone a chance to destroy evidence," he said.

"Really!" Edwina sniffed. "This is all beyond my comprehension, Chief Inspector. Suggesting that a member of this family might behave like a common criminal. Something like this has never happened in the history of the Altringham family." She turned to address Huxstep, who was still hovering in the background. "You heard the Chief Inspector, Huxstep. Please have everyone assembled again in the Long Gallery." She shook her head. "This is turning into a farce."

"Nothing farcical about murder, Your Grace," Fairbotham said. "I'll be in to speak with you in ten minutes." And he walked off down the hall toward Cedric's study.

"Should I help assemble the family, Your Grace?" I asked because Edwina looked stunned.

"No, no. Leave it to Huxstep. You may accompany me to the Long Gallery, Georgiana." I offered her my arm and she took it. "You're a good girl, my dear. I'm glad to have you here at this distressing time."

We entered the Long Gallery. Edwina looked around as if reassuring herself that she really was in her own home. "How can this be,

Georgiana?" she said. "How can it be possible that someone in this house poisoned Cedric? Surely not my own flesh and blood. I just pray that it is an outsider and not one of us."

I seated her in the armchair by the fire and took a place myself on the sofa opposite. Soon we were joined by the others. Darcy gave me an inquiring look as he came to sit beside me. It felt almost as if the cast of characters was coming on stage for the next act of an improbable play. Nobody spoke as Chief Inspector Fairbotham made his entrance.

"Your Grace." He gave her a little bow. "You asked me if I had discovered what poisoned your son. The answer is yes and no. The medical examiner has found traces of cyanide in his tissues."

"Cyanide!" Edwina exclaimed. "Where would anyone have got their hands on cyanide in this house?"

"You'd be surprised," Fairbotham said. "Cyanide is used for all sorts of things. Destroying wasp's nests, for example. My men are searching the house and outbuildings right now, and I expect we'll turn up something."

"So the murderer would have to be someone who knew how to use cyanide," Darcy said. "Dangerous substance, that. Could kill the would-be murderer if he breathed in the fumes."

"Now we come to the interesting part," Fairbotham said. "There was cyanide in his tissues, but the MO reckons there wasn't enough to kill him."

"Then what did kill him?" Edwina demanded.

"Tell me, Your Grace—did your son have a heart condition?"

"A heart condition? Absolutely not."

"Does anyone in the family have a heart condition?"

"As a matter of fact, I do," Edwina said.

"And you have been prescribed medicine for this?"

"I have. Some form of digitalis, I understand. From foxgloves."

"Interesting." Fairbotham nodded. "Because a significant amount of this chemical was found in his body."

"Somebody used my digitalis to kill my son?"

"Again it probably wouldn't have killed him."

"I don't understand," I said. "Are you suggesting that someone administered cyanide and digitalis to the duke, but neither in sufficient amounts to kill him? Why? If someone wanted him dead, why not feed him enough of one of these substances?"

"Why not, indeed. Good question, Lady Georgiana. And they weren't the only substances found. It seems there was atropine from eyedrops and certain other chemicals in his system too. So either he was a hypochondriac who administered various treatments to himself, or someone fed him a deadly cocktail. The MO reckons that he wasn't in the best condition—lungs damaged by too much smoking, heart not too strong—and thus it was the combination of substances, coupled with a brisk walk on a very cold morning that killed him. Rather ingenious in a way, although surely the killer realized that the substances would show up in his tissues."

"Perhaps the killer thought the death would be taken as a heart attack," Darcy suggested.

"And probably would have, Mr. O'Mara," Fairbotham said, "if someone hadn't chosen to plunge a great, big knife into his back while he lay there."

He looked up as one of his men came in. "What is it, Finch?" he asked.

There was a muttered conversation then Fairbotham turned back to us. "It seems that we've found our cyanide in a photographic darkroom."

"That was my son's darkroom," Edwina said. "He was much interested in photography."

"Fingerprints were found on the bottle," Fairbotham said, "and we'll be comparing them to the prints we took earlier from everyone here. And, Your Grace, I'd appreciate it if you let me take a look at your medicine cupboard and showed me your heart medication."

"Certainly, Chief Inspector," Edwina said wearily. She led him from the room. She reminded me of a splendid balloon that is slowly deflating. I wondered how many more of these unpleasant surprises she could take. And how she'd handle it if the culprit turned out to be a member of her family.

Princess Charlotte rose with effort to her feet first. "I could do with some coffee. All these shocks are not good for the system."

Virginia stood too. "There will still be coffee in the morning room. Maybe Mr. O'Mara will accompany us to protect us and cheer us up. There has been far too much gloom and doom in this household recently." She fluttered her eyelashes at Darcy in what she thought was a sexy manner. Darcy was gracious enough to offer her his arm, and led her out of the room.

I stood alone in the deserted room, trying to think. A clever cocktail to induce a heart attack—surely none of the people present had a sufficient knowledge of chemicals to concoct such a thing? It had to be an outsider. But who? And why?

I think we were all relieved when the luncheon gong sounded. It provided a moment of normality in an Alice-in-Wonderland world. Edwina had not been with us in the morning room, but she joined us as we made our way to the dining room. I approached her. "Did you want your grandchildren to join us for luncheon today?" I asked.

She reacted as if she had just come out of a trance. "What? Oh, yes. Please. By all means. If you'd be good enough to escort them down. I can see this nightmare has overexcited them. Not good for them to be alone too much."

I nodded and went up the stairs to the nursery. As I opened the door, the twins and Nanny looked up at me, openmouthed.

"Oh, your ladyship," Nanny said. "I'm so glad to see you. It was awful. The children should never have been put through something like that."

"Like what?" I asked.

Nicholas and Katherine rushed over to me. "The police came and took away Mr. Carter," Nick exclaimed, his eyes as wide as saucers.

"They found his fingerprints on the bottle of cyanide in Uncle Cedric's darkroom."

"He made an awful fuss," Katherine added. "He told the police he had helped Uncle Cedric with his photo developing, so of course his fingerprints would be on the bottles in there."

"He started crying!" Nick exclaimed delightedly. "Can you imagine? A man, crying. Papa would have been disgusted."

"He was shell-shocked in the war," I said. "You have to make allowances for men who were in the trenches."

"That would explain it, then," Nanny said. "His mind has gone. He's not responsible for his actions, poor soul. I always found him a nice enough man—pleasant and polite, and so patient with the children, who aren't the easiest, let me say."

"Us? We're angels, Nanny," Nick said.

"Well, I've come to bring you angels down to luncheon," I said.

"Good-oh," Nick said. "I'm awfully bored with nursery food."

"What about Sissy?" I asked. "Is she in her room?"

"She is, poor thing," Nanny said. "Very upset about Mr. Carter. I don't think she'd want to be taken downstairs. Could you ask for her luncheon to be sent up on a tray?"

"Of course. And tell her I'll come up and see her," I said. "Come on, you two angels."

They ran ahead of me along the hall and then down the stairs. Nick swung himself off the banister post; Kat didn't. She was rather quiet for her. I suspected that the arrest of Mr. Carter had upset her more than her brother. Perhaps she was secretly fond of him.

By the time we entered the dining room, the news of Mr. Carter had obviously reached the rest of the household.

"Sit down, children," Edwina said. "I understand that your tutor is being questioned by the police. Remember, in this country a man is innocent until proven guilty. You are not to come to judgment."

"No, Grandmama," the children muttered as they sat down, their eyes already on the food.

"See, what did I tell you?" Princess Charlotte said. "The spirits were correct all along. It wasn't Castor, it was Carter. One of us clearly pushed the planchette to the *S* rather than the *R*. So easy to do with many fingers on it."

"But I don't understand," Virginia said. "Surely the man was a tutor. Hired help. What could he possibly have to do with Cedric? He was nothing to our family."

Edwina cleared her throat. "Actually, he was connected to us in a way," she said stiffly. "He was at Oxford with Johnnie. Johnnie brought him here once during the holidays. He was very bright, I gathered. I rather suspect he helped Johnnie with his papers."

"But that hardly constitutes a family connection," Virginia said.

"He enlisted in the same regiment as Johnnie during the war," Edwina said. "From what I've been told, he completely lost his nerve in the trenches. Refused to go over the top with the rest of them. Johnnie was going to have him shot for cowardice, but then Johnnie was killed that day. Then a mortar landed in the trench where Carter was being held. Apparently he was rather brave in taking care of the wounded and dying, and Johnnie was dead, so the charges against him were dropped. But maybe he felt betrayed by a man who had been his friend."

"Still, that wouldn't make him want to kill Cedric, surely?" Irene said frostily.

"He came to Cedric after the war—asking for help—a job, a recommendation. His nerves were completely in shreds, and Cedric couldn't or wouldn't help him. Then when the children needed a tutor, I remembered him and offered him the post."

"And he repaid you by killing your son," Charlotte snapped. "That's gratitude for you."

"I think we have to be charitable and believe that he was not entirely responsible for his actions," Edwina said.

After luncheon, I took the children back to their nursery. Jack and Darcy came with me.

"Do you think Mr. Carter will be hanged?" Nick asked.

"If he is proven not to have been of sound mind, he will be committed to an insane asylum," Darcy said.

"How awful for him." Kat sounded near to tears, and I realized that my hunch was correct: she did have a soft spot for her tutor.

We recounted to Sissy everything that had happened, and then Jack and Darcy took the twins out to play ball. I sat with Sissy in her room, watching the four of them laughing as they chased a ball.

"I shall miss Mr. Carter," Sissy said. "He was kind to me and he didn't treat me as if I was soft in the head because my legs won't work."

"It's very unfortunate," I agreed. "I suppose we can't know what goes on in the head of someone who has been badly shell-shocked."

"I'm so glad it wasn't Jack." Sissy's eyes were on him, his blonde hair blowing in the breeze as he ran ahead of Nick and Kat. "I never believed he could do a thing like that."

"I'm glad too," I agreed.

We sat and talked together for a while. Sissy looked up at the crunch of tires on gravel below us. "Look, Georgie," she said. "Mr. Carter has come back." And indeed he was being escorted back into the house by a policeman. From Nanny we learned that he was still under suspicion and was being held in his room until he was formally charged. He had requested the presence of a lawyer. When I went downstairs for tea, I noticed that the mood had improved considerably. It wasn't one of them after all. It was a stranger, an interloper. Life could go back to normal. Even Edwina ate two cream cakes.

It was a cold, blustery evening and we pulled up chairs around the fire. Edwina brought out embroidery. As we were a household in mourning, neither cards nor music were acceptable, so we sat, watching the flames dancing up the chimney. Suddenly there was the sound of running feet upstairs. Doors slamming. Raised voices. We all looked up as a young policeman came into the room.

"We've called for an ambulance, Your Grace," he said. "Mr. Carter has tried to kill himself."

Chapter 32

Darcy was on his feet immediately and followed the constable out of the room. Edwina stood too, as if unsure whether to follow them. I wished that Darcy hadn't gone because a disturbing thought had crept into my mind. What if Carter had not tried to kill himself? What if he was innocent and the true killer had tried to silence him?

We heard the bell as the ambulance arrived, the tramp of booted feet as Carter was carried out. Still Darcy didn't come. Then one of the maids came up to Irene. "If you please, my lady," she said, "but your daughter isn't feeling well. I thought you should know."

"My daughter?" Irene looked up. "Elisabeth is not well?"

"No, my lady. Katherine. She is vomiting, if you'll pardon the expression, and she looks awful pale. I think you should get the doctor to her."

"Oh, God." Irene stood up.

"Don't upset yourself, Irene." Edwina reached out to her daughter. "The child has probably got herself into a state over what happened to her tutor."

"No, Your Grace. She seems really ill," the maid said. "Nanny is that worried."

"Have Huxstep call the doctor immediately," Irene said. She

rushed from the room. Edwina followed her. I'd like to have gone too, but I wasn't a family member and had no excuse to go with them. I couldn't believe that Kat had just "got herself into a state." It had to be more serious than that. Poor little Kat, so inquisitive, so keen to play detective. Had she found out the vital clue that pointed to the killer?

The rest of us sat there, not knowing what to do.

"The child obviously ate some food that was too rich for her," Princess Charlotte said. "I told Edwina I thought it was a stupid idea to have the children present at the adult's luncheon. In my day, children ate bread and milk and lightly boiled eggs for their midday meal."

I found I was holding my breath, waiting for doom to fall. My gaze went around the room, watching the others, wondering.

I noticed that only two of the Starlings were in the room: Julian and Adrian. Simon was missing. I realized I knew nothing about him. Did he, like Carter, have connections to the family that none of us knew about? I should find Darcy. I should find Chief Inspector Fairbotham. I got up and left the Long Gallery. I stood all alone in the great, marble foyer wondering what to do first. Had they summoned a doctor? Was Fairbotham still on the premises? Where was Huxstep? I decided to go up to the nursery. They should know what I now suspected. As I made my way up the grand staircase, I was conscious of those nymphs and satyrs and Greek gods laughing down serenely at me. Suddenly they looked menacing—the fates mocking us. And then I stood, rooted to the spot. I had to grab the banister or I would have fallen down the stairs.

Greek gods. I remembered the book I had had in my nursery and the picture of Castor and Pollux, the heavenly twins, children of Zeus, in Greek mythology. Princess Charlotte and her spirits had been right after all. And I realized something else . . . Charlotte had dreamed of the cuckoo, coming into Kingsdowne, and she had dreamed of the dangerous panther among us. The black cat.

I started to run now—up the stairs, up to the second flight and along the hall to the nursery. I opened the door. Kat was lying in bed, her eyes closed, looking deathly pale. Nick was perched at the end of the bed, looking terrified. Sissy was in her chair in the corner. There was no sign of the grown-ups. Nick's gaze fastened on me as I came in.

"She nearly died," he said. "She was puking and puking. It was horrible."

Kat opened her eyes. "I feel awful," she said. "I want a drink of water."

"Nanny's gone to get you some barley water," Nick said.

"What do you think happened, Katherine?" I asked. "Did you eat or drink something bad?"

"I think someone tried to poison me," she said. "Someone mixed poison with my tea."

"Or did you take a sip of the potion you made—the one you gave to Mr. Carter? The one you gave to your uncle Cedric?"

"Katherine!" Sissy gasped. "You didn't. Please say it's not true."

"It was only an experiment." Katherine tried to sit up. "We didn't expect it to work. We just mixed up a drop of everything deadly that we could find and then we brushed it onto an envelope on Uncle Cedric's desk."

"It was Kat's idea," Nick said. "We never thought. . . ."

"Uncle Cedric was being so beastly to us," Kat said. "He wouldn't give Mummy any money. He didn't want us in the house. He wouldn't let us go to school, or let Sissy's legs get better. Mummy kept crying."

"We never wanted to kill anyone," Nick said.

"What about Mr. Carter? You didn't try to kill him?"

"No. I swear it wasn't us," Nick said. "We didn't go anywhere near him."

"Then he must have made the ultimate sacrifice for you," I said. "He realized what you had done and he drank your potion."

"I know." Kat was crying now. "I don't want him to die."

"He's gone off in an ambulance. They may be able to save him,"

I said. "But it will mean that you two have to tell the truth to the police."

"Will we go to prison?" Nick asked in a quavering little voice. "Will they hang us?"

"I'm sure they'll take your age into account," I said, "and the fact that you didn't really intend to kill anybody."

"What's this?" Irene stood in the doorway with a glass of barley water in her hands.

"We made a potion and put it on Uncle Cedric's envelope, Mummy. We thought he'd lick it and feel ill. We didn't think it would kill anybody. And then when Uncle Cedric died, we were so frightened. We decided to keep quiet about it and they'd never think it was us. But Georgie worked it out . . . she's really clever."

Irene put down the glass, shut the door behind her and came into the room. "Who else have you told about this?"

"Nobody," I said. And as I said it, a cold shiver went down my spine. I remembered what she had said, that time in the Long Gallery: she was the mother lion, ready to fight to protect her cubs.

"Where is this potion?" Irene asked calmly.

"In the schoolroom. It's labeled copper sulfate. At the back of the shelf."

"Go and get it, Nicholas."

"But Mummy . . ."

"Do it."

She was cold and frightening, and she was standing between me and the door.

"I'm sure any judge would understand that the children didn't realize what they were doing," I said.

"If they believe the children acted alone."

The penny dropped. "You were the one who stabbed Cedric. You wanted everyone to suspect Jack."

"Nasty, common, Australian brat," she snapped. "How can he possibly be the rightful heir? Cedric should have adopted Nicholas.

He'd be a proper heir . . . not an Australian, and certainly not a French servant."

"But you were sound asleep. They couldn't wake you," I said, and then I added, "Oh, I see. You stabbed Cedric and then you took your sleeping draft that morning. No wonder you were so deeply asleep. You'd only just taken it."

"I made up my mind to go up to town early and see our solicitor before Cedric could get in touch with him," she said. "I wanted to find out whether he could really go ahead with this stupid adoption and how we could stop him. But I didn't want anyone to know. I told my maid I had a migraine and she was not to wake me. I slipped out through the secret passage we used to use as children."

"Mummy, there really is a secret passage, then!" Nick exclaimed. "We've been looking and looking."

"It comes out into the folly," I said. "Right above the glen. You saw Cedric lying there, did you?"

"He was dead," she said. "He had a letter clutched in his hand. A letter to our solicitor. I took it. It was hard to prize it out of his dead hand. Horrible. I was going to go for help. I started back toward the house. Then I realized what a chance this was. I crept back through the bushes up to the tack room, took the knife and went back to him. But I wasn't strong enough to stab him through that jacket, so I had to take it off. I thought everyone would believe that Jack did it." She took the bottle that Nick was holding. "Hold her hands, children."

"What are you going to do?" Nick asked.

"Make her drink it, of course. We'll tell everyone that she tried to poison you. We caught her and she drank it herself."

"No, Mummy," Nick said.

"Don't be stupid. This is the end of everything, don't you see? They'll send me to prison. They'll take you away to some awful institution. Is that what you want? Grab her hands."

"Let go of me," I shouted and shook myself free. Irene was still between me and the door.

"You are not leaving this room alive," Irene said. She looked almost insane, with eyes bulging and face distorted. "No one is going to take my children from me." She came at me with the bottle. I backed away. Suddenly she buckled and slumped to the floor.

Sissy had thrown the clock at her head. She looked stunned at what she had done.

"I haven't killed her, have I?" she asked.

Chapter 33

As you can imagine, the next twenty-four hours were utter chaos. Irene being hauled off, looking regal and stoic, the twins crying and saying that they hadn't meant any harm.

"What were you thinking, handling cyanide?" Darcy asked them. "You were jolly lucky that you weren't killed yourselves. It doesn't take much of the vapor to kill someone."

"We used Uncle Cedric's special gloves," Nick said. "And we only took a tiny drop. We only took a tiny drop of everything. It was only a bit of fun. We didn't think our potion could possibly do any real harm."

"Let's hope that your bit of fun doesn't wreck both your futures," Darcy said.

"Did you take some of your own potion to make you sick?" I asked Katherine. "You're lucky it didn't kill you."

"It wasn't the potion," she said. "I ate soap. I just wanted people to think I was being poisoned so nobody would suspect us."

"Do you think we'll go to prison?" Nick asked. His face was completely white and his eyes looked huge.

"Your grandmother has telephoned her solicitor. He's an important man. He'll know what to do," I said. "I don't think they send eleven-year-olds to prison."

"They may send you off to some kind of strict school," Darcy said.

"Good-oh. A school. That would be brilliant," Nick said, and he ran off happily with Kat.

"WHAT HAPPENS NOW?" Jack asked.

Darcy, Jack and I were walking in the grounds. It was the day after Irene had tried to kill me. Edwina had made an urgent telephone call to Mr. Camden-Smythe, the family solicitor, and he had arrived first thing next morning. His Rolls-Royce stood parked on the forecourt now and he was in conference with Edwina.

"I don't know," I said.

It was a glorious, bright, spring day, with a gentle breeze stirring the daffodils and occasional puff-ball clouds drifting across a blue sky. Swans glided across a still, blue lake. Birds were twittering like mad in the trees. It was almost as if nature was mocking our present turmoil at Kingsdowne.

"Do you think the twins will be sent to some kind of reform school?" Jack asked. "They are too young for prison, aren't they?"

"I overheard Mr. Camden-Smythe saying to Edwina that he thought it would be all right. He said there was clearly no intent to murder. It was just youthful experimentation and the court would understand that two bright children, cut off from normal life and encouraged in scientific experiments by their tutor, were horrified at the result of their experiment. He said he was sure any judge would agree to sending the children to separate boarding schools where they could be well supervised and continuously occupied."

"So they will get what they wanted," Jack said. "But their mother won't get off so easily, will she?"

"She didn't actually kill anybody," I said. Although she tried to, a voice in my head whispered. I remembered her blazing eyes—the lioness protecting her young.

"She'll probably be charged with desecrating a corpse, I should think," Darcy said. "That is, if she can convince a jury that she knew Cedric was already dead."

"But deliberately using my knife and trying to pin it on me," Jack said. "She shouldn't get off with that, should she? I could have been waiting for the gallows by now, if Georgie hadn't figured out the truth."

"That's true," I said. "But I rather suspect that a jury would think she did it to take suspicion away from her children."

"But she didn't even know they were responsible at that moment," Darcy said.

"All the same, I suspect that is the tack that her solicitor will want to take. Sympathy, you know. A mother doing anything to protect her young."

"What a family," Darcy muttered.

"Poor Edwina," I said. "I feel sorry for her. Whatever happens to Irene, this family is broken. Things will never be the same."

"And what about Sissy?" Jack asked suddenly. "She'll lose everybody."

"She has her grandmother," I said. "And she has you."

"And you're a rich duke," Darcy said. "You could pay to send her to Switzerland for the expensive treatment."

"Is that right?" Jack's face lit up. "Crikey. I could do that, couldn't I? She might walk again. And I know she's only fifteen, but what does English law say about cousins marrying?" His cheeks went rather pink.

"It's quite legal. Royals do it all the time," I said, laughing.

"You've got a lot of learning and a lot of growing up to do before you think about things like that, my lad," Darcy said. "You want to become a man of the world first. Find out about life beyond the sheep station."

"I don't suppose I can go back home to Australia now, can I?" Jack said. "I'm stuck here whether I like it or not."

"I wouldn't say that being the owner of all this is such a hardship." Darcy smiled as he looked up at Kingsdowne, its stone glowing in the afternoon sunlight.

"If Mr. Carter recovers all right, I hope he'll stay on and give me a bit of book learning," Jack said.

"I think it's quite hopeful that he will recover," I said. "They got to him in time. Funny, isn't it? He was branded a coward in the war but he's just shown us what a brave man he is."

"How do you mean?" Jack asked.

"He worked out that the twins must have killed their uncle and he took the blame for them."

Jack nodded then looked from Darcy to me. "You'll stay on for a while, won't you? I still haven't got the hang of which fork to use for what."

"I'll be happy to stay," I said. "Your poor grandmother is going to need our support in the coming weeks. She has essentially lost her family."

"What about you, Darcy?" Jack turned to him. "Are you going to be here?"

Darcy's eyes met mine. "I can't say how long," he said, "but for the immediate future, anyway."

And after the horrid events of the past few days, I felt a bubble of hope and happiness forming inside me. Darcy was going to stay for a while. Everything would be all right.

We looked up as we saw Edwina coming across the forecourt to meet us. "Mr. Camden-Smythe says he'll sort everything out," she said. "Those poor children. My poor daughter. If I didn't have you, Jack . . ." and she left the rest of the sentence hanging. Jack went over to her and took her arm. "Don't worry, Grandmama," he said. "We'll get through this."

She nodded. Then she looked up at us. "And do you know what

Mr. Camden-Smythe told me? He said that under the terms of the entailment, the title can only pass to an heir of the body, and failing that, to the next male in the line of succession. So all this stupid talk of adoption was for nothing. So stupid. Such a waste."

We watched them go back to the house. I went to follow them but Darcy held me back.

"What's the rush?" he said. "They don't need us in there, and it's a lovely evening."

"What had you in mind?" I smiled up at him.

"I know Edwina wouldn't approve," he said, "but I was suggesting a stroll down to the local pub."

I laughed as I took his hand.